THE MUSEUM OF ETERNA'S NOVEL (THE FIRST GOOD NOVEL)

MACEDONIO FERNÁNDEZ

TRANSLATED FROM THE SPANISH
BY MARGARET SCHWARTZ

THE MUSEUM OF ETERNA'S NOVEL (THE FIRST GOOD NOVEL)

MACEDONIO FERNÁNDEZ

PREFACE BY ADAM THIRLWELL
INTRODUCTION BY THE TRANSLATOR

OPEN LETTER
LITERARY TRANSLATIONS FROM THE UNIVERSITY OF ROCHESTER

Copyright © Ediciones Corregidor, 2007
Published by arrangement with Ediciones Corregidor, 2008
Translation copyright © Margaret Schwartz, 2010
Preface copyright © Adam Thirlwell, 2010
Originally published in Spanish as *Museo de la novela de la Eterna*.

First edition, 2010
All rights reserved

Library of Congress Cataloging-in-Publication Data:

Fernández, Macedonio, 1874-1952.
    [Museo de la novela de la eterna. English]
    The museum of eterna's novel : the first good novel / Macedonio Fernández ;
translated from the Spanish by Margaret Schwartz. – 1st ed.
    p. cm.
    ISBN-13: 978-1-934824-06-1 (pbk. : alk. paper)
    ISBN-10: 1-934824-06-2 (pbk. : alk. paper)
    I. Schwartz, Margaret. II. Title.
    PQ7797.F312M813 2010
    863'.62—dc22
                         2009048625

This publication is made possible with public funds from
the New York State Council on the Arts, a state agency.

NYSCA

Printed on acid-free paper in the United States of America.

Text set in Bodoni, a serif typeface first designed by Giambattista Bodoni
(1740–1813) in 1798.

Design by N. J. Furl

Open Letter is the University of Rochester's nonprofit, literary translation press:
Lattimore Hall 411, Box 270082, Rochester, NY 14627

www.openletterbooks.org

A PREFACE FOR MACEDONIO FERNÁNDEZ

BY ADAM THIRLWELL

I.

The Museum of Eterna's Novel, written but never published by Macedonio Fernández, is a novel that is half made up of prologues.

These prologues can inspire contradictory conclusions. It is a novel which does not want to begin. Or, perhaps, it is really a novel which does not want to end. Then again, it is a novel which does not want to be a novel at all. It will not become its own future. And yet if a novel exists as its own museum, then the reader must in some way presume that it has once existed, in the past.

Here are some usual facts involving time. Macedonio Fernández was born in 1874; he died in 1952. He began this novel around 1925, and worked on it in five drafts until he died. And this novel was a machine to prove that none of these facts had any sense at all.

Yes: Macedonio Fernández's novel would like to refute the ordinary ideas of time. And this is complicated. This is an invention whose conclusions have not yet all been noted.

2.

In Argentina, in the early part of the twentieth century, experiments were made with fictional reality. It is Macedonio Fernández's friend and protégé, Jorge Luis Borges, whose investigations are most famous. But it doesn't really matter about the provenance of the investigations. The consequences are more important; and the consequences are still unstably active. And I think of two moments where more recent Argentine novelists, writing on Borges, have tried to define this new relationship to reality. In his book *The Borges Factor,* Alan Pauls comments that for Borges "to lose is not a fatality but a construction, an artefact, a *work* . . ." It forms, in fact, writes Pauls, the basis of his style. And Pauls goes on to relate this sensation to Borges's technique of inventing his works as immediate and imaginary classics: "to put in practice *in the interior* of his work the mechanisms of a process (access to the category of a classic) which are traditionally *exterior* to the work . . ." This is one way of approaching the new relation to reality. While in his essay *The Last Reader*, Ricardo Piglia writes that "Borges's greatest lesson is perhaps the certainty that fiction doesn't only depend on the person who constructs it but also on the person who reads it." And he adds: "What is particular to Borges (if such a thing exists), is the capacity to read everything like a fiction and believe in its power. Fiction as a theory of reading."

3.

Late in his novel, Macedonio Fernández interrupts with a dialogue between Reader and Author. And the Author laments: "'Reader, sometimes your presence is requested in my pages and you are absent: your face comes close, and mirrors the dreaming in these pages, and you are absent. What bothers me is the reader: you're my problem, your existence is invincible; the rest is just a pretext to keep you within earshot of these proceedings.'" Macedonio Fernández was the first novelist for whom the problem of writing was so explicitly the problem of the reader. This is the basis of his discoveries. He developed techniques to dissolve the reader's invincible existence as a continuous entity. The aim of Macedonio Fernández's novels is to convert all reality into fiction (or the other way round): and the only way of doing this is if the reader is converted into fiction first. "It's very subtle and patient work, getting quit of the self, disrupting interiors and identities. In all my writing I've only achieved eight or ten minutes in which two or three lines disrupted the stability, the unity of someone, even at times, I believe, disrupting the self-sameness of the reader. Nevertheless, I still believe that Literature does not exist, because it hasn't dedicated itself solely to this Effect of dis-identification, the only thing that would justify its existence . . ." This technique of disruption has a precise aim: the real conclusion is immortality: "If in each of my books I have two or three times achieved an instant of what I will call in homespun terms a 'suffocation,' an 'upset' in the certitude of personal continuity, a slippage of the reader's own self, then that's all I wanted as a means; the end towards which I'm working is liberation from the idea of death: evanescence, mutability, rotation, and spinning of the self make it immortal, which is to say, release its destiny from the body."

This is the grandest aim of Macedonio's fiction. In fact, it is only through fiction that such an aim, he believed, could be realised. He just wants, he says of the reader, to "win him over as a character, so that for an instant he believes that he himself does not live." And this is only possible through the elastic techniques of novel-writing—only the novel has this ontological power: "It seems to me that there isn't any one else who has used this method, or that it would be applicable to any other genre but the novel."

4.

It is possible, however, to look at this another way. The pressure under which this novel is written is the infinite, the eternal. "This novel is not content to be separate from eternity; it wants to feel the breeze of the eternal on its face . . ." A novel written from the perspective of infinity will contain some unusual premises: everything is repetition ("A Romanian woman once sang me a phrase of folk music and I have since found it tens of times in different works from different composers of the past four hundred years. Indubitably: things do not begin; or they don't begin when they are created. Or the world was created old"); which means there is no such thing as death; which means there is no such thing as the self; and so it is impossible to distinguish between different levels of reality—"they're all real; any image in a mind is reality, and lives . . ."

But the eternal, of course, is not quite true. The infinite is an invention. And Macedonio knows this too. With the metaphysical, he is trying to console himself. He is intent on the construction of "an interior world so strong that no Reality can have the power of sadness or impossibility or limitation for him that it has over someone who hasn't managed to construct thought-fascinations to accompany him always."

Macedonio's formal play with the idea of the novel has a void, a melancholy, which is its movement. Because what is the eternal a compensation for? What is the pressure which leads to the invention of the eternal? The answer, dear mortal reader, is obvious.

The only things that can't die are the things that haven't begun. This is true of novels; and it is true of humans, too. And because this is true, there is a related hurt. Love, being an attachment to a mortal animal, is an irrational pleasure. It can only lead to pain. Transience invalidates all happiness: "suicide occurs in the moment of pleasure." And yet we carry on living, and loving.

Against this, Macedonio performs this manic, grief-stricken experiment with fiction: because if he can turn the reader into a fiction, if he can deny that anything really lives and dies, then he can save love as a meaningful emotion.

The real subjects of this lightly playful novel are the grave ones of death and love.

In one of the prologues to the novel, "The Essential Fantasmagoricalism of the World," Fernández writes: *"You believe that death awaits us, a termination of our persons and our love, and I don't believe that totalove can flourish in beings who believe that they are fleeting."* This is the novel's sad centre. Just as the President "doesn't believe in Death, but he can't love what he believes to be mortal, or what he does not know to be immortal . . ." And so using the game of fiction, Macedonio Fernández tries to invent a place of non-existence, where death no longer has meaning:

> In the construction of my novel, my fervent hope was to make of the novel a home for non-existence, for the non-existence necessary to The Lover, the Gentleman Who Doesn't Exist, to effect his very real hope, by putting him in some region or locale worthy of the subtlety of his being. His exquisite aspiration is to have a place somewhere in my novel while he waits for his love to return from the other side of death . . .

In his Museum, Macedonio Fernández invents a laboratory for investigating whether every philosophical question can be observed through the condition of falling in love. "Sexual love," wrote Freud in his paper "Observations on Love in Transference," "undoubtedly has a prime place among life's experiences . . . Everybody knows this, apart from a few weird fanatics, and arranges his life accordingly . . ." But Fernández knew this already. In his novel, he tests the possibility that all philosophical questions are only meaningful in relation to human relations: that all questions of infinity are really questions about love. Eterna is the beloved, after all: and she is also the eternal itself. "In other words, my novel has the sacred vocation and the allure to be the Where from which the Beloved will come, fresh, returned from a death that couldn't best her . . ."

And who else is a novelist in love with, if not the absent reader?

5.

And so it is that the process called fiction, the object called a novel, the entities called characters, will all be entreated to undergo various transformations.

And the playfulness of this novel is identical to its sadness. If Macedonio could truly carry out these experiments, if he really could make the reader doubt his own reality, then maybe he would have a chance to create the conditions for his happiness. But, of course, he can't. And yet the experiments are enchanting.

A character can be discontinuous ("this novel resembles life more than the 'bad' or realist novel, that is, the conventional novel. Continuity (identity) of the characters makes sorcerers out of the bad or conventional novelists: this continuity was never shown in a novel nor does it exist in life . . ."). There can be extra characters ("The reader should not entertain himself with the aforementioned security guard; he isn't ours; the one that belongs in our novel is standing on the opposite corner."). There can be characters borrowed for a single use and then kept on for fun. There can be a character who appears fleetingly in the novel before her official first appearance. And through the prologues, a proleptic novel will take place in hints, in the background—"a frightened General hesitating in the darkness on the basement stairs of the house, called 'La Novela,' while Eterna guides him, his trembling prompting her to say: But General, take hold of my skirt and walk confidently, I won't lead you astray." Yes, this novel will contain "loose pages, a total novelty for novels, as well as a model page and an exhibition of a day in the estancia 'La Novela,' a cast of discarded characters and a sort of character internship, and an absent character . . ."

As for the novel itself, Macedonio thinks that it should take place in the street:

> It would be even better if I had put into action the "novel that went out into the street" that I had proposed to a few artist friends. We would have really increased impossibilities in the city.
>
> The public would have seen our "scraps of art," novelistic scenes unfolding by themselves in the streets, catching glimpses of one another among the "scraps of the living," in sidewalks, doorways, domiciles, bars, and the public would dream it saw "life;" it would dream the novel but in reverse: in this case, the novel's consciousness is its fantasy; its dream the external execution of its themes.

And I think this fantasy is important. It is one of the oldest avant-garde wishes, after all, to make a novel which is in fact a reality: that art only has a value in so far as it stops being art. And Macedonio Fernández was an anarchist. He believed in transformative action.

The way in which the novel does indeed go out into the street, where the characters are sent out by the President to undertake a succession of small practical jokes—"the deployment of jokes as conquest"—is reminiscent of Borges's comic homage to Fernández, "The Man Who Will be President," with its plot to create a nervous breakdown generally in Buenos Aires, to multiply annoyances: "barrel organs wouldn't ever finish a melody, cutting it short halfway through; the whole city would be filled with useless objects, like barometers; the handrails on trams would be loosened, etc." And so lead to the election of Fernández as President.

The novel that goes out into the street is an ideal of artistic suicide: of a novel that suddenly stops being a novel at all.

All his technique is designed to improvise confusion between what is fictional and what is real. So that one of his characters can discuss with another character a scheme for making them live: to write their own story about characters within the novel: "'It's a story about 'novel characters,' not living persons, and it was conceived this way because in it I found a magical method for you and I to have life and be people, because it seems to me that the moment a character appears on a novel's page narrating another novels, he and all the characters listening to him assume a reality, and they only feel themselves to be characters that are narrated in the other novel: whether the reader likes it or not.'" And once the characters' reality is doubted, then Macedonio can then doubt his own: "It seems the author has had a fright; he thinks he's a character, trapped by his own invention. Will he recover? What if he stayed that way forever! This is the tenth time it's happened to him: for two years running, he's been thinking more or less every day about these characters, and sometimes he's known the sweat and suspension of feeling himself to be no more than a character! Is he really more real than they are? What is it to be real?"

But Macedonio needs more than his own self to become unreal. He needs the readers to help.

This novel itself, he writes, must be finished by its readers, who will then become characters, unreal, in their turn: "By offering this opportunity I insist that the true execution of my novelistic theory can only be achieved by various people, who have gotten together to read a different novel, to write it—so that they are reader-characters, readers of the other novel and characters in this one, will incessantly create themselves as existing persons, not 'characters,' as a counter-shock to the figures and images in the novel that they themselves are reading." For the reader is a character in a deeper way, too. Every reader, after all, is a skipreader: a "Skip-Around Reader." No one reads in order. But since this novel is itself not written in order, the Skip-Around Reader becomes an Orderly Reader. Freedom turns out to be manipulation: we are always in the grip of a higher power—prevented in our assumptions by the novelist. Which is another way of saying that we might be a dream: "you are so uncomfortable with the disorder I brought you with my prologues, in which the disorderly author makes you a figure of art and dreams, that you have flipped and are now a continuous reader to the point that you doubt the inveterate identity of the disorderly self."

6.

And I love this, the grandeur of the experiment, but I am still not sure.

In a very early essay, "The Nothingness of Personality," Borges wrote that "Life is truthful appearance"—there is no deeper reality: "Reality has no need of other realities to bolster it." And as further proof he quoted a line of Macedonio's: "Reality works in overt mystery."

This collapse of the fictional and the real, the appearance and depth, is what was discovered in Argentina, in Buenos Aires, in the early part of the twentieth century: and it is still not clear what conclusions should follow. We still, for instance, believe that a novel is a description of the world. But if Macedonio is right, then every novel is simply a construction.

And yet, I sadly want to say: this world, however, is not a construction. A character is not a person. The conditions for each are different. But I love the fervour and the patience and the melancholy with which Macedonio Fernández tried to prove this wasn't true: with the full weight of his grief at the world, the gravity with which he tried to be precise to the trauma of love. And in trying to prove this impossible truth, he discovered the limits of fiction.

7.

Early on in *The Museum of Eterna's Novel*, Macedonio Fernández credits himself with the invention of certain novelistic specialities:

> The Novel That Begins
> The Frustrated Novel (a manufacturing defect)
> The Novel That Went Out In The Street, with all its characters, to write itself.

The Prologue-Novel, whose story plays out, concealed from the reader, in prologues.

The Novel Written By Its Characters

The Inexpert Novel, which sets itself the task of killing off its "characters" separately, ignorant that creatures of literature always die together at the End of a reading.

The Novel in Stages

The Last Bad Novel—The First Good Novel—The Obligatory Novel.

It is such a witty, and noble, list. It makes me, in homage, want to invent my own list of possible futures for the novel—possible experiments with the ideas of the real and the reader:

The Novel with Only One Copy

The Novel as a Rewrite of Someone Else's Novel

The Novel with Only One Reader

The Infinite Novel

They seem, I have to admit, unlikely experiments. And then I remember Borges's own description of the problem of infinity as the problem of fiction within fiction, where he refers to the 602nd Arabian Night: "On that strange night, the king hears his own story from the queen's lips. He hears the beginning of the story, which includes all the others, and also—monstrously—itself. Does the reader have a clear sense of the vast possibility held out by this interpolation, its peculiar danger?" And it strikes me that one homage is always possible, one immediate experiment.

Yes, everyone can write their own preface to Macedonio's great novel of prefaces.

London, 2009

I first encountered the archive of Macedonio's manuscripts, note-books, photographs, and diaries in 2002, in the closet of an apart-ment in Buenos Aires's Cabellito district. I had come to Argentina as a young Fulbright scholar in search of Macedonio's son, Adolfo, who was his father's literary executor and posthumous editor, responsible for the meticulous work of typing out and arranging Macedonio's chaotic longhand. Since the bulk of Macedonio's publication was posthumous—including *The Museum of Eterna's Novel*— it is only thanks to Adolfo's meticulous care and patience that this book exists at all.

Unfortunately, the elderly Adolfo had died just a few months ear-lier, and the archive was in limbo. Perhaps because North American pilgrims to the shrine of Macedonio are few, or perhaps because I had come so far only to face disappointment, I was eventually put in touch with a friend of the family, in whose apartment the archive was temporarily stored. I read the manuscripts, under supervision and in secret, every day for two months, as clouds moved across the Southern Hemisphere's winter sky to settle over the river at dusk.

I inhaled the musty, yellowed pages, stroked my finger across the indentations made on the page by a thick pencil and a heavy, elderly hand, obsessively catalogued marginalia, stains on the paper, fingerprints in the ink, and even a crumb of something stuck to the page—perhaps evidence of Maceodnio's famous sweet tooth?—the fun and the frustration is, one cannot know. An archive is in many ways defined by what it cannot contain.

The most obvious piece missing from the archive is the writings that are commonly thought to have been lost because of Macedonio's own neglect for them. The story goes that he wrote on crumpled café napkins, that he used to light the stove or his cigarette with loose manuscript pages, or that he piled them up in suitcases, only to abandon them when he moved from one flophouse room to the next. Though this neglect for his own written production is a cornerstone of the Macedonio mythology, the enormous number of writings that have survived (over thirty notebooks, and five full manuscripts of *The Museum of Eterna's Novel*) suggest that perhaps rumors of Macedonio's disinterest in his writings have been greatly exaggerated.

Less obvious, and more real, missing pieces are the notebooks full of undeciphered pages. Macedonio did not type: every one of the manuscripts in his archive is handwritten. The early notebooks, like the diary or so-called "Book for Oneself" (*Libro para sí mismo*) are written in ink in the lovely calligraphy considered a courtesy and a grace in the nineteenth century. As he aged, however, Macedonio's hand grew ever crabbed, and his utensil—in the later notebooks usually a dull pencil—more easily smudged and blurred. These later notebooks are thus often illegible for long passages. The object-quality of the notebooks, their stubborn *thingliness*, stands in this case as a kind of maddening tease, as the words, though they are there on the page in clear and obvious reality, do not necessarily give way to intelligible meaning, especially in an author whose hand followed his meandering and fragmentary thoughts with such obsessive fidelity. Like Poe's purloined letter, some of these thoughts are hidden in plain view, illegible.

As physical and thus mortal objects, these manuscripts have a lifespan. They were almost all written on cheap dime-store paper, and many were written with highly acidic ink. This ink is slowly breaking down the wood fibers in the paper, which will eventually disintegrate even if they are kept under ideal conditions. But the immediacy of the stroke of the living hand on the page leaves its trace on these manuscripts in a way I can only describe in metaphysical terms. The marks are not always intelligible or identifiable: they are ciphers. The only certainty is that Macedonio once held his living hands to these pages. It's like laying one's ear to a train track to listen for the vibrations of a train that passed fifty years ago. Microscopically, they are there—and knowing that is the thrill that keeps your ear pressed to the tracks.

•

Macedonio Fernández (1874-1952) is best known in his native Argentina as the mentor of a young Jorge Luis Borges, who later wrote of his friend, "I imitated him to the point of plagiarism." This confession, however, belies the longstanding anxiety of influence between the two writers, and gives some insight into why Macedonio—as he

is affectionately known—is more of a local folk hero than an interna-
tionally renowned writer. There exists a Macedonio of Borges's invention, and this invented character's reticence, or failure, to publish
tends to reinforce Borges's quaint mythology of a man dedicated to
meditation, stillness, and only incidentally to the written word. Nevertheless, Macedonio wrote thousands of pages of manuscript in his
life, most of which remained unpublished when he died, in 1952. His
son, Adolfo de Obieta, organized and published these manuscripts,
serving as literary executor, editor, and high priest of the cult of
Macedonio until his death in 2002.

    The Museum of Eterna's Novel is Macedonio's most important work.
This is the first time it—or any of his considerable oeuvre—has been
translated into English in its entirety. He began what he called the
"first good novel" around 1925, at the height of his involvement with
the avant-garde literary scene in Buenos Aires. He would labor over
the book for the next twenty-seven years, producing five full manuscripts in total, the first of which was written out in longhand by his
lover, muse, and companion, Consuelo Bosch. Although *The Museum
of Eterna's Novel* eludes categorization, its many prologues and self-
conscious use of authorial persona often lead to its characterization
as an example of proto-postmodernism. Macedonio himself would
have shrugged off this label, and insisted instead that the novel is a
sketch for a metaphysics wherein love conquers death.

.

    The Museum of Eterna's Novel is written for what the author calls the
"skip-around reader." In an often hilarious but equally maddening
series of between fifty-seven and sixty prologues—depending on
whether you count the dedications, the post-prologue, and the blank
page dedicated to the reader's indecision—the novel postpones itself,
thwarting both the reader who tries to skip ahead (where to?) and
the dull "orderly" reader's desire for linearity. There are prologues
of salutation, prologues introducing the author and the characters,
prologue-letters to the critics, prologues about characters who were
rejected, a prologue of authorial despair and, of course, prologues
about prologuing.

    The Museum of Eterna's Novel is also dedicated to its main charac-
ter, the lovely Eterna, who has the power to change the past. She is at
once transparently allegorical, as the idea of eternal love against the
threat of death, and wonderfully real. *Museum* enshrines her laugh,

her changing expressions, black eyes and hair, her grace. She is also real biographically: in the manuscript dedication, the word "Consuelo" has been crossed out and replaced with "Eterna." Consuelo Bosch was Macedonio's longtime companion, patroness, and muse after the death of his wife; *The Museum of Eterna's Novel* is in a real sense the most earnest, complex, and heartwrenching of love poems. "I write this unnecessary book," he writes in "Introduction to Eterna," "because she wants to smile at her lover from outside this love, from the space of Art."

The novel takes place on an *estancia*, or country home, outside of Buenos Aires. The *estancia* is named "La Novela," and in it the characters share a domestic intimacy reflected in its prose. Much time is devoted to the small comings and goings of life at "La Novela," and the eventual abandonment of this placid domesticity in favor of the action of the novel—the conquest of Buenos Aires in the name of beauty. Thus *The Museum of Eterna's Novel* is also an ardent structure, dedicated to the suspension of time, its enclosure both still and fluid. The eternity it captures is intimate, domestic: kitchen conversations and stovetop kettles, the sound of eucalyptus leaves blowing against the eaves on wet afternoons.

The Museum of Eterna's Novel asks a simple question: how can we give ourselves fully to love in the face of the certainty of death? And it proposes itself as an answer, however awkwardly and provisionally, by creating a space where neither life nor death exist, only non-being and oblivion. Where there is love, there is no death, only forgetfulness.

As difficult and visionary and ambitious as the structure is, this concern is very simple, human, and understandable. Love opens all of us up to the possibility of loss. What makes Macedonio's story remarkable is how earnestly he wrestles with tigers that we all face. It isn't the felicity of his prose, or the prescience of his ideas—though his prose is often felicitous and his ideas often prescient. Rather, it's the open heart with which he takes up his pen and seeks, through its wanderings, to find a way to love the sound of the kettle on the stove, the crumbled *mate* leaves on the tablecloth, the arrangement of the furniture in the room—all the dull, pedestrian details of everyday life that clearly offer more irritation than fascination. And somewhere in these details, the tiny tinkerings that he inexhaustibly and minutely calibrates in every corner of his life, is the beloved. And in the beloved, in the other, there is passion, and death, and art, and eternity.

"I was born a *porteño*, and in a very 1874 sort of year. Shortly thereafter (though not at first) I began to be cited by a certain Jorge Luis Borges, and with such unabashed commendation, that, thanks to the risks incurred by his vehemence, I became the author of his best work."

—Macedonio Fernández,
in the Argentine literary magazine *Sur*

As Marcelo Ballvé recently observed, Macedonio invented Borges as much as Borges invented Macedonio. The difference is that it is more likely that a reader will have actually read Borges than Macedonio, whose prose is difficult and does not fit comfortably within any literary genre, and who has been much less widely translated. Like most people, I also came to Macedonio through Borges, in the wistful question that ends his prose poem "The Witness:" "What will die with me when I die? What pathetic or fragile form will the world lose? The voice of Macedonio Fernández, the image of a roan horse on the vacant lot at Serrano and Charcas, a bar of sulphur in the drawer of a mahogany desk?" Macedonio here is a voice—or the memory of a voice—that Borges alone possesses, and whose trace will disappear with him. The unusual name, and its casual inclusion in a list of vaguely eccentric, or perhaps anachronistic objects, catches the attention. It sets up a notion of Macedonio's voice as talisman, momento mori.

There is no easy way, then, to place Borges in an introduction to Macedonio's work that does not threaten to overwhelm or re-author the man he nevertheless called his mentor. Borges was a generation younger, and he "inherited" Macedonio's friendship from his father, who had attended law school with Macedonio. When the Borges family returned from Europe (where their stay had been extended by the outbreak of World War I), Macedonio was recently widowed, and his life was in airless limbo. He lived in a series of flophouses, having given up his law practice and sent his children to live with his mother and sister-in-law.

Before his wife died he was a regular, if somewhat eccentric, bourgeois man with occasional literary pretentions and an interest in philosophy, psychology, and music. A photograph from this time in his life shows a small man in a bowler hat with a severe, resigned expression, kneeling with his arms around two small children whose faces are blurred by motion. Now, in his grief but also in his freedom, he divested himself of all bourgeois responsibilities and dedicated himself to metaphysics. As a young man he corresponded with William James and read Schopenhauer and Kant—now he would begin his engagement with the mystery of consciousness in earnest.

Borges wrote that in those days he felt "Macedonio *is* metaphysics, he *is* literature." Nevertheless, the Macedonio of Borges's eulogy is not so much a man of letters as of conversation. His jokes, his observations, his anecdotes, and his cordial, almost quaint manner—this was his brilliance, not the writing he left behind. In Borges's construction, Macedonio was the Socrates to his Plato, the oral teacher whose words the disciple transcribed and transformed.

He was a *creole* Socrates, a New World Socrates, a founder of a new Argentine literature. Borges had spent his adolescence in Europe, and felt ill at ease, perhaps, in his homeland, which seemed backwards by comparison with the cafés of Madrid and Geneva. Macedonio, he writes, seemed to command a uniquely Argentine point of view on "certain eternal things." The humbleness of his surroundings, his fraternization with the prostitutes and confidence men with whom he shared his lodgings, and his age all contributed to this romantic image.

In his classic book of Buenos Aires essays, *The Man Who Is Alone and Waits (El hombre que está solo y espera)*, Raúl Scalabrini Ortíz writes: "Buenos Aires's first metaphysician and its only authentic philosopher is Macedonio Fernández." As the creole Socrates, then, Macedonio re-founded metaphysics and philosophy in an Argentine context. He's an archetype, a kind of distillation of what it is to think like an Argentine, of the particular poetics and mournful solitude of the South. That Macedonio is the only *authentic* philosopher of Buenos Aires implies that many others may pretend to the title. His reported disdain for publication and fame underpin that authenticity and add to his mystique. An authentic *porteño* philosopher discusses his ideas over a *cortado* in one of the city's cafés or bars, or over a *mate* in his home, at the kitchen table, on the porch of a country *estancia* while the eucalyptus trees rustle in the hot pampas wind. He disdains the pomposity of writing for publication, for he writes, as Borges once said of himself, for himself and his friends—as an afterthought to these cordial, lazy, endless hours of conversation.

In Argentina, Macedonio's people prefer to trade stories about his eccentricities rather than read his difficult books: how he gave his guitar away to a busboy who was passing on the street, how he founded an anarchist colony in Paraguay but gave up after one night of mosquitoes, how he slept in his clothes and fed sweets to the ants in his boarding house rooms. Very few of these stories are biographically true, or at least they cannot be verified—though what is known does support the image of an eccentric and a recluse. As his son and literary executor, Adolfo de Obieta once wrote, Macedonio's life is one of those "about which more will always be unknown than known," a quality that lends itself to literary gossip.

Borges wrote that "writing was no trouble for Macedonio Fernández. He lived (more than any other person I have ever known) to think. Every day he abandoned himself to the vicissitudes and surprises of thoughts as a swimmer is borne along by the current of a great river." The writing may have been easy, but reading Macedonio is often very challenging. Perhaps because they trace the errant line of his thoughts, his jokes and ideas and images are all presented at once, in rambling sentences with loose syntax and utterly chaotic diction. His ideas are complex, and they are stated in a complicated, ironic, and often contradictory way. He is consciously trying to make the reader uncomfortable and confused, and he was trying to publish at a time when postmodern literature was not yet a genre. As a visionary, his lot was to remain unrecognized in his time, except by a handful of avant-gardists who shared his vision. It may have suited him best—a man with more than his fair share of anxiety who became increasingly reclusive with age— to cultivate his mystique and work on his manuscripts in solitude.

•

In the mythology, Macedonio's role is not only as Socrates, but as grieving widower. His poem, "Elena Bellamuerte" (Elena Beautiful Death) is one of his few non-posthumous publications. It is a gorgeous, keening lament and celebration of the innocent, childlike quality of his dead beloved—she the occulted, the awaited. He likens himself to Poe, who also had a dead child wife at the center of his poetics. Here, too, was the motionless metaphysician, the prophet of artistic-non-being and the nothingness of death, the champion of oblivion and the prince of thought: a man utterly stunned by grief, overwhelmed by guilt, confused and frightened and unable to come to terms with life.

The Museum of Eterna's Novel, however, was written during a second chapter in this story, one that has long remained hidden, mostly because both protagonists wanted it that way. Sometime in 1925 Macedonio met and fell in love with a wealthy widow named Consuelo Bosch de Sáenz Valiente. They spent the next twenty-seven years as an artistic and romantic couple, though they kept this relationship a secret and never married. Twenty years his junior, Consuelo also died in 1952, meaning that the partnership lasted for the remainder of both of their lives.

Consuelo gave Macedonio back the experience of love and the desire to create. She gave him back his life and allowed him to re-shape it to better suit him—an artist's life, a thinker's life, not the life of a lawyer and family man. She came from a very old and wealthy family, and this position allowed her to support him financially. He lived on her country estate and also in her house in Buenos Aires. Nevertheless, she called him the Maestro and always used formal address when speaking to him in public, as he did to her. She deferred to him as an artist and creator, thus easing the awkwardness, for a man of his generation and background, of her financial patronage. Instead, she was the muse and the benefactress, and the secretary. She copied out by hand—largely from his dictation—the entire first manuscript of *The Museum of Eterna's Novel.*

> "The death asked for love's
> initiation is not
> the death lovers fear.
> Day through night,
> not night through day."

Borges remembers: "Two fears throbbed in back of Macedonio's smiling courtesy and somewhat distant air; the fear of pain and of death. The latter led him to deny the self, so there could be no self to die." The fear of death, or perhaps more accurately the inevitable *encounter* with death, is the core of *The Museum of Eterna's Novel.* The President gathers together his friends at an estancia in the countryside outside of Buenos Aires called "La Novela." This President is more like a spiritual leader, for he assembles his characters for the purpose of helping them see that they are only characters: their only death is artistic (at the end of the novel), their only being, novelistic. He gives them training maneuvers to practice this "artistic-non-being."

Non-existence and persona are the principle tools with which *The Museum of Eterna's Novel* builds this theme. In addition to the President, other persona are obviously stand-ins for Macedonio himself.

The Gentleman Who Does Not Exist, The Lover, and the Author are all characters in the novel and are used to express different elements of his theory of artistic non-being. The Reader appears frequently as well, voicing his concerns and confusions, yet all the while also drawn into the net of non-being and recognizing the "character like" nature of his being—that is, his non-being, his inability to die. The characters, meanwhile, demand to live and seek various escape routes from the novel.

Even as the novel denies the self and, by extension, death, it also despises novelistic pretention, particularly realism or what Macedonio calls "the novel of hallucination." Why should we want to dream the same dull things that happen in the real world? Novels are for novelistic non-being; they are also tools to elicit in ordinary people the sense of their own non-being. Thus the structure is mutually determining: the novel writes us, and we write the novel, and in this way death is transformed.

•

Let's return to *The Museum of Eterna's Novel* simple, even naïve question. How can we risk love when death is inevitable? Macedonio, for all of his many eccentricities, seems to be a man determined to take on questions that we all face. Even his quirks have their origins in everyday fears that characterized his life and times—fear of the dentist's drill, fear of tramcars, fear of dogs—and his quests are more Quixotic than heroic.

As a young man, Macedonio filled a diary with earnest exhortations and meditations on the abbreviation SFz—*ser feliz*, to be happy. He wants so desperately to find joy in the small and dull aspects of everyday life, and he holds his wife and his mother up as examples of good people who are not annoyed with these details. He writes that he suffered, between 1894 and 1903, a terrible period of desperation. He intricately calculates hours and days of *SFz*, fills pages with prescriptions not for joy, necessarily, but for contentment: *eat very little, wear your long underwear when the weather gets cold, don't complain, don't smoke too much, get enough sleep. Remember the good people, and do not make them unhappy. Stop touching your mustache. Make ample use of toothpicks.*

Don't we all wish we weren't irritable with those who love us, that we could keep from eating the things that make us feel bad, that we could be liberated from annoying tics, like talking too much or biting our nails? That we could be truly good, not in some abstract way, but in all of these little, maddening ways? And yet how few of us would turn these anxieties and preoccupations into art? How many of us would set down the world and take up another, in which these questions are the only passion? The method is madcap; the intent is desperately human.

.

Because *Museum* was transcribed, edited, and published posthumously, it's important to realize that there's a certain hypergraphic quality to Macedonio's manuscripts. Compulsive lists and fragmentary observations appear without any organizational structure and without respect for the linear form of the notebook or even the page. He obsessively traced the patterns of his psyche onto the page.

In the *Museum* manuscripts there is almost no editing. That is to say, Macedonio seems rarely if ever to have returned to a passage once it was written. Multiple versions of the same prologue exist, or multiple treatments of the same idea, and Ana Camblong's 1993 annotated edition of *Museum* traces these repetitions and their variations. But mostly one sees Macedonio adding, not subtracting: reading a passage, perhaps (towards the end of his life) one that Adolfo had typed up for him, he makes a few underlinings or minimal corrections and then writes another two paragraphs on the bottom half of the page. *Museum*'s logic is one of supplementarity as well as deferral: there's a kind of additive logic, wherein ideas, rather than being illustrated or explained, are repeated often enough that they start to take intuitive shape for the reader.

It is very much a book that teaches you how to read it. It's not so much a question of showing versus telling, since neither form seems to apply. The reader is simply thrown into the book as Heidegger (someone for whom Macedonio would have had only scorn, given the importance of death for his ontology) says we are thrown into the world: there is no point of entrance or origin, merely a *given world* that unfolds in its own time.

.

How to translate someone who deliberately tangles his words, uses antiquated language, and who writes at the speed of thought, without regard for syntax and punctuation? Macedonio was a famed conversationalist. Borges often identifies Macedonio not so much by name as by voice, tobacco roughened, distant, yet very genteel. Macedonio's voice becomes a metonym for his presence and his uniqueness—an ineffable quality, physically and temporally constrained by the body of the man himself. As a translator, therefore, my choices have consistently been to preserve this voice.

Macedonio's prose is best characterized as *baroque*, for several reasons. First, because it is complicated and ornate. Sentences may go on for pages, without any temperance with regard to punctuation, with open parentheses dangling and semicolons propping up impossibly convoluted clauses. An idea begins, only to be interrupted by a different thought, then the first idea returns without fanfare or apology. Secondly, the writing is baroque because the diction is antiquated, if not necessarily high-register. Wherever possible, I have tried to capture this quaint quality, almost as if there were lexical mothballs scattered liberally in the closet of his prose, giving it the air of your grandmother's steamer trunk. Macedonio was very aware of his *grand vieux* image among the young vanguardists, and it's possible he cultivated this in his writing. But Macedonio was also a man whose formative years were in the nineteenth century, and who was conscious that he was coming late, as he so often joked, to authorship. Like Chaplin's tramp in the film *Modern Times*, he is alternately befuddled, entangled, and irritated by newfangled contraptions, by the speed that characterizes modern life.

These persona—the Chaplin's tramp style of the Author, or the melancholy President, or the gallant Gentleman Who Does Not Exist—are one of *The Museum of Eterna's Novel*'s main delights. And, as I described earlier, they form the core of the novel's metaphysical project to promulgate artistic non-being. Wherever possible, then, I have made decisions that favor the development of these persona, inevitably at the expense of what I consider a misguided fidelity to each word on the page. For example, I have translated the character's name *Deunamor* as The Lover. Literally, *Deunamor* means "Of A Love," or "Ofalove," to preserve the neologism, as *Deunamor* is actually a phrase: *De un amor*. Of course the combination of words is much more felicitous in Spanish than in English (where indeed it's almost impossible to pronounce it as a single word), and their meaning would be obscured by the neologism in a way that it is not for Spanish speakers. By calling *Deunamor* The Lover, then, I have selected the most important part of his character—his love, the fact that he has only one love to which he dedicates himself—and emblematized it in the meaningful, but not necessarily perfectly "faithful," rendition The Lover.

Translation is an encounter with a textual other that both demands and defies an ethical response. Here the text is posthumous, and so it carries with it the sort of delicate intimacy of a draft: it was not yet ready for publication, if indeed its author would ever have thought it so. It demands a certain tenderness; just as it will teach you how to read it, it taught me how to render it, as I listened for the traces of the remarkable man who built an ardent structure of his grief and, ultimately, his belief in the redemptive power of love.

MUSEUM OF "ETERNA'S" NOVEL AND MELANCHOLY'S CHILD, THE "SWEETHEART" OF AN UNDECLARED LOVER

With a Finale of Academic Death: An artistic and realistic, though prudently deployed presentation of Absence; or, the voluntary equivalent of a death, sweetened.

And, a proceeding act of the Character's Training as gesture of respect towards the Reading Public, thus guaranteeing that for once its efforts are fittingly rewarded.

DEDICATION TO MY CHARACTER ETERNA

In Eterna I have known the maximum impulse to piety without vice, nothing confused or demented in the act of abnegation and mercy. Nothing that can be published, spoken, or otherwise evoked can prepare the mind for her fulminous and total impulse, her Act of Pity. The most gallant Promptness of spirit moves in Eterna's every step, a total and instantaneous impulse, an altruistic leap towards succor or engladdening or consolation.

In
A Flash
I encountered
The sublimely Swift

It was in Eterna; and nobody saw it.
Her light shone and nobody saw it, not in anything.

Reality and the I, or principally the I, the Individual (whether or not the World exists) only gives itself fully in the altruistic moment of mercy (and of satisfaction) without fusion, that is, in plurality. The end point of What Is, of World, and is its only ethic is the non-instinctive act of Mercy, keeping for itself the lucid discernment of plurality, without confusing the Other with Itself: to still be other, while living for another.

To
A Superlative Individual

Capable of stopping time. Of compensating for death. Of changing the past.

And, so obliging with her Self, to kill
  With her No
  With her forgetfulness
  With her comicalness
  With her reproach

But ever melancholy over her unrelinquished past, her unappeasable past.

3

WHAT IS BORN AND WHAT DIES

Today we release to the public the last bad novel and the first good novel.[1] Which one will be the best? In order to prevent the reader from opting for his preferred genre at the other's expense, we've arranged that these two novels be sold as an indivisible set; considering that we're unable to impose a mandatory reading of both novels, at least there remains the consolation of having devised an obligatory purchase of what one does not want, because it cannot be untangled from what one does. Therefore, the Obligatory Novel will either be the last bad novel or the first good novel, depending on the reader's taste. There is one absurdity that must not be permitted: that the reader thinks the two novels are equally good, and congratulates us on such comprehensive "good fortune."

The Bad Novel deserves its homage; this is mine. This way, nobody can say I don't know how to do things poorly, that I didn't have the talent for this novelistic genre; that is, the bad. Thus I'll show the full scope of my capacities in the same day. It is true that I have run the risk of mixing up the bad thoughts of *Adriana Buenos Aires* with the good ones that constantly occurred to me for *Eterna's Novel*, but it's up to the reader to collaborate and sort out the confusion. Sometimes I found myself perplexed, especially when the wind blew the manuscript pages around the room. Then I wouldn't know which page belonged in which novel because, as you know, I wrote a page of each novel per day; nothing could help me because the pagination was the same, the quality of ideas, paper, and ink were all equal–I had made an effort to be equally intelligent in each, to keep my twin novels from quarreling. How I suffered, not knowing if the brilliant page before me belonged in the last bad novel or the first good one!

1. Already in *The Newcomers Paper and the Continuation of the Nothing* (1944) these novels were so announced. As the Warning to *Adriana Buenos Aires* says, with its publication the original plan was restored, because although they were not sold as a set, the two novels have nevertheless appeared almost simultaneously. (*Editor's Note–Adolfo de Obieta*)

Let the Reader take charge of my agitation and trust in my promise of a forthcoming goodbad novel, firstlast in its genre, in which the best of the bad of *Adriana Buenos Aires* and the best of the good of *Eterna's Novel* will be allied, and in which I will recollect the experience gained in my efforts to convince myself that something good was bad, and vice versa, because I needed it in order to finish a chapter of one or the other . . .

PROLOGUE TO ETERNITY

When the world hadn't yet been created and there was only nothingness, God heard it said: it's all been written, it's all been said, it's all been done. "Maybe that's already been said, too," he perhaps replied out of the ancient, yawning Void. And he began.

A Romanian woman once sang me a phrase of folk music and I have since found it tens of times in different works from different composers of the past four hundred years. Indubitably: things do not begin; or they don't begin when they are created. Or the world was created old.

PERSPECTIVE

There's nothing worse than sloppiness, unless it's the facile perfection of solemnity. This book will be eminently sloppy, which is to say it will commit the maximum discourtesy possible to its readers—except an even greater and all too common discourtesy: the perfect, empty book.

I've done what I can to hide the seams in the patchwork passages of my novelistic prose, which brings with it inexhaustible swatches of revision; and I do myself the service of confessing what no one will notice, because if ever a book demanded hard work it's this one, and I believe that all art is labor, and very arduous labor at that.

But I know that a highly personal, compensatory immortality awaits me: Generations of readers will pass the shop window, and nobody will stop to buy the book.

This will be the novel that's thrown violently to the floor most often, and avidly taken up again just as often. What other author can boast of that?

A novel whose incoherencies of plot are patched together with *transversal cuts* that show what all the characters of the novel are doing at every moment.

An irritating read, this book will annoy the reader like no other, with its false promises and inconclusive and incompatible methodology; nevertheless it's a novel that will not cause reader evasion, since it will produce an interest in the soul of the reader that will leave him allied to its destiny—it's a novel that needs a lot of friends.

In the end, the final organization and revisions took me three frenzied days; happily, I wear detachable shirt cuffs, and I had kept all of the ink-stained ones ever since I began to conceive of the novel; about a thousand of them have all of my notes, in addition to twelve thousand composition books and notepads and loose pages: I threw it all into a corner of my room. Once I made it out of bed, I flung myself to the floor, where I stayed for three days; I raved and I cried, a hundred times over I howled: This is the last time I write for publication.

If Eterna had seen me, she would have laughed so hard it would have almost made her sick. It's unhealthy to laugh when you don't want to laugh, and this is the way she laughed in the face of this Hysteria. She never understood Hysteria—what a hopeless creature!—and I appreciate it so much, and it's so essential to me that I procured for her an expensive and extremely ornamental cigarette holder made of vinagrol, a material whose discovery I commissioned. When it solidifies, it may be made into cigarette holders for smoking hysterics. It is this characteristic of Hysteria, so typical of the male of the species, that particularly excites the fatal explosion of Laughter in Eterna. "My my, what a tantrum!" she exclaims, and thus can't help but make it worse. One could be on the point of death, choked with passion by the dexterity and patience with which, during a long telephone call that she herself initiated and which began with words of soothing kindness, one has been brought to the ultimate in ridiculous desperation, making one feel he had indeed been quite intemperate.

This is the mystery of Eterna that only I know: she finds more goodness in the sentiment of men than in the soul of women, yet she would like to correct this defect in the male character. There are therefore two Mysteries of Eterna: her felicity in turning a distant phrase; her felicity in her perception of the Ridiculous, to the point of making not only herself but others ill with her own Laughter. Thus she is a Mystery I have never grasped.

Later:

All human suffering, without a father and son having to fall in love with the same woman, without desire between a brother and sister, without kinship, or aberration, or blindness, or madness—all human suffering makes Tragedy and

All the blessings of human life, without the millionaire marrying the factory girl, without a happy marriage between a blind man and an ugly woman; without power or glory, but for Passion, the only certainty.

PROLOGUE TO MY AUTHORIAL PERSONA

The greatest risk one runs in publishing a novel at this stage in life is that nobody knows your age; mine is 73, and I hope that it will rescue me from a potential judgment such as: "For the First Good Novel, it isn't bad at all, and since it's the author's first novel, we predict a brilliant future, if he perseveres in his aesthetic conjurings with strong will and discipline. In any case, we'll await his future work before rendering a definitive judgment." With this kind of postponement, I'll be left out of posterity, and prematurely at that. It's not flattery at every age when the critics postpone the judgment reserved for novices and squander all confidence on our future.

Moreover, I had planned to publish this novel twenty-two years after the earth completely exhausts its supply of petroleum, because a fortune teller once told me that at the same moment the world will run out of the ample supply of readerly yawns on which we presently rely. Unfortunately, the World Readers Union has promised to take revenge on a certain writer, reserving for him—he just announced his forthcoming work—all the abundant yawns at its disposal and thus severely limiting the available supply for my no less anticipated novel. So you see what good luck it is to be a writer. With this guarantee— which nobody until now has enjoyed—who wouldn't happily hurl himself into the public eye?

Also I've noticed, since becoming an author, how grateful I am to the man who says, "I've read everything." I'm counting on him to come through at an opportune moment, as this melancholy item just appeared in *La Razon*: "On The Impossibility of Reading Everything." I'm hurrying to publish my novel so that it may appear before the commencement of this exasperating impossibility.

ONWARD

This is a celebrated novel in press, so often promised that the author himself isn't willing to bet on when it will come out.

Nobody dies in it—although the book itself is mortal—since as people of fantasy, the characters all die together at the end of the story: it's an easy extermination. Just as the sacristan puts out the candles at the end of mass, authors run the risk of forgetting things and repeating someone's death, because they take upon themselves the unnecessary task of meting out a little expiration to each protagonist—so as not to leave the fish out of water, the "character" out of the novel.

What's more, I'm sure no living man was ever in a narrative, since physiological characters, besides being hampered by fatigue and various indispositions—which is why one never sees protagonists falling ill and taking cures, because their job is only to represent falling ill, and to continue with an active performance of illness and death—are of a realist aesthetic, and our aesthetic is creative.

This is a work of the imagination not lacking in plot—so much so that it runs the risk of exploding out of the binding—and it's such a precipitous plot that it's already started in the title, to allow time to fit everything in; the reader comes late if he comes after the cover.

In this novel everything is known, or at least confirmed, so no character is forced to publicly display his ignorance, that is, that he doesn't know what is happening to him, or that the author doesn't know what is happening to him, or that he is maintaining the character's ignorance out of a lack of trust. You never see our protagonists exclaim: "Dear Lord, what is this? What should I think? What do I do now? When will this suffering end?" The reader doesn't know what to answer; distressed, he gets it wrong, and restricts himself to giving notice.

This must be what happens to authors:

1) They haven't publicized their novel enough.

2) They don't know how to render "the unsayable" with "ineffable" style.

3) They still believe that sonatas, paintings, verses, and novels all need titles.

In this Novel, the Impossibility of situations and characters, that is, the sole criterion in classifying something as artistic (without the complications of History, or Physiology), has been so cultivated that nobody—no one versed in daily impossibilities, or anyone with even a passing acquaintance with the impossible—could, by alleging that facts or characters were as familiar as their neighbors, deny the relentless fantasy of our tale.

It would be even better if I had put into action *the "novel that went out in the street" that I had proposed to a few artist friends. We would have really increased impossibilities in the city.*

The public would have seen our "scraps of art," novelistic scenes unfolding by themselves in the streets, catching glimpses of one another among the "scraps of the living," in sidewalks, doorways, domiciles, bars, and the public would believe it saw "life;" it would dream the novel but in reverse: in this case, the novel's consciousness is its fantasy; its dream the external execution of its scenes. But we would need another theory in addition to the one we just sustained, that of Impossibility as the criterion for Art.

This novel's very existence is novelesque, thanks to having been so often announced, promised, and then dropped, and any reader who understands it is novelesque, too. Such a reader would make himself known by the label of fantastic reader. This reader of mine would be very well-read among all the many reading publics.

THE AUTHOR ALSO SPEAKS

I sometimes anxiously wonder how this sublime and difficult novel—difficult now for the reader, but first for me—could be forgettable, considering it contains a frightened General who's hesitating in the darkness on the basement stairs of the house, called "La Novela," while Eterna guides him, and his trembling prompts her to say: But General, take hold of my skirt and walk confidently, I won't lead you astray.

Also you will read how it happened that Eterna, one windless day in Buenos Aires, sent a messenger—with one arm in a sling and a paralytic hand—to cross the whole city with a lighted candle pressed into a contraption in his hand. He was on the point of burning himself because nobody had volunteered to blow the candle out, and he didn't have enough breath to blow it out himself because he was a character in this novel and was consequently exhausted by the "efforts" that the dignity and glory of appearing in such an indubitably sublime novel so imperiously demands. Reduced to heroic ashes, the messenger was left in a reliquary, not because the *porteño* (as the inhabitants of Buenos Aires are known) isn't the most benevolent and pious of men, but because so many scholars, writers, journalists, politicians, capitalists, communists, religionists both old and new, and penicillinists, have the *porteños* so full of promises and so lacking in a sense of reality and sincerity that—they didn't trust the messenger! They didn't trust Eterna! And so they begrudged the most endearing messenger that ever lived even a breath of assistance.

Also it will be discovered that I gave life to the nonexistence of the Lover,[1] just as Posterity has given life to such illustrious nonexistences

---

1. In *Índice de la nueva poesía americana* (*The Anthology of New American Poetry*) (1926) there appears a "Salutation from the Lover to the Non-Existent Gentleman—Novel of Hope," included in *Miscellany* (volume VII of the *Complete Works*). The Lover appears again in *Not All Consciousness is Wakefulness*, which bears precisely this subtitle: "A Compilation of the Papers Left by a Novel Character Created By Art, the Lover, the Gentleman Who Doesn't Exist, the Student of His Hopes;" in "Solution" and "Conclusion" the aforementioned persona explicates his metaphysical doctrine, which correlates with that of the present novel. (*Editor's Note—Adolfo de Obieta*)

as authors, making them out of nothing in the name of glory. Another nonexistence given life by operas, novels, and poems is unrequited love, which, if it is actually love, is a structural impossibility. Innumerable nonexistent things have been invented: today there is a whole other world of nonexistences (the Unconscious, duty, synesthesia, lots of "Gods" from various "religions"). Permit me just this one inexistence in my novel: The Gentleman Who Doesn't Exist; it's necessary to endow a work of art with such a character, so that the others can show off their existence. The one nonexistent character gives life to the others by contrast.

And the Lover agrees to put at our novel's disposition all of his nonexistence, as long as it lasts, without the fear of putting it at risk by entering into a "life of art;" this life enchants him less than his nonexistence, and to this he prefers the "altruexistence:" existence for others, which is to say, love. The only thing he won't risk is to live for the sake of living, or longevity, with birthdays.

With such rich elements I intend to make the first "novel," and not only first of the day it appears, in the morning, the moment when all novels have their minute of primacy. I have tarried too long in Literature; I must urge myself to get up early, since the slow-footed are always hurrying towards something: that is, to get to a place that isn't behind. It's not yet late in the genre "novel:" I will start behind. I repeat: I aim to write the first genuinely artistic novel. It will also be the last of the protonovels: mine will make last of what came before it, since it no longer insists upon its own past.

For all this I believe, as Author, to have credited myself with the following novelistic specialties:

The Novel That Begins

The Frustrated Novel (a manufacturing defect)

The Novel That Went Out In The Street, with all its characters, to write itself.

The Prologue-Novel, whose story plays out, concealed from the reader, in prologues.

The Novel Written By Its Characters

The Inexpert Novel, which sets itself the task of killing off its "characters" separately, ignorant that creatures of literature always die together at the End of a reading.

The Novel in Stages

The Last Bad Novel—The First Good Novel—The Obligatory Novel.

TO THE CRITICS

Suicide has made more than one mediocre author glorious before he's able to achieve that sobering "second edition:" making his a suicide that waits until it's justified. But I've taken more precautions against true suicide, which is to survive in the face of failure. Success is mostly editing, that's what makes things nice. To edit is the other great Power; thus, this novel, started at age thirty, continued at fifty and at seventy-three, has finally achieved supremacy: a person of Good Taste as the third author and as a result the editor of all three. In the end I'll be the author of a letter to the critics, a sort of "open letter" but for the living: suicide is not something you can edit out.

LETTER TO THE CRITICS

I'm the only one who understood you, gentlemen; the first who grasped your basic vocation: those eternally in hope of Perfection, who are daily reduced to eulogizing book binding, driven to it by the continual failure of the poem, the novel, the printed word, one after the other and day after day; you, gentlemen, are the only lovers and connoisseurs of Perfection. No such thing for the writers, the publishers of sketches, hasty books, opportune books, party books; someday Perfection will come in the form of a book, just as you rightly hoped and planned: until now Perfection has only been seen in the grace and moral power of certain men and women, known to all of us, who will never gain either historical or name recognition.

But it's good that you wait, and I'm sure the day Perfection appears as a Book you will all applaud, unanimously and immensely gratified.

Writers have always understood that for some time now we should have been in compliance with this critical attitude. But knowing how terribly fatiguing it is to construct a novel according to strict artistic standards, and what little hope there is of getting it right, not only do we suffer, but we also waste our talents since we don't write the Book, and in waiting to write, we forget the nicety of waiting to find perfection in the efforts of others.

I didn't find an easy way to execute my own artistic theory. My novel is flawed, but I would like to be recognized as the first who has attempted to use that prodigious instrument, the commotion of consciousness—that is, the novelistic character in its proper efficiency and virtue. By this I mean the total *commotion of consciousness of the reader, and not the trivial occupation of the attention with a particular, precarious, ephemeral topic: itself. With this and some other thoughts formulated in the course of the book, I approach this Perfection you gentlemen expect, and set an example as well: a rigorous doctrine of the literary art.*

If I'm wrong, I won't be the first, or the last. You may give me the maximum sentence.

I know very well that my work will keep you waiting in your quest for

Perfection, but perhaps I may succeed in whetting your appetite. If your appetite is whetted, then my book was good enough.

I realized that all you really know is what Perfection is not.

—*M.F.*

INTRODUCING ETERNA

Hesitation.

I've had some days of my own like those winter days of storm and sunshine, tremulous days that burn out for moments at a time and make the world a spectacle of the turn of Indecision's screw. After I first met Eterna I wandered in such darkness and depression that I vacillated between her, Art, and Mystery. Now resolved to be unlost, I have since lived for discovery.

Even when I was able to achieve faith in myself, only faith in her was always ready at hand.

And I write this unnecessary book simply because she wants to smile at her lover from outside this love, from the space of Art.

The book is not hard to write at all if it is of little importance. I already did it a long time ago, as an initiate in skepticism, not in art but that which would conserve for us some kind of reference for Art.

The storm birds will not hover over our love, they will not cross its path.

But a certain shadow of the End, of concealing . . .

When it comes we'll narrow ourselves, drawing in our bodies and our clothing so that the pale terror that surrounds us cannot touch them.

All that is sad in her eyes is exalted in my being, my being of hope. And the instant passes. And passes again, and I did it, I had to split open this shadow, so it never returns.

You still don't believe it. I didn't see you coming either. The impossibility that you are. The impossibility of an Answer to death, yet I have it. The all-love that you are; the all-knowing that was mine.

Whether you exist or not, I dedicate this work to you; beauty eternal, you are at the very least what is real in my spirit.

A HOME FOR NON-EXISTENCE

In the construction of my novel, my fervent hope was to make of the novel a home for non-existence, for the non-existence necessary to The Lover, the Gentleman Who Doesn't Exist, to effect his very real hope, by putting him in some region or locale worthy of the subtlety of his being. His exquisite aspiration is to have a place somewhere in my novel while he waits for his love to return from the other side of death, the one he named Bellamuerte, beautiful death, she who made death beautiful when she smiled at its coming. Only her Beauty died: a beauty made of separation and concealing, for death engenders all the beauty of Reality: it separates lovers, there is no other death. One does not die for oneself, nor is there death for he who has not loved; nor is there beauty that does not proceed from death, nor death that does not proceed from love, since death is what accounts for the exaltation of the Idyll-Tragedy, the idyll exalted because of a fear of death and the tragedy made of the deep sorrow of an idyll destroyed.[1]

In other words, my novel has the sacred vocation and the allure to be the Where from which the Beloved will come, fresh, returned from a death that couldn't best her, that didn't need Her to purify itself. It only needed her to worry the Lover, which is why she'll come fresh from death, not resuscitated but reborn, smiling just as she did when she left, as if her years-long absence lasted only an instant.[2]

---

1. Cf.: "The Idyll-Tragedy" in *Miscellanea*, as well as other references in this novel. (*Editor's Note—Adolfo de Obieta*)

2. M.F. had thought of consecrating a book to the "Ella" named or alluded to in various passages and who he later characterized as "character with the being of being awaited." In a letter written in 1932 to Ramón Gómez de la Serna (in the *Epistolario*) he says: "I'll soon finish my *Novel of Eterna* and my metaphysics *Ella* (theory of the Eternity of Figure, Feeling, and Memory)", and from here I'll start with a new page:

"Explanation. Having lived from a young age among poets, thinkers, musicians and statesmen, the inclination to occupy the public's attention and to leave a public record neither dominates me nor repulses me. For the first time, already in the shadows and the superfluities of so-called life, the impulse to publish and

The droning bees of Life will alight on the new smile of the returned woman, just as they did in her departing smile, finding for a time that both smiles were fresh and united in an ever-present time, an adamantine time that breath cannot corrupt.

The vigil of The Lover was also pure and singular. His non-existence, which is purer than death, gives him the power, "among equals," to marry her again—as if she had died without confusion, or shame.

---

perpetuate a public persona and a public action has appeared to me, which probably won't happen again. So it is that I enter the world of professionals in the expression of thought and feeling just in time to leave it without any pretension possible, neither possessing nor mourning the tact and vigor of the profession; it's better to beg pardon and aid beforehand so that my ambition to win a bit of glory for this name (an ambition that She will look upon with disapproval and pity) and principally, to win a bit of sympathy and knowledge of this person, her character and her actions." (*Editor's Note—Adolfo de Obieta*)

WE ARE A LIMITLESS DREAM AND ONLY A DREAM.
WE CANNOT, THEREFORE, HAVE ANY IDEA
OF WHAT NOT-DREAMING MAY BE

Every existence, every time, is a sensation, and each one of us is only this, always and forever. Where does a feeling or a sensibility get any notion of what might be a non-feeling, like time without passing? Only things that happen in our states of consciousness and senses exist. Only our eternity, an infinite dream identical to the present, is certain.

But you will say that there are dreams that end, or rebel dreams that we cannot recover: there are dreams that conceal themselves, concealments, perhaps, of those who once existed but who we will never see or know again.

These concealments only exist for a hesitant Dreamer: there are dreams that clamor to return to the plenitude of the overflowing soul, itself a shadowless certainty as soon as we dream it.

In our hesitant dreaming, who knows how many times we have bid farewell to a fantasy of those who may return to us, how often have we disbelieved, denying the full and eternal vision that someone Returning from Concealment can bring![1]

---

1. Cf.: "Majesty" in Miscellanea. (*Editor's Note—Adolfo de Obieta*)

FOR READERS WHO WILL PERISH
IF THEY DON'T KNOW WHAT THE NOVEL IS ABOUT

(In which it is observed that the readers who skip around in a book are nevertheless complete readers. Moreover, when something like skip-around literature is inaugurated—as it is here—they should exercise caution, and read in order, if they want to continue being skip-around readers. Equally, the author is surprised to discover that although he is an out-of-order man of letters, he likes skip-around readers just as much as the ones who read in order, and to persuade the reader he has found this good argument: he who reads everything to the end (since it's lazy to read out of order and disrupt the frame) will be mortified by this novel, saying to himself: "I read it in bits and pieces; very good novel, but a little disjointed, very truncated.")

Disorderly reader, I do not ask you—unconfessed—to read all of it, or to stop reading all of my novel, what with the pagination having been unraveled in vain for you, but you should know that in the book in which the reader will finally be read, *Biography of a Reader*, it disconcertingly happened that with such a trench-riddled book the disorderly reader had no other recourse than to read in order, so as to maintain the disorder of the text, since the book was out of order before . . . I do not ask your forgiveness for giving you an out-of-order book that, as it is, would be an interruption for you, because you interrupt yourself on your own and you are so uncomfortable with the disorder I brought you with my prologues, in which the disorderly author makes you a figure of art and dreams, that you have flipped and are now a continuous reader to the point that you doubt the inveterate identity of the disorderly self.

If you have to read all of it, a bit of forewarning. Don't go around trying a little bit of my novel here and there to see if it's finished, if it needs sugar or if it's too cold; you'd do better to do as my butler does when he ties on a napkin and takes up knife and fork "just for a taste," as he meekly tells the cook.[1] I've made you an orderly reader thanks to a work full of prefaces and such vague titles that you have finally been trapped by the unexpected continuity of your reading.

Now I can't keep you happy any longer. I've already advanced you all the postponements that I've been able to cook up: I don't have any more prologues until after the novel. How it oppresses me, this artistic endeavor to which I have committed myself! I still don't have any true comprehension of the theory of the novel, let alone an aesthetic or plan for my own.[2]

Very well, as for the point of the title of this prologue, which is to say, as for the reader who is bothered because he doesn't know everything in the novel:

It's true that "the Traveler then uttered a few words, inaudible from this novel, and, waving goodbye, *went away*" (travelers tend to do that). My novel also waves, but it is mortified that one of its characters hasn't finished reading everything. It's curious about the story it's going to tell, a reading of itself, or better a narrative of itself, since self-love is inherent in Art (for Art, and to Art). Art is that which is written without knowing what will happen, and thus has to be written while docilely discovering and then resolving each situation, each problem of action or expression. As an author, I despair of my novel every time I am slow to finish a scene. The novel is enamored (and Eterna is not) of itself (Eterna's not in love with herself, either: in a disregard of self that is immensely beautiful and which fills me with sadness and reverence, she also disregards my daily pleas that she love herself. Is it that neither she nor I should love ourselves or love at all, or is it a supreme error that clouds her vision of herself and of the grandeur of her destiny? I'm not uncertain about this: Eterna, our passion is as plain as can be; but you don't care that passion

1. "The best dessert is often tasted but never served." "He who stays in the kitchen is both guest and regrets at table." "Hardworking guest, invisible yet."

Some of my own ingenious refrains, designed to irritate the disorderly reader who goes around saying that he can read my novel halfway, and stop reading the disorderly middle, which nobody can resist doing with my lethargic and prolonging novel. I have so dominated the disorderly reader that he will be the first of his kind to read disorder itself.

2. There's no lack of texts more difficult than mine: which is to say, there are those that are found lacking. Nevertheless, ever since this morning I've been listening to Maruca singing while she combs her hair, and now this afternoon it seems that both things are coming to an end: it isn't only difficult things that remain undone.

exists, you don't admit it is even possible in this phase of your life; and despite all this, you love Art, without loving yourself) . . .

This novel is enamored of itself and it is the sort of novel where mishaps and adventures happen, artistic indecisions, whether to get lost in art, to be silent, to be ignorant; even as it relates events it is swept away by others; it contains accidents and it is the victim of accidents. We see it today, in streetcars with internal warnings in the form of drawings of transients being run over, even as the machine metes out shock and alarm. It is curious about itself, like children in costumes who shout "Trick or treat!" and ecstatically run away. What is disguised is that they are children with an audience. Going around in costume is for them a disguise: the mask is the disguise. I, the author, am principally public even now, in publicity. I am always searching, and I'm missing knowledge and living because there's a kind of living that I'd still like to experience even though I think I already understand it: the finality of Art as the end of life, of the individual aspect of life: the Tragedy-Idyll that is Love, which is itself made from Beauty by Death which makes of love as much tragedy as idyll, since the certainty, along the path of life, of the personal destruction of lovers (also there are those who aren't in love who, although they have death they don't have the Beauty of life, an individual matter) exalts, makes love just as it makes its tragedy. Death is only death of love; there is only the death of the other, her concealment, since for oneself there is no concealment. But there is much for me to learn about love in its execution, about how to slake its daily thirst, about its delicate and implacable congress.

So it is that even as I write, I inquire and hope for things to happen, just like the reader. And when I think of the unruly skip-around reader, I notice that I'm obliged to imagine what I should have the Traveler feel after what's just happened, in order to deduce what he likely said—since it was inaudible. What he would have said would be what I just told you. It's not improbable either that he would have said, "I'm a Traveler in a Novel, in a story that's already underway: I shouldn't dally then, I've been in this scene too long already. Let the reader always see me boarding a train or setting sail; he has to see me leave so many times that I don't even know what it's like to be around, and now I fear I'll have to leave the novel in a flurry of departure."

In reality, the Traveler was still finishing up with his sticking around when, at first sight of the reader, he took off. In the interval, that moment that remained before he had finished sticking around, he got an urge to stay, but the reader—never inopportune—intervened.

I think the latter will be happy with the phrase I put in the Traveler's mouth as if he had just learned it: it's all that he thought, and yet he said nothing about it that anyone could hear.

With that, I think the passage complete, and thus I make good on the promise I made to my novel that I would relate everything, even what I don't know, which I do sometimes in the novel, and sometimes skirting away from it, to which effect I have arranged these ample outskirts, these suburbs: my prologues.

This Traveler character, whose arrival is always awaited during the novel, garners me more and more sympathy. The words I attribute to him show that he occupies himself above all with his role, sacrificing his own desires (that people hear everything he says, and stay in one place) just to obey me. He was recommended to me for his obedience, and his practicality, and because of a lack of personnel I gave him the job of traveling constantly; there has been so much hurry in the preparation of this book that even delays in returning, arriving, answering, coming to a resolution—which figure in the entire story, and which do so much to move it along, have had to be invented in a hurry. So we've given the role of always going away in the book to a character who, just because he sticks around, is stuck with nothing. This frustration in vocation is just as true in life as it is in novels that, in striving to contain even a little truth, offend with its mere mention.

If the reader still finds any imperfection in this compensatory passage, I ask him to appreciate in the present explication the tranquility of reading that my efforts have spared him until this page. At the moment, these forces are focused on keeping the Boy with the Long Stick out of the novel, and we wouldn't want to beg because that would make everything uncomfortable. We can't let him drop into some quiet passage of this story, brandishing the long stick of catastrophe in this scenic place, making a drag race of the story, his very apparition clearing out all my characters. He'll throw himself on the sofa in the end and, observing our frown, will ask nicely, indicating the stick: Would you let me whack it every once in a while? He'll ask your forgiveness for not having come sooner and your permission later to leave, as if this were all very necessary; he'll act very solicitous, with promises to get in the way somewhere else; after you give him permission he'll stick around just the same, he'll straighten some picture frame that he had knocked with his stick. You would have left during all this, since generally wherever he goes, everybody leaves, who knows why.

His being-in-the-world bruises, but on this planet we haven't yet found a not-being-in-the-world for him. His not-being-in-the-world is still too near. Places where he can't be found—very sought after places—can't be gotten even from the resellers of his absence, and it's doubtful whether it's even possible for him to be absent. And he used to depart with such velocity, as if leaving quickly were somehow leaving more, and would thus diminish the time he spent somewhere; this left him so drained that what was left over ended much earlier. His "far away" lasts for no time at all, and meanwhile what you had to put up with from him increased exponentially. He needs to learn to stay somewhere quickly; everyone wants to figure out how to do this, and then teach him how; his retreat isn't leaving so much as still leaving. And there's even hurried bruises left by his absence. His is a most occupying presence.

We do not condemn his brusque departure as inopportune; let's be indulgent: it must be attributed to when he realized "all of a sudden" that there was one wall in the town from which he had yet to fall, and he ran off to occupy himself with falling off of it. The world suffers when he's near and there's not a place far enough to throw him. But he has found a new space in this doubling of the world that is the fantasy of a novel. I figure that if I let him come in to my novel, people will suspect that I value him only as a nuisance deployed to distract the reader from an imperfect passage. Moreover I know that in not coming, or wherever he isn't, he's well behaved. That's why my advertisement says: "the only novel where boys with long sticks are not allowed," and, "it's the novel that holds the boy at bay."

It would behoove a novel that wants a readership—my novel is currently bored with me, it would like some guests to come, to have a bit of conversation, it would like to be read—to begin its narrative with an accident, or a good screeching of brakes. The public gathers at such places in such numbers that nowadays lots of books would like to have the same readership as the average fender-bender.

Ever since I've been an author I've looked on in envy at the audience there is for auto accidents. I sometimes dream that certain passages in the novel had such a throng of readers that they obstructed the progression of the plot, running the risk that the difficulties and catastrophes of the interior of the novel would appear in the forward, among the mangled bodies. You will understand that if the novel had stopped for even an instant, I would have at that point inserted a new prologue in the hole thus produced in the narration. And I would make that prologue with dignity, which is to say with so many decorative ruckuses, rushes, insults, orders, chases, bells, breaks, guards, and inspectors, plus a security guard who comes to read about the accident in front of the window of the passenger who's reading my novel. In short, with proper homage to the inverisimilitude of the event, which will be entirely dissimulated, like they do in those "Companies" that never admit to the verisimilitude of their tram accidents, a sticking point at this late date in the locomotive narrative. Moreover, I'll stick my arm out of the window of my novel as a signal to the other novels coming after mine, so they don't hit it. The reader should not entertain himself with the aforementioned security guard; he isn't ours; the one that belongs in our novel is standing on the opposite corner.

Let's bid farewell to the boy, adding that if he has any absence it is so diminished that his first arrival is already frequent and in its fifth edition of presence.

A NEW PROLOGUE TO MY AUTHORIAL PERSONA

This is what I imagine here: non-death; also the artistic work involved in the transformation of the self, routing the stability of each person in his self.

I'm working with various persons here, which is to say, I'm tempted in every book to transformation: Ella, Eterna, William James, The Lover, and the Author. In my humorous writing, I attempted the irrationality of the author and of his identity.[1]

"Ella" is the most radical decentering: here and in "La Eterna" I work in contradictions on her decentering: not the minor kind, to be one living being instead of another, or one dream figure instead of another, but the radical decentering, to be pure image, to be and to appear not to be real, and vice versa. Eterna is also fully decentered, because she is the one with the power to change others' pasts (Sweetheart will come asking to change her past, since hers is the most unfortunate). She hasn't the power to change her own past, before she met the President, as she wishes. The Lover is the suspension, the caesura of identity, and Sweetheart is the expectation of being. She suffers from that tendency, the poor girl.

I take credit for having lived to construct a metaphysics of the total-lover, without interesting myself in my own metaphysics: as I am, I don't deserve either explanation or eternity; I don't deserve Ella or a metaphysics; The Lover deserves both Ella and metaphysics.

It's very subtle and patient work, getting quit of the self, disrupting interiors and identities. In all my writing I've only achieved eight or ten minutes in which two or three lines disrupted the stability, the unity of someone, even at times, I believe, disrupting the self-sameness of the reader. Nevertheless, I still believe that Literature does not exist, because it hasn't dedicated itself solely to this Effect

---

1. This doctrine is included in "Towards a Theory of Art," in "Theories," and the exercises in *Newcomer's Papers* and *The Nothing Continues*. (*Editor's Note—Adolfo de Obieta*)

of dis-identification, the only thing that would justify its existence and that only Belarte can achieve. Perhaps Painting or Dance could also attempt it.

I don't believe that Metaphysics is the direct pleasure of an exegesis: it's a task that brings second-hand pleasure only gained from a position of power; it's a power one seeks out: the direct power of love. If this power were a first cause (since if it were mediated, all virtue and aspiration would be frustrated because the intermediate links can also be frustrated) in the mechanical world, it would bring total presence (visual, tactile, audible, thermal) of the beloved to any present in time, to the same present in time, to the same present of this desire, and with it the details of an actual state of perception. The mechanical world is the world in which material appears: only the body of the beloved appears as a first cause, the sole apparition in a psyche of fervent hope, of desire.

If in each of my books I have two or three times achieved an instant of what I will call in homespun terms a "suffocation," an "upset" in the certitude of personal continuity, a slippage of the reader's own self, then that's all I wanted as a means; the end towards which I'm working is liberation from the idea of death: evanescence, mutability, rotation, and spinning of the self make it immortal, which is to say, release its destiny from the body. (For others, this Body is no more than a complex of images in my sensory apparatus, which itself seems to be tied to this Body, or another sensory apparatus associated with another Body.) Just as I sometimes asked when I was corresponding with William James forty years ago, I ask for your consent, that you let me present a demonstration here of these extremely difficult attempts to confuse and immortalize the "I." In a note to The Perception of Space in his "Psychology," James says; "let us see whether we cannot push our theoretic insight a little farther. *It seems to me* we can" (*Principles of Psychology I*, Chapter 20, "The Perception of Space. Crude Extensivity," note 28). I underline, and I leave underlined, James's *it seems to me*, who will exist and be read even a hundred years hence; and I write at the foot of his page. This "it seems to me" is a pre-state that James felt forty years ago at a precise moment in his efforts to work at thinking and writing; he pre-felt that he was going to unravel the tangled argument that he was developing. And noticing this excites in me today—April of 1931, in Buenos Aires—the consciousness that for a short time now I've been irritated reading for a feeling of nonconformity, of expectation, trying to make out in what moment of those laborious lines James would give us a glimpse of the explanation of space by movement (transfer, muscularity, the evocation of either), and I held out hope that he had seen, as I had, the possible explanation of the localized "affliction" by muscular evocations.

But with some distance, I can now emphatically assert that nobody is stronger, more rigorous, more serious and specialized than I in non-discursive metaphysics, the metaphysics that Hegel forgot and which, I would argue, is given artistically. I don't think that the genuine metaphysicians, nor the bibliographers, the historians, or the teachers of Metaphysics would disdain the force of the intellectual attitude here achieved. I don't think that anyone who has felt the Mystery (the Mystery of feeling, I would say; James would say the mystery of feeling) has come up with anything clearer than the illumination I will have attained. The truth in these pages will not be resented even if they appeared in an edition of Kant or Hegel as a part of their work.

I think I resemble Poe, and even though I've begun to imitate him a bit, I believe I am Poe all over again. And it's extraordinary that as an author and as a persona that it was a Peruvian poet, Mario Chabes, who discovered the resemblance. It's not a resemblance, it's . . . who knows? A reapparation. In the poem "Elena Bellamuerte" I approached Poe in feeling, but I don't think the text shows much similarity in literary style.

I wouldn't make these assertions if it weren't to encourage the young reader to maintain himself in a defensive stance against the impression that the I is a shipwreck on the isle of bodily death.

Follow me then, reader: I seek "one" eternity that has yet to be found, although others had the Desire as strongly as I, they lacked hope, and the notion of a way to proceed.

Many people, maybe all people, are certain of their personal eternity, their souls, but nobody believes that love could eternally retain one's personal human being—his body. And without this corporeal permanence each person would only know his own personal eternal existence, an existence where neither the eternity nor the traveler matters, where a minute is indistinguishable from a million centuries.

You'll see that I share with the anxious and mentally gifted William James an indefatigable exploration of what he held was death before truth (which will perhaps be what happens to me). He nevertheless reached the truth of the Act, without the foreknowledge and the felicity to "die" (bodily concealment) knowing it. Surely temptations and entanglements of circumstance will prevent him from always using all of his thought for this investigation. I am only confident in "knowing" before "being" if analogous circumstances don't prevent it.

I dignify this quest with Passion, without which neither life nor quests are worthwhile.[1] And in the name of its dignity I have labored to arm myself with the maximum of information; no one, I think, has ever studied more thoroughly, been more calm in his preparation, or more self-critical. Only overwhelming reflection can impede me now, since I already possessed absolute certainty of personal eternity when I undertook this investigation, directed solely towards the search for corporeal eternity, without which Companionship ends: love and Memory are retained in both and, even more lacerating, the certainty of existing concealed from one another, without hope of Knowlege or Recognition.

I hope that the Man of Supreme Misfortune alone gives himself over to the certainty of the beloved's eternal existence, that which we can only have by means of permanence, an eternity of the spiritual figure as much as of the personal, physical figure. But, also, I assume the responsibility to continue seeking this certainty for others.

---

1. *Not All Consciousness is Wakefulness* presents itself precisely as a pro passion discourse against exhausting intellectualism. ("Passion, the supreme suitability of Being!") But in addition to the metaphysics of passion with its correlative issues of Being, Non-Being, Death, Persona Eternity, Body, etc. initially allude there to the being of a character of art and its metaphysical operation ("Solution," "Fantasy is a formality"). (*Editor's Note—Adolfo de Obieta*)

PROLOGUE THAT THINKS IT KNOWS SOMETHING, NOT ABOUT THE NOVEL (IT'S NOT ALLOWED THAT), BUT ABOUT THE DOCTRINE OF ART

The present tentative aesthetic is a provocation to the realist school, a total program to discredit the truth or reality of what happens in a novel. Only the subjection of truth to Art is intrinsic, unconditional, and self-authentic. The challenge that I present to Verisimilitude, to that deformed intrusion of Art, Authenticity—this is already a part of Art, it makes anyone who has recourse to fantasy and wants it to be Real absurd—this challenge culminates in the use of incongruities, to the point of forgetting the identities of the characters, forgetting continuity, temporal order, forgetting to put effects before causes, etcetera, thus I implore the reader not to detain himself disentangling absurdities or reconciling contradictions, but to follow the course of the emotional pull that, molecule by molecule, the reading promotes in him.

In my attempt there are various ideas that are, most likely, original. I'm interested in method: I seek to distract the reader for moments, even oppressively, when I want to impress him with the emotional subtlety that I must engender in him, little impressions that concur with the emotional purpose of the whole, which is to obtain in him a unique, final, and general state enabling me to unexpectedly trap his senses when he isn't on guard and conscious that he is dealing with a literary campaign. He won't expect, nor later realize, that he has been conquered.

There is a reader with whom I cannot reconcile myself: the reader who wants what all novelists have coveted, to their shame: Hallucination. I want the reader to always know he is reading a novel and not watching the living, not attending to a "life." The moment the reader falls into Hallucination, that ignominy of Art, I have lost rather than gained a reader. What I want is something very different, which is to win him over as a character, so that for an instant he believes that he himself does not live. This is the emotion for which he should thank me, since until now no one has thought of procuring it for him.

The reader should know that this impression, never before achieved for anyone by the written word—this impression that, along with my novel, seeks an introduction into the human psyche, in the natural consciousness of man—is a benediction for all consciousness, because this impression obliterates and liberates the mental or emotional fear that we call the terror of ceasing to exist. Whoever experiences even a moment of the state of belief in not existing and later returns to the state of belief in existing, will forever understand that the whole content of the verbalization or notion "not to be" is the belief in not being. It's not possible to believe that one does not exist without existing. For example, Descartes's metaphysics had to begin with "I don't exist" in order to substitute the lamentable "I exist." In sum: existence is frequented just as often by the belief in non-existence as it is by the belief in existence. Whoever believes, exists, even if his belief is that he does not exist; whoever exists can in effect believe that he does not exist and, alternatively, believe that he exists. "I think" never had anything other than innocent consequences, but it can be said lazily or even distractedly; or, it can be a fact and a judgment that is *felt*. To exist is a fact, but *I* exist can never be a "felt" judgment: it is a mere juxtaposition of words, as it does not contain a *moment* of belief; it just happens that words come together. He who assures you of all this is one who laments it, in contrast to all of those great readers of Kant, who understood him too much, which is to say, had not a single doubt that Kant was a metaphysician. (The French demolish a deified painter every twenty years, a deified poet every fifteen, and a deified novelist every ten; at a hundred and fifty years it's high time Kant were thrown into doubt. This isn't daring, it would be more daring to call him a metaphysician. With these antecedents I anticipate future arguments for the demolition of my Art.)

It seems to me that no one else has used this method, or that it would be applicable to any other genre but the novel. Besides technique, there is a series of contrivances of in-verisimilitude and denials of the reality of the story. This is the doctrine, and it is executed most notably when it explains expositionally, not artistically, a fact that never happened, but which was fully deliberated in a living consciousness, (Sweetheart's father's consciousness), and which constitutes the defining fact of her destiny.

Even if I have invented the novel-museum, it won't matter if I'm able to raise interest in the story if all the while the reader believes himself to be only a reader. If to him the characters are only characters in a novel and in the prologues (although delicate, smokily glimpsed and in truncated actions and facts, I believe that Eterna, Sweetheart, Maybegenius, and The Lover will be unforgettable even though I've barely put them in the story) I'll have failed to effect a "shock of inexistence" in the psyche of the reader—the shock of being here, not reading, but being read, being a character, in favor of the conscious carelessness obtained by interestedness.

If the novel fails as what is called a novel, my Aesthetic will save the day: I admit that it could be taken as a novel, a good fantasy, a substitute novel. So if the novel fails as a novel, it could be that my Aesthetic will make a good novel.

I have entrusted the execution of my novel to the following characters, having selected them carefully based upon their conduct in
other novels. I have indoctrinated them in everything a "character
of art" should know, I've made them read my prologues, which are
studies in Aesthetics. If the novel turns out badly, don't blame me. I
did everything that as an author it was incumbent upon me to do: to
prove the characters' discipline by means of their previous conduct,
and give them a theory that they didn't have before, of the character
of art.

Every *character* only halfway exists, because none was ever introduced who wasn't taken by half or more from "real life" people. That's
why there's a subtle discomfort and agitation in every character's
"being," since there are several humans wandering the world that a
novelist used partially for a character and who feel a discomfort in
their "being" in life. Something of them is in a novel, fantasized in
written pages, and it can't truly be said where they really are.

All the characters are under obligation to *dream of being*, which
is their proper way of being, inaccessible to living people, and the
only genuine stuff of Art. To be a character is to dream of being real.
And the magic of them, what possesses us and enchants us about
them, and what only they know as the form of their being, is not
the author's dream, but the dream of being, in which they avidly
participate, that makes them act and feel. Only realist art—which is
not Belarte—the art of Anna Karenina, Madame Bovary, Quixote,
Mignon, lacks "characters," which is to say, these characters don't
dream of being, because they think they are copies.

What I don't want and what I've tried to avoid twenty times over
in my pages is that a character seems to live, and this happens any
time the reader hallucinates the reality of an event: the truth of life,
the copy of life, which is my abomination, and certainly, isn't that
the genuine failure of art, the worst, perhaps the only frustration or
abortion of a character, that he *appear* to live? I can admit that they
want to live, that they attempt life and even covet it, but I cannot

admit that they appear to live, in the sense that events seem to be real; the abomination of all realism.

For my pages, I want constant fantasy, and faced with the difficulty of avoiding a hallucination of reality, which is a blemish on the face of art, I have created the only character ever born whose consistent fantasy is the guarantee of the firm irreality of this novel, which is irreducible to the real: the character who does not appear, whose existence in the novel makes him fantastic with respect to both the novel and the world, being—he seems real to us because daydreams exist. To him I have entrusted the vouchsafing of fantasy here, if all else fails; to the Traveler who in life itself perhaps never existed, since I don't believe in Travelers; the two sentiments that define the Traveler of quality are the faculty and desire to forget, and the desire to be forgotten. The magnificent Forgetter, complete with this latter faculty of indifference to being forgotten and even the valor and knowledge to want his image to die in the mind of others, a death more fearful than personal death, perhaps because we all sense that personal death does not exist. The death that exists in oblivion is what leads us to the error of believing in personal death. But this belief is very weak, that's why we do a lot more to avoid being forgotten than to avoid dying.

—And so, where does our Traveler wander and sojourn?

—My Traveler lives there, across the way. And he doesn't come out of his house except at the end of a chapter.

He functions exclusively as the extinguisher of the hallucination that menaces the story with realism.

PROLOGUE TO THE NEVER-SEEN

The genre of there-never-was, so frequently invoked, but without precedents, will make its debut here, since it has never existed itself, there never has been a there-never-was, yet there will be in the current year, and, as is only fair, in Buenos Aires, the first city of the world to present itself in this category, the only city that is equally good for the conclusion of a trip around the world as for the start of one, a city that serves this purpose for trips started wherever else, as various and continual world navigators have successively discovered, with any around the world trips—whether they start in Berlin or Rio de Janeiro—being consumed, without regard for its future plans, in Buenos Aires, where it lingers, whispering its disdain for the other legs of the trip, instead going off into the streets, tramways and public works of Buenos Aires, buying a little house, getting married, producing offspring, all of which has the fullness and heroism of the fulminous completion of the whole trip.

With this genre, humanity will finally lay eyes upon the never-before-seen, a display of there-never-was; it won't be a bridge that's always dry, a conjugal frigidity, a religious war between peoples without religion, or other things that haven't been seen. The never-before-seen will really be seen; this isn't fantasy, it's something else: the first example in this genre will be a novel. I'm just about to publish it, as the manuscript critics have already mentioned, admiringly, "it's a novel that has never been written before." And it hasn't been written yet, but there's only a little ways to go.

Such a collection of events is contained in the novel that there's practically nothing left over to happen in the streets, houses, and plazas; the papers, confronted with this lack of current events, will have to content themselves with citing the novel: "the following exchange took place in the middle of the afternoon yesterday in the novel of Eterna;" "this morning the Sweetheart is smiling;" "the President of the Novel, responding in person to the rumors circulating among his numerous readers, told us that today he will positively launch his plan for the hystericization of Buenos Aires and the conquest, in the name of aesthetic salvation, of our population by humor."

"After Chapter V of the Novel we can be sure that it isn't because of GWDE (the Gentleman Who Doesn't Exist) that Sweetheart's existence is saddened today." "This evening, the Novel will send its soloist orchestra—six guitars—to execute various obsequious polyphonies for the orchestras of the bars Ideal, Sibarita, and Real, so that they can listen to music for a change. The Polygraph of Silence will explain the reasons for this with erudite gestures, and he will circulate the bottomless collection plate of gratitude among the personnel of the orchestras, which will make the music of thanks as coin strikes against coin. The public will also serve as a harmony of contentment, as the listening orchestra, momentarily laying aside its instruments for calling-the-waiter in favor of its instruments of applause."

This is a novel that was and will be futuristic until it's written, just as its author is, until today he had yet to write a single future page, although he has left futurism until the future, as a proof of his enthusiasm, and doing so brilliantly from there on—without falling into the trap of being a consecutive futurist, like those who have adopted futurism, without understanding it, in the present. And, for that reason, they have declared much to come for the novelist, who has everything in front of him, including his own genial sense of haste, which arises from having thought that with the speed of progress, posterity has been left behind; each day comes quicker, almost completely forgotten, a series of contemporaneous events that exist in the last journalistic edition of the day it appears, and that's it. We all die already judged immediately, book and author, made classics or corpses in a day, and meanwhile they recommend us to posterity and complain about the present. And today, all of this is done with sufficient justice in 24 hours. The old posterity, with all the time it took to think about it, consecrated a multitude of nonentities as glorious artists; there's more equity and common sense in today's reporter: vacuous solemnity and moralisms were posterity's cheap and effective bribe, born until yesterday. I will look, trusting, for posterity's universal judgment of my novel in the 30th of September 1929 edition of *Critique and Reason*, the day the novel will appear, a date which could not have been postponed, since all the postponements had already been used up in promises, with the most literary postponements having been used for prologues.

For the consecrated future literati that does not believe in, nor is able to estimate, posterity beyond each day's night; it won't make sense for authors to feel a sense of urgency to write promptly for a prompt posterior judgment: with the speeds that posterity can reach today, the artist will outlive his posterity and will know the next day whether he should or should not write better, or if he has already written so well that he should content himself by contemplating the perfection of his writing. Or if he has no literary accolades left to seek, other than the one that's most difficult to find—the reader's. The actual ease of writing makes the legible scarce, and it has reached the point of superseding the injurious necessity of having readers in the first place: writing is for the fruition of art and at best is for knowing the critic's opinion. In all sincerity, this change is lovely; it's art for art's sake and art for the critics' sake, which is art for art's sake all over again.

Horrible art and the accumulated glories of the past, which have always existed, are a result of the following: the sonorousness of language and the existence of an audience; without this sonorousness, only thinking and creating would remain; without a clamoring public, art would not be drowned. Under these conditions, Literature would be pure art, and there would be many more beautiful works than there are at present: there would be three or four Cervantes, the Cervantes of the *Quixote*, without the stories, Quevedo the humorist and poet of passion, without the moralizing orator, various Gómez de la Sernas. We'll be liberated from the likes of Calderón, the Prince of falsetto, from lack of feeling, which is poor taste itself; from the likes of Góngora, at least from time to time, with his exclamations of "Ay Fabio, o sorrow!" We'd have three Heines, each of sarcasm and sadness, or D'Annunzios to limitlessly versify passion. Happily, we would have only the first act of *Faust*, and in compensation various Poes, and various Bovaries—with their sad affliction of loveless appetite, despicable and bloody—and this other, lacerating absurdity: Hamlet's lyric of sorrow, which convinces and breeds sympathy, despite the false psychologism of its source. We'll be free of the scientific realism of Ibsen, one of Zola's victims, and this magnificent artist for his part will be dismantled by sociology and theory of heresy and pathology, and instead of a dozen master works we'll possess a hundred, of true, intrinsic artistic worth, not mere copies of reality. These works will be typically literary, works of Prose, not of didactics, without any musical language (meter, rhyme, sonorousness) or paintings with words, that is, descriptions.

With this I'm publishing a prologue of such a novel, since I hope to guarantee that in special rehearsals its characters, events, and jokes will all prove its utter seriousness; and even publishing it is a rehearsal, anterior to the reader. But only the prologues after this one!

I'll rehearse the upcoming prologue instead. Also, there's a new German word in Spanish that I consulted with Xul Solar about in his workshop: "Languages in repair." It's an amended adjective, but new, not like mended boots.

The "for-all-of-us-artists-gifted-with-daydreams" Reader.

The "often-dreamed-of" Reader; The "who-the-author-dreams-is-reading-his-dreams" Reader.

The "who-the-art-of-writing-wants-to-be-real-more-than-merely-real-reader-of-dreams" Reader.

The "only-real-that-art-recognizes" reader of dreams.

The "less-real, he-who-dreams-the-dreams-of-the-other,-and-stronger-in-reality,-since-he-does-not-lose-it-although-they-won't-let-him-dream-them-but-only-re-dream" Reader.

I believe I have identified the reader who addresses himself to me, and I have obtained the proper adjectivalization of his entire being, after so much fragmentation and some false adjectives. "Dear" reader does not modify the reader but the author, et cetera.

The adjectivalization read above—conveniently, I speak before the novel of that which is not read that the book contains; but the rest, here, is before everything and I leave only a little of it; by means of prologues I have the refinement to privilege the readers who know the entire book, something only my readers have found in an abnegated author—I give the book to the public just to turn around and put it through the linguistic workshop of that singular artist, Xul Solar, who will make it into one, definitive word. And, already in its fourth edition, my salutation to the reader, which you'll have to pardon me, will today be served decaffeinated.

To your health, reader. How sad we are in our books, and how distant. I, the most often mentioned and identified of the unknowns, find myself in a predicament with my Complete Works, to start with, in such a way that the entire future, my whole literary career, will be posterior, in my case, to the aforementioned Complete Works; only because the public has not stopped to wait for me and hasn't given me the name of a great unknown. So now I am obliged to deserve it, composing myself a past as an author in one fell swoop, so that later I'll be able to write. This is a new situation in the life of writers, and isn't it adverse to success?

For those who have read me before I began to write, if you have a problem like mine, by now I won't have it any more. I've finished my Complete Works. In my satisfaction, monumentally incapable of understanding difficulty, I can give you a distillation of long experience in art, collected in the present Complete Work.

Let art be limitless and free and all that is intrinsic to it—its handwriting, its titles, the life of its exponents. Tragedy or Humorism or Fantasy should never have to suffer a Past director, nor should they have to copy a Present Reality, and all should incessantly be judged, abolished.

It's an axiomatic error to define art by copies: I understand life without getting a copy of it first; if copies were necessary, each new situation, each new character that we encountered would be eternally incomprehensible. The effectiveness of the author derives solely from his Invention.

I leave only the title finished, since:

A prologue that starts right away is really sloppy: it loses the perfume of its preceding, just as I said that the only genuine way to practice futurism is to put it off for later.

I will also have said, earlier, that this is one of the twenty-nine prologues of a novel that's impossible to prologue, as a critic, who surely born in that tranquil country of "ask questions later," has recently predicted; there's another, more sympathetic, book, that is, one that's more given to length and limited in prologues—which can still be remedied—which was going to be called "The Man Who Would Be President But Wasn't."[1]

Or, an equivalent:

"Buenos Aires hysterical, torn between the hilarious faction and the faction of eternity, and saved by a splendid compatriot, who unifies humorism and passion." But the title I've got left for "the novel permitted a beginning," which although it begins late has no less of a beginning, and, if he reads it, the reader will wish it were all made of continuations, such as "Novel of Eterna, and of the Child of Melancholy, Sweetheart of-an-undeclared-lover."

1. This "Man Who Would Be President" (in the novel) and who wasn't (in history, where who would want to be?) is connected to a possible political-fantastical action alluded to in the notes to "Towards A Theory of the State," in *Teorías*. (*Editor's Note—Adolfo de Obieta*)

This last is the title a certain gentleman preferred; he began to read it and promised to come back right away, to finish finding out how the novel is named.

This is the only novel that tells everything and that, nevertheless, has nothing added, although the obligation to tell everything leads to telling more. I got hung up reading Arabic stories in my adolescence, because I didn't know there were only 1,001, so I kept reading them after I'd finished: I was warned much too late, and so I continued devouring stories, which I found abundantly scattered through Morality, History; there are stories of Progress, the abnegation of statesmen or martyrs or propagandists of some selfless cause, like the happiness of the good, repentance of evil, the ultimate concordance of the general and the particular, or Utilitarianism, the order of the Universe and other miracles of the abundant "faith" of the men of science, which is so demanding of vulgar miracles!

This is a novel with two beginnings, depending on the reader's preference.

It has a lot of sadness and a lot of enthusiasm, but no death, only the words The End, written much later, long after you have finished reading the title. It's only written once, although the prologues need it (not all of them, but a few need endings), and even the title, when it ends: I've abolished The End of the title, The End of the prologue, so as to show just how little the novel depends on death for its existence—but neither does it rely on life (truth, realism)—.

It has two almost-impossibilities that are almost resolved: how to narrate the *ultimate* and what to do with a bungled joke—how to regain one's composure after having laughed at a tragedy because the title gave no indication that it was not a comedy.

It interrupts its reading and narration once, so that Sweetheart can get dressed, during which the reader should have no pretext to read, as that's his way of looking.

It has twenty-nine prologues written to prevent it from beginning.

It has the exclusive use of three new mathematical tenses. These are "novel tenses" which have never, before today, been spooled out in narratives and novels, as if time didn't flee and flow during events of fantasy. The aforementioned tenses are: the tense of *porteño* or Buenos Aires-style courtesy, which dictates that no one be disposed of or denied, but that one simply wait "until there's a new tango" to look for work or improve oneself. Second, the tense of the interval (on the floor) between two falls of the Prince of Wales: this surveyor Prince is very nice, he acquired his title by measuring short stretches against the length of his real persona, but I hope this won't reinforce the hobo inclinations of the skip-around reader or encourage him to read by the illustrious example of this skip-around pony. Finally, the minimal tense: the one that's left over now to make the first overcoat for the first cold of winter, or measuring this tense by another standard: the tense of rescuing a black hat which had been forgotten on the black seat of a chair, during the forthcoming visit of a recently arrived guest. Or, if you like: five minutes of film in which the entire cast of Hollywood has to run, falling over themselves to convert all of the disgraces in two hours of film—marriage, kissing, the unmasking of false virtue—into happiness.

It has characters from three different ages, measured by Oblivion: the age in which we leave a cigarette burning in Papa's new cigarette holder and forget it in the maid's room; the already advanced age when we forget a baguette that's been left on a polished desk; and the desperate age in which we forget everything, including age, even forgetting a hat that's been left in a soup tureen—a horrible turn of events. (The age in which we take the stairs in leaps will predominate, that age in which we tangle our last kite or our last fishing line, and the first game of billiards emerges, and the first night of forgetting one's house keys.)

With the melancholy of the child, whose beautiful love remained unrequited.

And the valor of the quest of the Gentleman Who Doesn't Exist.

All of which is stocked with indescribable confusion—but for the forbearance of the Novel we would describe it now—for a bank employee who doesn't know whether he is a genius.

Once the prologues are finished, the novel will begin all of a sudden, opening surprisingly with "An executed novel, which has gone out into the street," insistently insinuating itself to the point of the full extent of the "Novel of impediments" and ending with all the rest that the author found out in "What to cry about," a chapter that will procure for the reader a list of what is worth crying about, plus the impossible death of the "Man who Feigned To Live," here played by the barber who pretended he was awake and able to see, although he was sleeping at the moment, as he almost always is. His accursed sleep does not prevent everything from coming to be known and told, without being said, however, nothing that isn't in the book, that comes from outside the novel or has the formality of an End, will impede this novel. It has its end in the same place as every other novel, that is, the point where the book is left with nothing to say, throwing into doubt everything it said in the first place. We assure you that very few eras have a forthcoming novel, even the ones who by the end have been more lauded, been as concluded as ours, written entirely before the end and not leaving behind a single continuation.

To conclude, this novel is sure to appear, since it's been promised three times already just to fulfill the first promise. It does not contain any trips abroad, nor does it neglect to continue; both of these things are mere pretexts to leave the reader without characters, since obviously the story cannot move ahead if various protagonists don't leave for Europe or are simply forgotten for pages at a time, obliging the reader to wait until so-and-so returns so that the forgetful parts will slap their hands to their foreheads and remember. That's why I already said, or I will say, that we do not accept among our kitchen characters those that want a degree in mending buttons or making sure the pots on the stove don't boil over and burn their bottoms with rice and milk.

SALUTATION

What I have here is, strangely enough, now the promised Novel, which certainly had the instinct of assuring itself a state of effective non-existence—it hasn't emerged from non-being because a promised book traces the border between being and non-being, and from a distant perspective, such as the mind of the author, its place in existence is being prepared, and energy, curiosity, and attention are reserved for it; even promising it so much existence that juries have reserved prizes for it—and it had the instinct of maintaining itself in this non-existence for a half-dozen years, so that it can appear as if its being had never known nothingness, which, doubling the virtue of its reality, makes possible such an abundance thereof that, in a fantasy, non existence lives in the person of the Gentleman Who Doesn't Exist, whose insinuated substance is only effective, can only breathe, whose slender shadow can only have a place in a novel whose existence is as strong as this one, whose beginning has not been preceded by a nothing.

I'll say goodbye here, too, reader, not because you can ever forget me—you can't, this is an unforgettable novel—but because I'm just a poor novel, ardent, but short on tremulous dreams, a little curtain of shadows that has decided to pull itself back so as to reveal everything, assuming you begin to read it: Sweetheart, the President, GWDE–Eterna is not on the same path—the sad being-characters only live in the minutes that someone spends writing them: once their making is concluded, they are concluded, they are nothing, they're even sadder now because the ticklish feeling of being read ran over their dead figures like a butterfly, or disquieting peals of laughter, or even the piety that you will disgorge it gave them goosebumps all over their bodies because they never had access to Life.

My Novel has been executed without life, and yet it's not to be forgotten. It's worse that way, even sadder, even more pitiless. You who are eternal, the living, are those who can weep for it, since you have touched Life and there's no death when there is a present, a single instant of Life is followed by eternity; you can cry, your tears burn your face, they run, they wet your cheeks; I, the Novel, am only made of daydreams, and the day you dream me you'll forget me; I'll be over forever, and I'll end each time that, because he's happy, because he's triumphant, he doesn't dream me; meanwhile you will never forget existing.

ANOTHER ATTEMPT AT A SALUTATION

Why not? And why not call it a salutation, even if it doesn't end up being one? I haven't promised you my mental continuity and congruency as a man, but only as an author—to give a novelistic definition. Here I am, with all of the cravings that happen between the self and the intimate movements of every day; I live my day before the reader's eyes. The reader is by definition a sympathizer, and I can be interesting to him in what I show of my doubt and inconstancy.

Knowledge is a deep and complex thing, nothing like the melancholy thing which is to know words. That's the worst thing that can happen to us, and at the same time, it engenders such infatuation. I say that we live with very little knowledge, as if to convince ourselves we don't need it. And if it were true that our knowledge is very small, it would be doubtful if it were true: if we know scarcely anything in depth, it's probable that our vast ignorance includes ignorance of whether it's certain we know nothing.

This isn't what I wanted to say. I wanted to say that everyone has deep knowledge of two or three complex truths, but that our experience with life embraces a thousand more aspects, so that we live almost all of our lives in darkness, something that is not conducive to constant misfortune, not least of which because pain tends to engender pleasure on its own just by ceasing, and vice versa. What's certain, knowledge, counts for very little in light of this rule.

But if we lived in constant surprise; almost totally in the unexpected. We don't know a single scrap integrally (*integrally, scrap*, these words denounce the fragility of human mental labor), not even a total fraction of our lot in life, unless we dedicate the better part of our lives to learning all the motivations of every action and passion, which is rarely possible. We like to reconstruct the beginning of effects and events that continue a long time or a short time, and connect us, but rarely do we find the stamina for a methodical evocation of an effect or event.

We also rarely know whether we are dealing with ideas, or with conduct.

In music, for example, if we were to document the immensity of the small melodic labor of artists who were contemporaries of Bach, or who came before him, the common people of the past and of the present, and of Bach himself, it's possible to doubt regarding Beethoven that we have really, even now, been dealing with music; or if we only consider music to be this remote music which is not artistic in itself (even less so with earlier music). Maybe all that we call music, starting from Bach, and fragments of song which these musicians and people left behind in an immense number is nothing but the elaboration of an obsession tied to fear. Perhaps genuine music has never, or almost never existed: it's the traffic of the state that the individual artist feels and its direct and personal expression, the search for a means and the desire to express oneself. What I have here is how we work for a long time in darkness and then give our work a name that it has not earned.

So now I also ask myself: What has motivated the idea and the will to make a novel? Do these last two or three years of my life not show me any one of these motivations, not because nothing should be mysterious or inaccessible, but because inquiries are tiring or troubling, even though we are all interested in the search for origins in our history and in schemas of the whole motivation for an action or a sentiment.

At first, I wanted to express myself, and also I wanted to look at life psychologically, and I wanted to commit myself to a general study of aesthetics, and I wanted to better myself economically, and thereby make a bit of a reputation for myself which would facilitate my means in difficult circumstances. All of this was erased by a great, new motivation, which coincided with my unexpected meeting of a person of such elevated influences on my spirit, such incredible grace, that sometimes I don't know if I only dreamed her.

To show my gratitude—or to keep her dream alive—I began the manuscript. This remained the main motive, though there was one other, smaller motivation, which will interest the public more: to execute a theory of Art, particularly of the Art of the Novel.

So it is that we even write a letter to this novel in darkness, and in darkness the person to whom it is dedicated asks to read it, and a consternation arises in her that she cannot define. She also cannot guess Eterna's motives, because she does not know herself well, and so she writes this missive for unknown reasons.

The reader will have equally confused impressions of this Novel. I don't believe I've made a novel that's faithful to the doctrine that it expresses. If both were excellent, the reader would still have plenty of time to form his impression, finding much to doubt, to declare vague or contradictory or inartistic, since in order to justify these imperfections I've just argued that it's difficult to really know motivations and impressions.

Goodbye, reader! . . .

HOW, IN THE END, THE PERFECT NOVEL IS POSSIBLE

We are now able to present the model novel, thanks to a curious upheaval in the circulation among the literati of the character named John Mountainclimber, who as everyone knows—even Socrates, who didn't know anything, and even those who only know what he said—has appeared in literature for two or three thousand years, since the days of Greek and Roman literature, and in every truly sensational, modern novel which resembles no other, not even in having Mountainclimber as a character.

This protagonist has always been known for his invariable position, which makes him afflictingly interesting: John Mountainclimber, driven by love to a life of adventure, on a mountaintop with novelistically opportune precipices, has fallen several meters from one of the same, something that's always a pity, and even more so in those moments when the story can't be put off; proof of this is that the story begins by describing his accident, which serves as the impetus for the novel and as the imperilment of the life of Mountainclimber, and for the reader as a way of maintaining suspense and worry, and in the story to move things along: it's the only effective contrivance for confounding the skip-around reader.

Mountainclimber is at a great height and in great danger, but the story continues, like those crime serials that need something to happen in order to get going; and Mountainclimber's enthusiastic mountain-climbing only begins to enthuse the reader and the author when they see him miss a step and incur great danger. He's holding on by a twig, toes clinging to some tiny outcropping of insecure rock, mortally exhausting himself, struggling and shouting at thirty or more unknown meters from the bottom of what we must already begin to call the abyss.

The whole novel happens while he's in this bind, I'll leave the reader to decide how he was rescued in the end. I can't think of a novelistic device that can more assuredly hold the reader until the end in suspense and uninterrupted interest, there's no novelistic procedure that yields a better value per page; even if the book were blank between the first and last pages and the promise of others—which are almost always as follows: plot, denouement, characters, unity and congruity— were not kept, the reader wouldn't skip a single one. Therefore, there's nobody like this John Mountainclimber for a model novel that is unlike any other; he's all characters in one, since he's plot personified: beginning and end without anything in the middle to unravel, or wrap up with a simulated solution.

Suspended in the air as he is, the attention of every reader cleaves to him; I needed him for the hardest part, the beginning of a novel, where the reader begins his task. It may be because Mountainclimber successfully procures both of these difficult beginnings—though the reader thinks his is the most difficult—or it may be because he's made us believe these things are difficult. With him, author and reader together take up their respective burdens on uncertain ground.

Uncertain ground and suspensions in the air helped in this case. When the Newcomer entered, he hung up his dog on the hook in the vestibule; the workers at Ford hang up their hats, which according to Ford is a type of movement as slight as the ones that later make up the day's work in the factory; I hang up a borrowed character and I fetch him on my way out so I can return him, but in the interim he grips the reader with such intense interest that he regrets any Skipping Around in the future. Any future author will be grateful for this method.

THE LOVER

The Lover came about because of the most important discovery that human intelligence has made: Hodgson's conception of automatism. At the first perspicuous discovery of psychological automatism, the author of this novel was led to formulate his theory of integral automatism, which could be considered one of the world's most audacious ideas and clear perceptions.

Departing from Hodgson's supreme example, the author was not afraid to raise it to its most extreme systemization. As we say, the novelesque author of this novel, by means of whose magic we promise to make of you a novelesque reader, discovered: that it's never been proved that a man or a woman who laughs or cries, who wrinkles his forehead, shouts, gets agitated, attacks, defends himself, searches, finds, plays, delays, writes, or seems to read, or pay attention is feeling or thinking anything in particular; that in this man or woman states of sound, color, odor, and pain exist—everything that the senses encompass. In sum: the fact that a "state of consciousness" does not exist does not impede anything—nor would the presence of consciousness help anything—from playing out exactly the same way an identical situation would play itself out in a person without consciousness and sensibility.[1]

It's in the interest of the physical organism to carry on living: it's not interested in being, or having perceptions. Automatism takes incessant charge of everything we do, and this automatism is totally acquired by individual experience (experience that does not necessarily have to be felt or perceived to produce the modifications we call adaptation), except perhaps in two fundamental reflexive impulses, which are congenital: flight from pain (which is what could destroy the physical organism, not psychic pain), and the retention or pursuit of pleasure. With this basic, congenital automatism experience goes on recording the physiological sequences of every emergency: a man

1. The reader is whispering with Hodgson and the author perceives that both are making marginal annotations.

who is assaulted by a furious mastiff may not see or hear or have any *sensuous* memory of a dog or his wound; or if we like, we could say: a man who today awoke with a total loss of consciousness would defend himself or run automatically, provided that at some point in the past a dog had wounded him, even if he had no memory of this. It will be said that I should admit it's necessary that once, at least, this person had a psyche, intelligence, emotion, felt sensory perceptions. But it's not like that: a child may be born absolutely without sensibility and develop in exactly the same way as his little brother, who has it (the halo of psychic sensibility).

The hurts that the body suffers have been associated with the sensations of the visual and auditory nerves, because of modifications in the nervous system provoked by the figure and the barks of the animal, without it necessarily being the case that these neural alterations have been translated into psychic facts of vision or audition. (Psychologically things are like this; metaphysically, all material phenomenology, the human body, sound and light waves, are nothing more than psychic states, or sensations in a psyche.)

What the author has tried to ascertain, unsuccessfully, is under what circumstances what we call the total domination of consciousness in a physical person may be produced; but it's enough to caution that the location of a consciousness in a body is an absurd idea, because the psychic is not malleable in terms of space: an emotion, a felt visual perception, this doesn't happen in my brain, although there might be a discernible causal relationship between sensations and cerebral alterations . . .

The author knew the Lover for many years, seeing him often, and he noticed that after the death of his wife, whom he seemed to love immensely, there was an almost imperceptible shift in the shading of his conduct and expressions, which was troubling, although hard to define. (The author professes in this professional novelist paragraph, but he retains the right to ask that the reader believe a little bit in novelistic miracles, something I've consented to believe in for many years, as a reader of a considerable number of less explicable and congruent novels than my own.) And so it was that little by little the Lover lost his sensibility, until he was reduced to a body without consciousness.

If the reader is also unaware of everything I'm ignorant of (and I thank him for his company), he won't know how to fully and satisfactorily explain Hodgson, or should I say the incomplete automatism

53

that he discovered. It's only possible to understand the basics of what I'm explaining. For that reason I'd swear that the Lover stopped being a personal consciousness years ago, and I myself observe that his conduct in the novel is that of a man who does not feel anything, who neither thinks nor sees, but who lives in an attitude of hopeful waiting, without feeling hope, for his beloved to return and with her, his happiness. In other words, he is actually an insensibility with the perspective of a sensibility. This is very mysterious, and it would be censurable in a person who didn't know that in this world there are movies, and Conan Doyle novels.

The tone of what surrounds him operates on his automatism without the Lover feeling it, that is why he participates in the movements of the novel.

The body is the dominant party, and it does not need sensible collaboration; it can live perfectly without consciousness, and when there is consciousness, the body can oblige it to live, even when it doesn't want to; it opposes itself to suicide in man as the most intolerable pain and will dispense with all feeling in order to maintain the integrity of a personal body: the Body has no other plan than Longevity, not Hedonism.

The novel does not have the Lover as a character, but as an insensible but automated body coordinated with a character. We're not bragging about any great novelty in introducing an automatic person (who would run for a month, perhaps, on clockwork) to the novel, because the Lover is not an automaton by birth; he had consciousness, and he can have it again . . .

The novel hopes that the visual, tactile, and auditory tone of a revived and returned beloved will bring about the miraculous recuperation of the Lover's consciousness.

And the Lover, for his part, will show his tenderness to the novel, enriching it with his beloved. How will he resuscitate her? By being the only man who does not deny his dreams. The Lover revives his beloved because he believes in his dreams and he's happy, because he has faith in lovers' eternity.

A CHARACTER, BEFORE HER FIRST APPEARANCE

"I want to know what kind of people I've ended up with here."

"Nobody who isn't worthy of it. Eterna, the Lover, the President."

"But you should know, Mr. Author, that I can't learn any more, and I can't teach anything to anyone else. Sometimes I'm called Mignon, in *Wilhelm Meister* . . .

"But if we have Eterna here, who was called Leonora in Poe; and the one who was called Rebecca in *Ivanhoe*, and our own Eterna finds herself in Lady Rowena."

"When will I find my own great novelist?"

"Haven't you found him here?"

"But look, your novel doesn't have a 'hermetic seal,' but it leads the way to another novel, because I'm a transmigrating character and I arise not from readers' posterity but out of authors' posterity."

"Let's leave it at this: behave yourself for me. For the rest of it, I don't believe that the authors of the future will be content with used characters, but this isn't my concern. We have an understanding."

ALSO A PROLOGUE

I would have liked this novel to have something of a daydream about it, the most subtle kind. I dreamed in 1928 (*dating* dreams, these can be dated by their concomitance with the series of wakefulness, and also by reference to other dreams which came before or afterwards): 'I found myself in a house where the floor was in shadow or covered with a curtain, either dark or half-opened, as it appeared to me alternatively. And there was a woman whose face I could not distinguish, only the vague contours of feminine dress; and I knew who it was, I felt she was someone I knew without really seeing her; I felt her cordiality, her company, that her soul was not my enemy; also at moments I wasn't sure whether or not I saw and recognized her. Upon my subsequent awaking, or the state that we call awake, referring to the idea or concept, I could not remember her face.' I use quotation marks for dreams, and I'll use them for everything I write specifically about them, so that if I, who am a dream for others, at one time appear in the reader's mind, I'll have the quotation marks to distinguish me as such. All art could be set in quotation marks, and everything I wrote, my three books: *Not All Consciousness is Wakefulness, Newcomer's Papers,* and *Museum of Eterna's Novel,* in each I wanted to evoke or feature the state of recent wakefulness, when we are not yet fully free of our dreams. It's the state that we should conserve to confront pain, and the presentiments of passion, since the ideal of passion is that we create for ourselves a hyper-wakefulness, even though passion is already such a state.

It seems to me that this dream, which I only had once, has a certain divinity, or mysticism, a sense of auto-existence: a certain slippage of personal identity, the eternal escape of individual continuity and its recognition, confirmation.

Outside the state of passion (only passion is altruistic), which is always a state of certainty, the only state of reality for dreams in which both lovers converge and in which everything must be risked, everything must be promised in full awareness, all happiness, all pain—outside of this, we must live in half light, and with half-actions, half-awake, without entirely knowing events and states, since outside of passion the probability is that suffering will prevail; the dream I remember here is the formula of the state of half denial of all certainty and effectivity.

METAPHYSICAL PROLOGUE

This novel is not content to be separate from eternity; it wants to feel the breeze of the eternal on its face; its metaphysics have not abandoned it, and they are as follows:[1]

Exceptions: First. Only about one million "civilized people" have experienced an instant of Radical Unfamiliarity, which is total unfamiliarity: therefore the metaphysical explanation in these pages will be of little importance to them.

Second. Moreover, man is a very small thing, he has very little time and energies for thought; and even the rare man who can dedicate some space to think, the man we call a sage and a genius, is overwhelmed with small or large distractions which demand thirty percent of the muscular and attentive energies of even a man favored with large amounts of free time, not to mention that his patience is drained by this suffering. That's why "sages" and "geniuses" are only condescendingly compared with the very muscular, who for their part are not obligated to think. There's also the sum of mental but automatic things (History, Languages) and apart from that, the irritating task of preparing pages, composition, etc. In summary: all those we call sages have lived and expired in darkness and they are only remembered by their specialties, which surprise us when we compare them with muscular or common men; of themselves, they only know that they've managed to clarify about ten percent of what they hoped. Let's be modest, those of us who are called *intellectuals*: in any trade or muscular life there's a healthy coincidece of net intellectual energies.

Having frankly stated the facts, I now invite myself to offer opinions.

Materialism is a metaphysics; it's not science; its concern is the same as that of Idealism, the essential metaphysical quandary: the astonishing inexplicability that anything "exists." .

1. This metaphysical doctrine is stated principally in *No toda es Vigilia la de los Ojos Abiertos y Otros escritos* (*Not all Consciousness is Wakefulness and Other Writings*) (*Editor's Note—Adolfo de Obieta*)

Science is a pastime that describes Being, with practical ambitions, and without the astonishment-of-being. Materialism, like idealism, and like all clearly-defined metaphysics, concludes by declaring the complete intelligibility of being, its absolute knowability. In this it differs from positivism and science, which attend to the how of the world, of being, and declare the *how* of how being is possible inaccessible to Intelligence, how being is given and not nothing, whether it is given in the first place, how something can happen, be, or feel. It's equivalent to a belief, to conceive that there could be a non-being, that one morning, space, things, and sensations could stop, or that one day they began, out of nothing.

When physicists constructed their visual-tactile world out of atoms, they believed that they could say something, understand something, with the invisible and the impalpable. In the same way they unconcernedly invented the apparition of the consciousness in the heart of these precious recombinations of the insensible and the unconscious: matter. It's not that such unintelligible verbiage calms them; it's that they weren't worried, there was not yet any astonishment: Metaphysics had not so easily been born in them as consciousness was born out of the Unconscious. On the other hand, they found it senseless that idealism should deny Time, Space, the Self, Matter; that it should affirm the sensible state, my current sensory state, as its Only knowability, it's only object of intellection; this is how I name and define being: eternally auto-existing, the eternal, mystical in the intellection; which is to say the category "being" is not fleeting, and cannot be lost.

I don't conceive of an instant of my not-being, of my not-sensing; what I am, which is to say my sensibility, didn't begin, nor will it end, nor will it be interrupted for even an instant, nor will individual identity ever be discontinued in my memory. A time without world, a not-being of being, is an impossible notion.

What is this Mystery, this Happiness and Pain, this existence from which we never escape, this inexorable, mnemonic personal eternity, this Pain towards what we would like not-to-be, and which will always wound us, this Happiness which comes and goes, this inseparable always-existing, this blissful hope, which is not of the moment, for what we would want to be in the moment?

There's only one man who asked himself, Can I not be? He's the man: he existed. When someone leaves, when *another* conceals himself, the man who exists is the one who asks himself, Does death exist?

As shocking as this utterance may be, it must be repeated: Is the one who exists the one who believes or who asks himself, Was I born today, did I not exist before? I can say this myself and yet it won't appear to be an utterance: When I want to think of nothing, does some image arise in my mind that can capture this thought? If an image arises, then I am thinking of something and not nothing; if there isn't an image, I'm not thinking. It's true that we have the word *nothing*, which alludes to something: it's a conditioned negation, or a partial, conditioned existence—that such-and-such a thing is not there, or felt in such-and-such a time or place—which is to say that it is combined with the determinations of other things: there's not anything on this table; or for there not to be in perception what there is in images: the sweets I'm thinking of are not in the house. *Nothing* has no other meaning.

Space is unreal, the world has no magnitude, given that what we can encounter with our widest gaze, the plains and the sky, fit in our memories, that is, in an image. They fit totally and in all their detail in a point of my psyche, of my mind; this does not have extension, points, and it contains images. It's sufficient that the material can make an image of itself without a position or extension, when I invoke it in my mind—it can represent itself totally and exactly, it can *see itself* (since only by this concept are we able to say that in this case we aren't seeing, but *recalling*) and the proof is the fact that in a dream, or in a waking evocation that is very intense, the image is equally alive and gives rise to the same emotions, acts, words, and gestures. Thus it is shown that 1) the Exterior is not intrinsically extensive; 2) the mind, psyche, consciousness, soul, sensibility—all essentially synonyms for subjectivity—has no extension, position, or station anywhere; 3) that immensity, the Cosmos, is therefore a point, or better, the autonomous, *involuntary* Image, the contingent and spontaneous that we face with our will.

In other words, everything that exists is an image, some voluntary, others involuntary, dreams and reality intermingling and giving rise to the same emotions and acts when they are equally vivid.

Given all this, it may therefore be said that the world is inextensive. But sometimes an object presents a different size, depending on the position it takes relative to ourselves; the sounds emanating from it with an identical rhythm would vary in their intensity, and to get a different kind of feeling from it, a tactile feeling, we'd have to effect some kind of translation. We thus have the only thing that's effective about Space: the *effect*. Distance, or given the perception of an object, sound, or perfume, we can make the size, the detail, or the intensity larger depending on the case and by means of our own work, which we would call getting closer, and in a certain moment of this task we could obtain a tactile sensation from this visual object. That translation is required, so that an object that we call distance can offer us a tactile sensation, is an *effect* of "space" and its only reality.

Likewise, with regard to Time, its reality resides in its *effect*: that a waiting is required, which is to say a series of events, so that there is a desired or feared outcome after one of those changes or states of things which we call the *present,*. When something pleasurable is desired, it's in the *future*; if pain is feared, it's the *future* also; if something painful is not feared, it's *past,* and the same for the pleasurable if it does not give rise to desire or joy; in each case there's always present effects of the past or present states that would be in the future. A student, who is two or three months away from his exams might have alternative representations of the same scene: imagining himself in some classroom near a table where four professors are seated; this scene could correspond, with the same details, to the anatomy exam he sat for in March or the one coming up next November: Which one of these scenes is future, or past? The intellectual fringe is exactly the same: sometimes it gives rise to a feeling of fear, and sometimes a pleasant feeling. In the first case the event is future; in the second it's past: the exam that I passed is pleasant for me to recall, the one I am *about to take* intimidates me.

Size (space) and duration (time) are not real, but inferences with respect to the effect of the muscular work of transposition or the mental work of hope, uncertainty, desire. Duration is merely the sum of the changes that must occur, that make themselves actual before another change happens; and this *before* and this *make itself actual* are not temporal implications, which would be tautological in this case, but psychological correlatives: so the *actual* is a state when the feeling—fear or desire—which is tied to it culminates in insensibility: the fear of something as fear is naturally always actual or present, but the represented or perceived scene is only real when the fear reaches its limit.

I've said all this to establish the nothingness of Time and Space. These are abstractions which only can tell us what happens in terms of representations of scenes or events which in perception or reality bring us pain or pleasure and which nevertheless are given in our minds several times, sometimes giving rise to emotion and drives and sometimes not. (In the first case the image is of a future reality;

in the second, of a past reality.) Such is the case with all that happens in our psyche with respect to Time. *Distant* and *proximal* (Space), in its turn, are differentiated because of the possibility of obtaining a better view of some object, or of other sensations of it, and in some cases, this demands a kind of work of translation: I see a flower and in order to obtain from it a tactile sensation and the sensation of aroma, I must initiate a muscular action, or another person must do it for me. This is all that matters about Space.

The nothingness of Time and Space, which is correlative to the nothingness of the Self (or personal identity) and of material Substance, situates us in an eternity without conceivable discontinuities. This is the metaphysical certainty of my novel.

THE MAN WHO FEIGNED TO LIVE

(THE ONLY CHARACTER WHO NEEDS EXPLAINING. HE'S ALREADY BEEN EXPLAINED TWICE:[1]
HE LACKS EXISTENCE, BUT HE ABOUNDS IN CLARIFICATIONS.)

1. It could be that I'll only give him two explanations, though I've promised two.
Yet another inconsistency! But I already said, or I'll say so later on, that I use
any recourse, including inconsistencies, to confront the artistic or verisimilitude,
childish verisimilitude, and I will signal each recourse and justify them all. It's a
more frank way of proceeding and a great labor that I undertake on the public's
behalf, much greater than the comfortable and overdone practice of putting lunatics in novels. Quixote, Sancho, Hamlet, these are all characters who are admittedly
insane, like Dostoevsky's idiot, and one of Hamsun's protagonists (they awarded a
madman to this writer, if during a single page he behaves with any sort of logic he
doesn't get the crazy man and we say that the author has failed: the lunatic gains
the author an exemption from taking care with his absurdities). And nevertheless
these authors continue to believe that they are realists; to make a novel or a play
with lunatics in it is like doing science by negating causality, it's to opt for as
little work as possible since everything is explained by dementia, as if it were the
novel's coordinator, which makes realism impossible to verify for the reader, since
the disjointed and absurd are in fact a verisimilitude of dementia. Insanity in art
is a realist negation of realist art. The effects, consequences, and influences of
insanity for the sane characters might be realist art, but the conduct and character
of the lunatic character, which is what principally happens in these comfortable,
pseudorealist novels, amounts to an outrageous practical joke. Analogously the
sensory (the pleasures and pains of eating, smoking, of sexuality and physiology,
etc) is not a possible topic for art; the effects of sensuality on the non-sensuality of
a character, yes. Example: Bovary, whose life is entirely despicable for its sensual
despair, which does not interest art except as desperation, not sensuality. I don't
give you insane characters, I give an insane book, and with the precise goal of
persuading by artistic, not realist means.

In this novel the man who feigns to live is not seen, nor does anyone allude to him.
He's not in the novel. He's a character "like that," idiosyncratic; "he's like that,"
and so characteristically that no one notices that he doesn't appear in the novel.
He would have liked to appear more prominently, if he still could fit; to give him
an importance worthy of a non-existent; to say, for example, that he carried off an

artistically rendered Absence, an Absence finally realized in symbols and taking up space.

Or we could blame him for everything bad that happens to the characters, or for the style or lack of elegance in the idea and composition of our novel. Or use him as if he accumulated, in his inconceivable reality as a "absent character," all of the impossibilities which are openly used in all novels and films and, from there, the impossibility of the author's knowing what's going to happen in the future, what the characters think but don't say, and other small impossibilities that happen in stories.

But I will restrict myself to honestly saying that what's impressive about this person is that he shows such satisfaction in the simple detail that the first page dealing with him is the only one, and the only one he requires. This wasn't done intentionally, but by means of a rare strategy: a subtitle in parenthesis and a long footnote. Stories and poems are full of things that are much harder to explain than what happens here, which is the influential action of a character's absence, thus typographically signaling the efficiency and the substantiality of this nonexistent protagonist.

As I said, nobody would know—this is how the author would have it—that this character isn't in the novel, if it weren't for the character (who before this prologue had not yet kindly agreed to be called Maybegenius) (since the man who may or may not be a genius tends to get confused with the Man who Feigned to Live), asking questions, being surprised and demanding his presence, even though he's already been told that, because of his role, making him appear would be the end of him (not because he'd be bad company for the rest of the characters, but because with him Absence, which is one of the most lauded qualities of verse, would not communicate its enchantment in a novel).

This not-yet-named Maybegenius's obstinance has obliged us to seek out and finally locate the explication that would have the most eloquence for the Man who Feigned to Live. Each time that Maybegenius asks for him, the reply is that the Man who Feigned to Live is busy with the only thing left in the world today that is shameful, or that could cause someone to hide: he's tearing apart a box of matches to get to the Victoria Matches Company coupon. Maybegenius is entirely calmed by this news, and he sympathizes with the Man who Feigned to Live. He truly believes that this task is pleasant, but risky, and thus the only serious reason to keep oneself out of sight.

The Man who Feigned to Live does not appear because he thinks that a novel that itself failed to appear for such a long time must celebrate him, and he runs the risk of finding nobody who will praise him if he doesn't retain, in the novel's publicity, something of his invisibility, some trace of a future thing; it makes a novel which has waited a long time to be written, to exist—which rarely happens; a book's non-existence is obtained between its being promised and its being published; a book that is not announced lacks non-existence—to maintain such a character in the state of being partially realized. But it also is convenient for the rigidity of the absolutely fantastic that we want to reign in this novel, that the services of a person with unassailable inexistence are guaranteed.

All of the events and characters in novels are pleasantly impossible, they are fantastic with respect to reality. The Man who Feigned to Live, in his pleasant inexistence, which is how he will gain the public's respect, is fantastic with respect to the novel: it's not only that he doesn't appear in life; he also doesn't appear in the book.

The reader will say if he and I are happy with the conduct of all the characters, and we don't know how to thank him for sticking with us until the end, which he's done so marvelously, running some of the characters over to whichever page the reader was on, so that they could be read. The Man who Feigned to Live has tirelessly attended to his nonexistent role, showing a real flair for non-being and a quite endearing proclivity towards absence; he must have had a lot of previous experience. Once the novel was finished, the ban on his being was lifted and he came to visit us like a newborn, weak and grateful and incipient, without a mark on him. It's lamentable that this prodigal visit wasn't part of our lovely novel, but it was already finished. It doesn't have the talent of always continuing the way the reader would like and the way the Sunday editions of *La Nación* and *La Prensa* do. There's no defect that shows his nonexistence, not even the smallest detail, nothing to run the risk of existing at every moment, of being a failed non-being, the type of nonexistent character that so many books have expelled from their pages.

GUIDE TO THE PROLOGUES (WARNING PROLOGUE)

I'm furnishing a new Chapter for leftover characters and scenes. I must improvise some kind of accommodations, pages, facts, and redaction for them, since my characters are all extremely minor: the second I leave off writing they stop doing things; when I'm not working, everything stops. Here's little Juancito, "in floorless air of space"—a lyric that swells in me like a breath of relief in the face of the prologues that remain—in the middle of falling from a balcony, because yesterday I stopped writing, as any writer of conscience would do, to clear a space for his fall's inevitable end (and to prepare the description thereof). It wouldn't cost him anything to follow the action to its conclusion, but he doesn't do it! Another time they were looking for me all over the Novel because I had left Don Luciano while he was putting one arm into his overcoat, and this posture had resulted in unbearable cramps. And the President complained because I interrupted his redaction just when he was going to blow out the match with which he had lit his cigarette, so he spent the whole afternoon burning his fingers with nothing to smoke. This seems impossible. At any given hour in my novel there's someone with only one boot on, a young man with only one girlfriend, or some couple who wanted to be left alone except I hadn't finished sending Mama to bed or having Auntie nod off. Also I left off writing Don Luciano when he was being fitted for a new Moral Sense, and I was nowhere to be found when they wanted me to return it. And what's worse, though of a fortuitous consequence: I abandoned the entire audience at the christening of a new street name, and they were counting on getting some sleep as soon as the Minister got up to give his boring speech. I left him standing, and in the moment in which I was going to write about how the public was asleep, I was called away because of some curl that hadn't curled or because only one side of some face was shaved; since the public was a character in my novel and the Minister wasn't, he expounded at length all of his indispensable notions, and the public had to listen to it all, something which has never happened in a single inauguration, anniversary celebration, high school prize

66

day, or statue unveiling. The audiences in my novel will never again call for streets to be christened. In the end, the editors warned me that if I leave off writing someone who's going to buy my novel in that delicate instant of his unstable decision, I'll be unworthy of the thousand pesos they spent on postering the walls with assurances about the "Best novel since both it and the world began."

AT THE GATES OF THE NOVEL
(IN ANTICIPATION OF THE STORY)

HOW, AS A TRUE NOVELISTIC ARTIST, TO EXTRICATE ONESELF FROM THE READER WHO
SKIPS TO THE END. REMEDY FOR THIS READERLY BLOCKAGE.

You can make your own list of rejected Characters; I'm only rejecting one kind of Reader: the reader who skips to the end. Thanks to his procedure of giving substance in advance to the whole story and the ending, he's already quit the scene.

My tactic as a novelist is: the Reader only catches glimpses of the characters, but what he comes to know of them he knows so well that he is pricked by readerly irritation. He's left insatiable by his incomplete knowledge or "half-knowledge," yet loves their delicacy. Thus two mnemonic devices are at work in his memory (you can't remember without some sort of emotion, be it irritation or tenderness), rendering the characters unforgettable. This explanation anticipating the novel will make it so that the reader is not worried that he doesn't understand its imperfections; this way, he'll read comfortably and won't set himself the task of understanding the truncated or obscure.

Any author should candidly advise the reader right from the start: "This is a novel that will go like this:

A gentleman of a certain maturity, the President, is assembling all the people who were good to him during his excursions away from home, and who want to live with him, in a certain countryside locale.

This circle of friendship prolongs itself for a happy while, but the host himself is not happy, and he incites his friends to undertake a certain Action.

The Action is undertaken with success but he continues to be unhappy.

Having concluded the action they separate, and aside from other details and events, nothing more is known about anyone.

The essence of this tale therefore consists, reader, in the President, who does not feel satisfied with the life of friendship in the

Estancia, moving with a great effort to prove himself in the vocation of happiness and, departing from his perennial discontent with this movement, struggles to action, but once he fully attains it, he falls into disillusionment with the action and with the great desire to be happy in love, since before he formed his friendly group in the *Estancia* he held Friendship, Action, and Love in disdain and his only vocation was meditation on the Mystery.

Before and after the novel's narrative, what dominated in him was metaphysical meditation, which made him a failure in Friendship, in the happiness of Action, and the fullness of Love.

The only character in this novel who's got this kind of devil in him is the President; he comes up short in everything: love, metaphysics, friendship, action; he's deep into the Mystery, he loves Eterna very much; later he seeks friendship; unsatisfied, he decides on Action; again discontented and always one to make suggestions, after nights of deliberation and suffering he invites those companions that he made so happy, that he enlightened and filled with problems during years of communal life, to part ways permanently. So as to never meet again, deliberately, those who were once so happily united and who are now separated, so as to never know one or the other's fortunes, disgraces, finales. This Academic Death is a not a foolish decision for those without Faith—which is almost all of us. It's true that it would be better to be united, and with Faith.

With these vacillations, that great character, the President, imposes on this novel a disjointed disposition and redaction, but the denouement of academic death gives it grandeur, and the rehearsal of the characters that comes before it shows a respect for the reading public that no author has yet mustered: there won't be any more plays and novels without first putting the characters through their paces in full view of the reader.

To conclude, the President author ends up with two discontents: the personality of Eterna imposes itself upon him to such a degree that he's unable to use his evocative power in the service of what would have been Eterna's august sentiment in the Farewell and the mystery of her subsequent destiny. And likewise the author, just as much of an artist as he is believed to be, can't imagine or even mention how beings of such innocence and sweetness—Sweetheart and Maybegenius—are torn from each other's company by the resulting dispersion.

In summary: the Finale of the half-written novel by the best of the semi-novelists is left unrealized.

If you think there's a probability that a novel like the one thus synthesized might be agreeable to you, read it. And allow me to exercise my artistic talent while you read it, since this novel might be agreeable without having anything artistic in it or having any value for me. But it would be useful for me if I could exercise the only true artistic operation over your spirit. You will feel, first obscurely and then more clearly, an artistic emotion, the one I have sought to elicit.

The reader who won't read my novel if he can't know all of it first is my kind of reader, he's an artist, because he who reads only seeking the final resolution is seeking what art should not provide, his interest is in the merely vital, not in a state of consciousness: the only artistic reader is the one who does not seek resolution."

FREDERICO'S ENTRANCE IN THE NOVEL, AS PROLOGUE

He's so substantial that he is what's the matter and yet another matter entirely.

I don't labor under the illusion of keeping the Boy with the Long Stick out of the novel forever—he's the one you all know as a future character without a birth, yet confined in the novel as its resisted aspirant, plotting to be a part of the story—and in my squeamishness I've prepared titles in the eventual though undesirable case that a place must be made for him, so that although I've received him under duress he has not been denied all consideration in his *actual* reception, at least that he can discern (for all the characters of my invention—who make the plot using the combined existence that I've allotted each one—are beings whose births were mandatory, called to novelistic life by the lazy cravings of Fantasy, not like we who were consulted in the matter, and they nevertheless feel themselves so in possession of this casual and thin existence that they'll yield a place to this hooligan). I've consented to what he's sensibly asked of me: that I make antecedents for him, giving him access in a prologue that will ease his ingress in to the novel, when he's able to obtain it thanks to a moment of carelessness on the part of the powerful characters who have been assured existence in the novel from the beginning; they're like retirees from unreal existence, they have such an easy air about them, as though they've been accustomed to exist in this way even before they started, an ease which we the living also bring with us from birth, since none of us showed any surprise when we began living, which we wouldn't believe if they hadn't told us so—and I, like those who remember my birth but don't remember their own, have opted for not believing it necessary, thus affirming our eternity—.

Although Federico may cause more ravages than a critic, the possibility of his appearance must be considered, and prepared for, so as to best ensure the peace if he does appear. Putting this boy in the novel saves the critics the trouble of destroying it.

He has titles, books, the past; he's not a boy whom the author began writing only in the present book and edition (this popular author, recently settled in Literature, which is here inaugurated, isn't so well-known that he demands that the sale of his book begin with the fourth edition, the way that great authors do).

God, invented so as to author our birth, was instantly worried about keeping our good graces, and so he created the World to *make believe* (this isn't religious, but it's religion's first step) that he had been concerned with other matters before us; he called it the third, and believed that we'd ask about the others. "Yes, this one is number three, which I've given you in addition to the ones before." On the contrary, when we saw the number we said, "Third and last." If it had occurred him to leave a return address, we'd have sent it back.

The boy Federico tirelessly undertakes economic endeavors. He made a Noise Factory with all his friends. To equip the best rubble-flingers from amongst their workers they obtained metals, zinc, brass, or crystals treated with mineral agents. Easy transport and an available market assured prosperity. The financial crisis of 1921, the toppling of Stinnes, the colossal competition between Standard Oil and Dutchshell, the flood of paper German marks . . . all we know is that despite the great demand, there wasn't a single noise left in the area that was ready for manufacture; Federico's company couldn't keep up, and had found a way to provide the public with a racket that no one would notice, without making noise, and without anyone knowing where it came from. Each father found his boy and helped him to walk at a variety of accelerated paces, two hours from the inauguration of this Establishment, which was so acclaimed by the population for its prescience and convenience. All the staff members were tucked into bed and thus avoided declaring bankruptcy, which either the Stinnes perturbations, currency instability, unlimited German marks, or the obscurity of Wilson's 14 points would have made necessary . . .[1] or maybe the only coincidence was that in this city—and I congratulate them on their work in rounding up the boys—papas are larger than their sons. Before Federico could define, in his reflections, what the final mercantile determination had been, if it had been the Stinnes perturbation, the petroleum wars, et cetera, or if it were all of them, he began new individual operations as God's secretary or official note-taker, to make note for Him of all the invocations of "God's will" in reference to whether the patio would

1. An allusion to the troubled times in the postwar period 1914-1918 (commercial and bank competition, unlimited printing of German marks, and the proposition of the North American President Wilson for a League of Nations). (*Editor's Note—Adolfo de Obieta*)

be cleaned "by tomorrow," which the ladies of modest houses formulated when they were feeling mortified by their procrastination: "Tomorrow, God willing, we'll wash the floors," "Tomorrow, God willing, I'll clean my room." He kept careful observations, and calculated that each day God was forgetting to will some thirty thousand put off floor washings worldwide. He also had to record all of the "Tomorrow, God willing, we'll organize the closets;" another thirty thousand. All we know for sure is that Federico found himself that morning standing on the ground before the entrance of my novel, and it's not proper to ask him if his dealings with God ended badly, thanks to boredom and bad pay. Gods are old and crafty; what's more, God or the Devil (they're the same) knows more because he's old than because he's a devil.

But there's one more thing that we can't put off saying for another minute: the coming and going of Federico around the world. We'll say this at least: it was very slow. He left when it was time to shift Eterna's lips and flutter her pale eyelids for an animated smile at the President's ingenuity, and he returned when the smile disappeared because the President had suffered an impossibility of candor at the impossibility of sulking and he took hold of Eterna's skirt as a signal that he wanted to "go to the wardrobe," that is, be punished.

And with that we've introduced Federico into the prologues.

TO THE WINDOW-SHOPPING READER

After long experience in beginning polygraphy, preceded by an A-plus silence, the kind of authoritative silence or encyclopedic clamming-up that touches on everything and that everybody welcomes, I have come to suspect that the Reader has a very fragile disposition. But his evanescence is not so extreme that Titles and Covers, at the very least, cannot reach him. From this reflection was born my innovation: title-texts. This is how I want to explain the length of my novel's title.

Since the circulation of covers and titles is at the mercy of window-dressers, newspaper stands, and warning labels, the ideal Reader of Covers, Reader in the Doorway—Minimal Reader, or Unsought Reader, will finally here stumble across the author who had him in mind, the author of the cover-book, of the Title-Novel. And consider that "the hooked reader" must be the title of the Title that we're presenting of our novel, since the first plot point already happened on the cover, where the Minimal Reader is solidly hooked by the only thing that the booksellers (ever stingy with their time) have read: the title page, the only page that for most books anyone bothered to edit; truly Posterity, which everyone worships and which no one has met in person, will recognize this.

The Sunday editions of *La Nación* and *La Prensa* perhaps suggested to me the cover-text, since they are a species of Sunday edition, a Sunday edition of titles and, despite their length, a holiday of titles. As I have also observed, after a long time believing that these editions never ended—and that's a warning to everyone who leafs through these editions, thinking them endless—they do indeed end: you have to have a Sunday as desperate as I did during the times when I read them in their entirety, just to extricate myself from the error of believing them infinite, a belief that no thinking person should ever have about anything.

The origin and plan of my inauguration of the title-read is thus proved: to take advantage of the better circulation procured for the title by the shop window, compared with the bulk interior of the book. That part is later circulated by a cordial character, the man of letters, who operates like the match that lights more than one cigarette. One man alone, if he is able to obtain a pension from the "Promotors of the Book" and longevity from tonics (these are the only religion left to us, besides those two great Argentine religions: the faith that whoever goes to Paraguay will return with a parrot, and the faith that people come from the North bring Tafi cheese. Without these tokens no one will believe that they've really returned; you can't bring back another bird, like the way rich gentlemen and ladies bring back philosophers from Europe, taking advantage of the sales)—one man, then, can make a whole edition from a single book, and the buyer won't even notice when sales fall off, since the borrower leaves him far behind with his invisible trajectory. A hundred title-readers are calculated for each book reader; text-titles and cover-books do not mistake the reader; they are often brilliant Literature's only hope for a wide radius of influence, since these titles are not content with the modest title of cherished and secret Literature.

I therefore prevent my book from continuing on after those who have finished reading my title withdraw, since it does not belong to that species of facsimile books in wood that simulate full library shelves. This way if the reader does not continue reading, no one will blame me for not warning him. It's already too late for the author who doesn't write and the reader who doesn't read to come to an agreement: now I am decidedly writing.

TWO REJECTED CHARACTERS

In a novel as well-ordered as this one, the reader should know the characters. And they should be classified.

Ours are:

Real Characters: Eterna, the President.

Fragile Characters, owing to their vocation in life, because they believe they can be happy: Maybegenius, Sweetheart.

Nonexistent Characters (with presence): The Lover.

Perfect Character, owing to a genuine vocation for being content to be a character: Simple.

End of the Chapter Character: The Traveler.

Absent Character, or Absence as character: The Man who Feigned to Live.

Smart, theoretical Character: The Metaphysician.

Thwarted Character, and Candidate for Character: Federico, the Boy with the Long Stick.

Unknown Character (the only celebrity appearing in the Novel).

Awaited Character: the Beloved of the Lover.

Characters by absurdity: the Reader and the Author.

Characters rejected ab initio: Pedro Corto and Nicolasa Moreno.

Those last two won't be in my novel. Pedro Corto wanted to read it just so he could be in it—some Readers don't want to start reading a book if you tell them beforehand everything that's in it—and he demanded that the book finish before certain pies, which he had acquired just before the narrative began, could get cold; I believe his exclusion is justified without leaving me vulnerable to accusations of avarice in the number of characters. Nicolasa Moreno will not appear either, and although she accepted her role with great pleasure, she's obliged to leave the novel for periods during which she goes to see whether the milk has boiled over, or she lifts the lid every few minutes on the sweet pumpkin she'd set to boil a third time; both activities cut down on her appearances in the book, and I can't do anything about it, since everyone knows that God made a mistake when he prohibited ubiquity.

I hope that the lack of a Cook character will not give rise to the fear that I left all the characters with nothing to eat from beginning to end, something which would only suit the silhouette of the elegant Maybegenius. I fixed this difficulty, but I can't remember now just how.

I forgot because I also had something else around here that could get cold: a food item or perhaps something more spiritual, I'm not sure, or something that could boil over: perhaps an enthusiasm or clarity in the Mystery, a half-phrase that might make all things finally transparent, give me mystic perception: perhaps it was something higher: one of Eterna's gestures, leftover from yesterday, a new sublimity in her tenderness, a smile at her melancholy or of gratitude towards the present and fear for the future, for what will put an end to her; and I didn't want to stop gazing at her in my memory, I kept this image of her expression—a pleat in her visage—with me in my solitude, making it appear to me again in memory, just as someone repeatedly throws a stone into quiet water, making the reflected light dance on the surface as it ripples with circles in relief.

In the end, John Mountainclimber found a job with us. He wanted to be an employee, not a character in the novel; it makes him nervous to be read, to be tickled by the gazes of the eternally curious: your gaze, reader. This means that in the tangled thought of this Mountainclimber the reader's existence was the obstacle to fame. Mountainclimber is so ruined by charity that he thought I might pay him with five centavos and still want change. He's the kind of person who wants you to lend him a suit when he needs it, which is when it's raining cats and dogs; and he found himself with the sort of person that only offers to lend his umbrella when it's a beautiful day, and only to someone who has influence with the State Meteorologist, or to someone who will be sure to lose the umbrella so he has an excuse to get a better one.

The author told him everything without displeasing a single character; I haven't done harm to anyone, and the fact that not one of them has written anything against me proves it. Mountainclimber, you will soon grace our pages, but we won't let you speak before we do, which will keep the public from meeting with your sharp tongue.

Some of the characters in question wanted to appear, but didn't:

Nicolasa and the Boy with the Long Stick; others like the little Watchman and the Traveler hardly even know of the novel. Our characters are a "heterogeneous population" of pretenders, unknowns, aforementioned, and actual characters in the novel; there are even characters who vary in their appearance and others who appear under different names. And a non-existent character. And outside there's a character that dreams the novel and the character of whom the novel dreams.

What can you tell me about Identity? Here all adventures transpire and all the tomes of metaphysics can't tell you a thing. What you think when you lie down to sleep, what marvels you dream of, and what you think on awaking—what do these states have in common? And we don't know that we've slept (we always believe when we wake up that we were awake at least several minutes before), and we wouldn't know if we had slept if other people (who could be just dreams themselves) didn't tell us, just as we don't directly experience our birth but are told about it by others, who don't know anything directly about their own births. And if they don't know themselves, how can we believe them? So it is that this novel resembles life more than the "bad" or realist novel, that is, the conventional novel. Continuity (identity) of the characters makes sorcerers out of the bad or conventional novelists: this continuity was never shown in a novel nor does it exist in life; these writers aren't very realist in this sense: they can't even say what continuity is.

We would have liked to talk about each type of character, but I will only explain one, this character who is missing, because he takes his role of Traveler seriously. He is always in the middle of an inexhaustible journey: he looks for a country or region whose climate and political system (I suppose it wouldn't be an electoral system) favors three conditions that are immensely advantageous for him: a clean shave lasts up to five weeks; and boots, usually so ephemeral, last as long as buttonholes.

We're doing this prologue while we wait for a certain uproar to quiet down: among all the prologues there has arisen the moveable prologue, which, they tell me, is going around changing pages; there should be no disagreements between prologues of the same novel; this unstable prologue is the one that looks around for where it is missing, in a Novel that found where art and spirit were missing.

FIRST PROLOGUE OF THE NOVEL
FOR THE ABRIDGED READER

There are two things I want to make public: a drawing that Sirio or Audivert made me, showing with some persuasiveness the ladies and gentlemen pounding on my door, demanding to appear as characters in my novel; thus I have brought upon myself the anger of so many people, who leave in a huff because I cannot accommodate them. You'll recognize also that only material impossibility and not a failure to recognize their talents is what obliges me to refuse admission. They will all read my novel (not because I am proposing to reserve them as readers since they are unfit to be characters), and they will be the only readers who are entirely entitled to their predisposition against the novel (because they aren't in it). I have the same experience: I've never appeared in a novel and so none has seemed perfect to me, and there are lots of authors who have managed what I've managed (or will have managed, in what I write), which is to keep the Boy out of the novel.

And another drawing, which might be of the same moment, but with a hundred times more people, which gives me an idea, however remote, of the throngs of readers awaiting my novel.

Everyone has noticed my widespread success as an author, or anyway it behooves them to know it. But someone says that while there's always a crowd of readers gathered around my novel, it's not because they want to read it so much, but *because there must be* near my novel, or across the street, some notice from *La Prensa* that says (and this is pure conjecture): "Millionare gentleman, celibate and sentimental, seeks agreeable housekeeper to take exclusive care of his house and serve as his sole companion." They add what the critics of the hard school, who only concern themselves with fundamental merits and essential aesthetics say, when synthesizing their plaudits in the comparative conclusion of whether the statement "My novel has more of a public than one of the most enticing personal ads from a great newspaper" is a concrete reality and not an unfair comparison; they've lazily commissioned the personal ad's efficacy to attract the crowd that was already there. They also explain that there's a difficulty in syntax in the aforementioned personal ad: it's not clear whether the millionaire seeks a housekeeper or the housekeeper seeks a millionaire, and this is why half the crowd is female, seeking the millionaire, and the other half are millionaires looking for a housekeeper.

What must be recognized here is that I've used the incentive of appearing in the novel with a few people whose sympathy or consideration I wanted; and that sometimes I'll withdraw someone from the novel because he or she made me angry, either justly or unjustly, or because of an inconsistent fidelity in the character.

FOR THOSE NOT EXPERT IN METAPHYSICS

I can't give the anxious young person what he longs for: a certain understanding or a certain power to achieve an ambition, or a steady, secure direction in the darkness of Being, nothing concrete, just a sign in the sky, a tree in Africa, a strange affinity, a turned stone, a shadow profile that, raising or retaining itself in the mind, will signify to him that the act or intuition that he had in his mind in the moment he found it must continue on, and is in fact what led him to the attainment of this desire. But I can send him down the path of such promising thoughts, so ripe with the totalpossibility that is eternity, so heady with mystery, that they will create for him an interior world so strong that no Reality can have the power of sadness or impossibility or limitation for him that it has over someone who hasn't managed to construct thought-fascinations to accompany him always.

We can all cultivate this constant and powerful daydream that dulls the sharpness of an adverse reality. Religions, patriotism, humanism, all do this in some way; most of all religions. The notion of honor is perhaps a voluntary combination of an anti-Reality analgesic.

But for someone who has not obtained Totalove, which is the Highest form of Daydream, because it is hedonic in two senses: in itself and aesthetically (which is to say in thought, in what appears to it when we contemplate it in ourselves or in another)—there is a still stronger base than these analgesics for construction of Daydream: the mystic's attitude—the opposite of the religious attitude—which is only achievable by touching the limitation of the Intelligence on all of its limits, the unthinkability of Being, not the small-minded unthinkability of antonyms—a prolific emptiness—but unthinkability itself.

While we await Totalove, let's emancipate ourselves from the absurd notion of the Unknowable, which is a vestige of that infantile veneration of Reality, the vague fear of Man faced with the World (physical and psychical) derived from a vulgar conception of Intelligence as just one tool among others, just as incapable as any of them of perceiving causes and effects and formulating causal laws for well-being and eluding, anticipating, or preventing good or bad things. And let us emancipate ourselves from the Impossible, from all that we search for and sometimes believe does not exist, and, even worse, cannot exist. Nothing, therefore, should detain us in the search for a full, unrestricted solution, leaving no irreducible remainder.

Because psychical or spatial[1] Reality is full, just as full as its correlative certainty. Up to a certain limit, Certainty and Reality, despite the Error associated with them, are synonyms. It's not only that Reality is full, familiar, and certain, but also that our Certainty and Familiarity, the aplomb with which we manage or judge it, and all of the metaphysical jargon, cannot vary our conduct, whether or not we feel certain. Example: A worker who puts in eight hours a day breaking glass lands one thousand hammer blows during a given period, always with the fulfilled certainty that the blow of the hammer will break the glass: one thousand instances of Certainty in an hour. And if we put in his place a top metaphysician, the same thing will happen to him (although no metaphysician can clearly tell which is the Fundamental of Induction). Certainty, Fullness, Familiarity of Reality.

The theory of Eternity demands suitable exercises of Emancipation from absurd limitations. And for only one prologue, that's quite enough metaphysics. To each prologue its own speciality.

1. I don't say external because everything, psychical or spatial, is exterior to the attention or interest with which we perceive it. This attention can't go with every perception, not everything is double—subject and object—and that which was in the mind or sensibility without being noticed can be, later, in the image that it leaves behind.

DESCRIPTION OF ETERNA

(SWEETHEART SAYS SHE DOESN'T KNOW ETERNA; HERE I'VE NOTED WHAT
SHE'S LIKE, SO THAT SWEETHEART CAN MEET HER, SINCE IT PLEASES
ME TO APPEASE THE CURIOSITY OF MY CHARACTERS.)

*She has tangled tresses, just as my novel does, with which it binds itself
to the reader's heart. She's tall, shapely, with black eyes and hair. Eterna
cannot be described in any other manner than this:*

*Whoever comes before her loses the power of forgetting. And he who is
able to forget her is crippled.*

*Whoever cannot forget her remains, understands her and loves her
without resignation.*

*And whomever she gives her love is given what nobody has ever had
until now: a Past, what he most wanted, what changes his history.*

*She is so delicate, so just and simple, and her happiness is so without
infatuation, that any one, no matter how monstrous, can beg happiness
of her.*

She's farthest of all from sensation.

*Whoever sees her must by the second day understand her mystery and
his own Eternity.*

*Many can give you a future, but only she can give you a happy past.
And even then, she also gives you a future, because you'll never lose anything again, or know anything again.*

THE ESSENTIAL FANTASMAGORICALISM OF THE WORLD

Beloved, we feel the emptiness of the world, of the geometrical and physical presentation of Things, of the Universe, and the fullness, the unique certainty of Passion, essential Being, without plurality.

You'll smile, as if spellbound by this void, from a window that seems to look out over an immense and immovable External Reality that quickly reduces to a point, if you think for a moment how the image of a scene you dream or imagine when you think yourself awake might contain the entire world, and nevertheless it fits in your mind, or spirit, or if you like, in the vibration of an imperceptible molecule of your "gray matter," as the physiologists say. If, having taken in a panoramic view of sun, earth, sky, forests, river, seas, river banks, or buildings, later you'll think or dream that you have exactly the same immense image closed in a point of your mind, of your soul, or, if you like, in a microscopic nervous cell in your brain. Moreover, this same gray matter, and the entire brain, is an image in your mind, since you wouldn't know it existed if it weren't for the images you have of its form, color, divisions, sketches, or views, and your images of contact, of temperature, if you've studied anatomy. If the gray matter existed for itself, how could it think of itself? What we're devising is precisely the gray matter's thought about itself, the gray matter's own imagination of itself. That's what we are, with the simplicity of a circle, ourselves, the gray matter's own imagination of itself. How can an imagistic organ have images of itself? How can the gray matter, where thought is said to reside, think of itself, while the eyes cannot see themselves directly; we see everything through the brain, and yet we don't see the brain itself?

If inside my mind there's no extension and yet I can represent in any image I make the entirety of what I've seen, it's simply because there is no Extension, the entire Universe is no more than a single point, or less even, it's no more than an idea, an image in my soul.

This extension is what creates the illusion of plurality that isn't applicable to the only reality of being: Sensibility.

I'll stop here; I think these words could bring your sensibility to the abyss of being and from there to the recognition that everything is psyche, and thus immortal. Because I already insinuated, in my many attempts to move your melancholy belief in death, that I feel that the obstacle that dominates me, keeping my love for you from being the totalove that you deserve and which is reality's entire worth, is this discrepancy that separates us: you believe that death awaits us, a termination of our persons and our love, and I don't believe that totalove can flourish in beings who believe that they are fleeting.

PROLOGUE OF INDECISION

The past, art, and the present offers four marvels: cold, fatalism, negation of the Human as a possibility for happiness and intellection, and indirect affirmation of the hedonistic and intellectual failure of the Human, which is Cervantes's attitude in Quixote and Sancho's, the only great and genuinely ironic attitude, the only authentic pessimism presented in literary art, where so many cardboard pessimists seek to persuade; Rabelais's negation, which is equally rotund, happier, and not as sentimental, since it's sometimes direct and as if deliberate, doctrinal, thus less secure; Beethoven's *Joy and Torment*, whose joy is rarer and more prodigious, never joyful in itself, but in sympathy, opening itself in the storm that, in his music, is always approaching; and one of Eterna's Gestures which I haven't yet seen, yet I know how it will be, and I'll see it in her face the day I make a certain request, if I ever make it.

One can live well on a single Story, and, in truth, totalovers live on only the news of Being, of the Mystery that one is for the other.

And even when I found Eterna in fantasy, I discovered, and I now am certain, that I could live on only one of her gestures, and there are others in her, so many, just to live on one. This gesture is so immense, so full of personal and total signification, that without having it, but feeling it possible in her, and knowing that it must show itself before a demand that I have yet to make, I find myself in the fullness of being.

This is entirely another prologue, I haven't begun it anywhere but here, and only those who still don't know what I say in it can assert that it contains nothing of what is proper and necessary in a prologue: a reader can't always get by just by making there be less pages of Literary Art (i.e., that there's no prologue).

I'm going to enumerate the books that I planned to write when I was twenty-five. I will use a prologue, a few pages to demonstrate how much the public has been spared because the circumstances of my life denied me the means, my pen and ink, for thirty years. The page that gives the public a clear idea is a page well-employed; just as it seems to me that this page is nearly as genial as Maeterlinck's three-hundred-page eulogy to silence; it's a pleasure to read any number of pages if they dedicate themselves to sufficiently praising precious Silence. Few virtues merit more than silence the application of the belarte of the Word—Prose—in their recollection and explanation to the public.

The books I was going to write are: *A Lawyer's Health; A Lawyer's Guitar; Theory of Being; Doctrine of Science; Theory of Beauty or the Aesthetic; Meter, Rhythm, and Rhyme; Art's Sophisms; Theory of Effort and its Hedonic Personal Influence; Theory of the Idyll-Tragedy; Tragic Poem; Individualism: A Theory of the State; Critique of Pain; Music as Mere Case of Respiratory Pleasure.*

People who understand that pleasure is merely suffering avoided, readers who are part of the public and have the psychological acumen to recognize this as hedonic truth—won't they hasten to discreetly dissimulate any irritation that reading my present book might cause them, which I modestly give in exchange for all those I didn't write, considering the amount of reading I've spared them in these thirty-five years?

In this way, then, dear reader, an unknown, so notable that in him may be found all the unknowns of the world, has spoken to you in pages that in other authors' books, which are bound in the usual fashion, would be blank and which in my book, for the first time ever, detain the reader:

To speak about people who have written nothing.

THIS NOVEL BEGAN BY LOSING NICOLASA, ITS "COOK CHARACTER," WHO RESIGNED FOR THE NOBLEST OF REASONS

Nicolasa is leaving, and in this prologue the novel bids her farewell. More sad than ill-humored, Nicolasa and her corpulent volume leave "La Novela," having resigned, as we already said. She passes in front of the novel's little watchman, who, as a good friend, asks her in surprise:

"How do you feel about leaving the novel?"

"I don't know. But you're a man of good appetite, you can imagine what will come of a novel without a cook: a novel of fasters."

The novel regrets this deeply, but hastens to add that when all of the furniture shops in Buenos Aires found out that Nicolasa was available, they fought among themselves to employ her and her 140 kilos, to test the resiliency of chairs and beds via the application of a certain part of her body. The chair or bed that can withstand her is thus imprinted with that certain body part, and this seal makes for a ten-year quality guarantee.

Nicolasa quickly tired of this position, though it earned her a lot of money, perhaps because she missed her position in the novel; she went to establish an Empanada Shop near the station, where you can catch the train to "La Novela." The fact is that the aroma of those delicious empanadas was such a powerful enticement that she not only almost deprived the novel of readers, since everyone on their way there was waylaid by the Empanada Shop, but she also held up the locomotives, whom she had spellbound. This earned her a distinction from the Municipality, whose traveling public benefited from trains no longer passing through the station without stopping.

Despite her bulk, Nicolasa is very sensitive. She was mortified when she discovered that she might deprive the novel of readers, and she abandoned her enviable situation at the Empanada Shop and only worked in the winter, in the wide avenues of Buenos Aires, using her ample person to shelter transients from the wind and cold. So many took refuge there that space became very limited.

I can also add that the images (gustatory-olfactory-visual) of the last empanada we ate rendered us incapable of conversation. It was universal, in the world-village of Veronica, to launch the epithet "He's got his head in empanadas" at the distracted listener, or repeat the saying "Whoever thinks of empanadas is not thinking badly." So it was that business meetings or other urgencies were fixed for "before empanada-hour" and, having concluded business, the custom was to bet on empanadas and celebrate in the shop. The "empanada-and-a-half," a gastronometric of Nicolasa's invention, was a frequent betting prize: to put up a dozen "empanadas-and-a-half" was at times an acceptable solution to disputes and prognostications alike. An old resident of Veronica was known for his skillful way of drawing apart an "empanada-and-a-half" without damage; you "drew" them apart, you didn't use the words cut or slice with empanadas-and-a-half.

The empanada-and-a-half was a unity[1] that was used, at times, as local currency; it wasn't unusual for the clause "Against reimbursement in cash or in empanadas-and-a-half" to appear in written or verbal stipulations. Other times you might hear someone say, "There's a storm coming on, amigo.—Yes, not even empanadas can stop it now."

But, in resolution, we already said that Nicolasa, who loved the novel so, moved elsewhere so as not to deprive it of readers who passed by "La Novela." It's a quiet example of loyalty.

We want her to know that the novel sends its fondest regards.

But we can't say goodbye to so sweet a person so soon, we'll say something more. For example, we'll talk about Nicolasa's metaphysical theory.

The cornerstone of her doctrine was this principle: that there are in reality two massive powers: Soot and Electricity. But the Verity of the world is such that it holds back these powers: Soot is kept at bay by the feeble piece of paper, and Light and Lightning are held back by a pane of glass, wood, or rubber. So we must conduct ourselves with the proper fear of these potencies and constantly remember that the world provides us with unlimited methods to frustrate them.

But apart from her metaphysical doctrine, Nicolasa also has a long-standing grudge against geometers, because of a certain episode in her life. What is known for certain is that she had her vengeance by sweetly inviting them to a banquet of her preparation. She made delicacies so perfectly spherical, particularly the first course, that, in

---

1. This daring innovation was compared (by a "character in the novel") to the audacities of Causs, Riemen, and the Babylonian astronomer of the sexagesimal (or base 60) system, which were celebrated at least in their town, and those nearby. Soon it will be universal (*Author's note*)

their scrupulousness, the geometers couldn't decide where to begin eating them (having found themselves confronted with an infinity, which of course they had to respect). They didn't taste them, and not having begun the banquet from the beginning, they abstained from beginning on the rest, which only increased their mortification, since the subsequent delicacies did not present geometrical impediments to their gustatory pleasure.

And now it is finally time to leave Nicolasa in peace.

NOVEL OF CLOISTERED THINGS, OF MUTENESSES, OF SECRETS, OF HIDDEN FRAGRENCES, OF WORDS THAT HAVE NO SOUND BECAUSE THEY DEPEND ON THE LIPS OF A FACE OR SMILE TO SPEAK THEM AND THIS SMILE IS NOT GIVEN

The hanging light of siesta, in front of the little house on the Estancia, can hide only one thing: another light, a little flame that nobody living there saw, that wanted to exist but did not want to be seen.

This little flame—maybe Eterna's expression when she thinks of her dream of totalove, so dazzling that this expression vanishes in brimming, reverberating fantasy: she doesn't know that the Day and the Little Flame within it, which are in perpetual connection with the house, are in fact the totalove that Eterna thinks of, and the gaze with which she views it.

But when he said goodbye, the Lover said to Eterna: "I know the little flame of the gaze that you fix on your dream of love at the height of each day on the Estancia in the novel. I don't have the power, Eterna, to make your dream come true: it's already much to have talked with you, and you will never return to my thoughts after today. My sadness for you in this instance occupied my spirit for a minute; only you could have achieved this: nothing outside of Ella, not even you, will enter ever again into my spirit."

ETERNA AND SWEETHEART

(DURATION OF SCENE: THAT OF A FLOWER'S OPENING.)

In all this novel's time—which is the only time of artistic existence, and Eterna and Sweetheart's only artistic existence—only Eterna can know the rosiness of Sweetheart's cheeks, and only Sweetheart can know Eterna's black eyes and hair and pale forehead, from window to window in the light of afternoon. In the silence of the country night they only hear the other's voice, both lovely but very different, Eterna speaking to the unseen President, and Sweetheart and Maybegenius speaking by the window.

All that either knew of the other happened after this, on one day, and only one, fleeting encounter. Eterna held in her hands two roses, of different sizes, one white and the other red, that she had pulled out of a great hamper of flowers. Her gaze moved from one to the other, comparing them; later she tied them together and put them in a vase for the President; still later, she untied them and left only the white one for him.

Jealousy? That he could love them both? And in the end, love only Eterna?

And so it was that this certain morning Sweetheart tried dressing her hair as Eterna did, a style she never wore, and in the end she took it out and went back to her own hairstyle, saying to herself with generous admiration: "It only looks good on her, even though she's 39 and I'm only 19. Let him love her, and just stroke my hair sometimes."

Sweetheart and Eterna never saw each other a second time, nor knew about what has been recounted here.

93

PROLOGUE FOR A BORROWED CHARACTER

Novelists have long and lucidly understood that it does not discredit them to adopt the literary practice here proposed, which is to use borrowed characters. In this way they escape the ridiculous self-infatuation that happens when they try to develop brilliant, fully-formed character-geniuses. I have proved that this effort implies declaring the author a genius, and so they limit themselves modestly to taking a character from me. Maybegenius? Poor Maybegenius, the novels that await you!

The Maybegeniuses have procured for me some authorial respite during the nights of my grand initial program—a dubious distinction, the best kind. In this way I pruned myself down to a smaller project, when I couldn't further reduce the maybegenius of my character to my initial character genius's novelistic audacity.

TO THE AUTHOR (OF THE NOVEL) HAS NOTHING HAPPENED TO YOU?

I'll tell you, Sweetheart, about the "reader's accident."

Anyone who comes impetuously or unprepared to a precipice falls, violently: an author must take care not to excite the interest of the reader when he has already chosen where to situate the end of his tale. In a novel of such intense, sustained interest as ours, the author has been careful not to destroy the reader with a precipitous fall. Rather, he prefers to slow down the narration close to the end—so much so, and I fear you'll see this, reader—that he will finish the book smoothly, that is, asleep.

Not every author takes such precautions. I won't let the reader be so surprised by the limit-end of the novel, when his passionate interest is most fired by the devilish skein of the book, that he falls headlong from the fullness of the novel into an attention-vacuum.

Since nothing happens to the author of the novel, it seems right to me, Sweetheart, that nothing should happen to the reader, except for the violent mental accommodation that he must employ just to enter into such a great novel, an accommodation of unique intensity, considering that he must first divest himself of this bulk of bloodless prologues.

(I make the readers love the characters in the prologues so as to spare the latter any bitter reaction on the part of the incredulous and discontented reader, when they first appear before him in the story.)

PROLOGUE OF AUTHORIAL DESPAIR

The disorder of my book is the same disorder of all apparently well-ordered lives and works.

Congruency, or an executed plan, in a novel, in a psychological or biological work, in a metaphysics—in all cases it's a trick of the literary world, and perhaps the entire artistic and scientific world.

Congruency, or a planned-out work, is mystification in Kant, in Schopenhauer, almost always in Wagner, and in Cervantes and Goethe.

That there should be a continuity or congruency outside of some text or other treatment is just as fantastic as consistency in the reader or student of such works.

I would be remiss if I did not at the same time declare that there is nothing more delicious, yet maddening, than the integrally congruous work. I mean unity, continuity not by means of repetition but by development, by incessant variation in a kind of permanence (of a thought, of a feeling). The supreme specimen of this development in unity, in my judgment, is Beethoven's *Fifth Symphony*.

In a complete mystification of unity, Schopenhauer presents us with the three volumes of *The World As Will and Representation*, with many chapters, each numbered and in apparent order. This thinker, perhaps the greatest metaphysician, published a draft of his research as if it were a great book, solid and definitive. Kant's argument in the complex *Critique of Pure Reason* is like the rattle of magazines inside a paper bag. Perhaps Spencer was able to write true books without an interrupted reasoning, without a single useless word. Perhaps today Husserl is more methodical?

Although I said otherwise in the opening, I don't have anything to apologize for.

MAYBEGENIUS LAMENTS HIS NAME

Maybegenius: "How did it occur to the author to give my name the extravagant modality of the interrogative: Maybegenius? It obliges me to appear in dialogues in the following way:

Sweetheart: "What have we here? Maybegenius? Again today you're here in 'La Novela?'"

Maybegenius: "Today's birthday is . . ."

Sweetheart: "The business of having birthdays tarnishes this novice novel; to celebrate birthdays is to live counting, to clutch at life, marking it with a tendency toward the End."

Maybegenius: "I'll think about what you say, and I'll continue with what you didn't let me say. Today's birthday is Nonexistence.

"But I'll return to the matter of my name. The author thought afterwards that since I was destined to talk a lot and only with you, Sweetheart, it would be a bother to you to enforce the interrogative pronunciation of my name. I'm agreed, but I should be named Full-Character . . ."

Sweetheart: "This is fine, yet he still can't mend his ways."

Maybegenius: "It'll be the novel's only defect. But the truth is that the author is only worried about his own convenience, giving me a short name that says nothing. Saying nothing is here concise for the first time: until now it always required volumes."

FOR THE CHARACTERS IN MY NOVEL

They know that I'm extremely happy with their performances, but they're begging me to tell them so before the novel, and not wait until its conclusion. Although they don't show it, this is because they know I'm competent to finish prologues, and they believe me less than competent to finish novels. Seeing that I'm in the last prologue without keeping my promise, they have me cornered. The novel would already be starting if it wasn't for this exigency, which occasions yet another prologue.

But if I acknowledge that they have conducted themselves admirably—for example, the Traveler, who has always been by my side and who has constantly been traveling within the novel, perfuming the chapters with his scent of suitcase-leather—it must be recognized that I, for my part, have been faithful to his docile character. In this way, although I have suffered shocking budget shortfalls while I wrote my great novel, I have neither sold nor pawned a single character. How much could I have gotten for the President? Or for the character who makes himself a millionaire, complete with a Rolls-Royce? Anyone would have pawned himself for Sweetheart's life and happiness, but among ourselves we all found a way to avoid one evil or another, and if I've borne certain inconveniences so as to not have to be separated from them for a few weeks, the novel has not been totally frustrated.

Thus characters and author are mutually content and a joint reception is planned in their honor.

PROLOGUE READ IN RECOMPENSE FOR THE AUTHOR WHO FORBIDS A BOY FROM ENTERING THE NOVEL

All the characters—and the readers announced so far—warned me that they would judge the interruption of the Boy with a Long Stick in the novel as a kind of "reading bruise" on the forehead. That's a singular metaphor, of irritating intention; as if a stick or a cane could cause "hematomas" on the reading operation, which is the same as claiming that reading about bananas makes people slip and fall. I understand the warning if it comes from fathers of families who are incapable of achieving at home what I have done in the novel: keeping kids from running around and getting free from the little brats, who are kept outside. For a rest, these fathers resort to whatever reading is hooligan-free; they've let me know that they will only take up a novel that won't be mistaken by those brats as a staircase, a wall, a cornice, or a tree branch, which all function as things to climb, only to fall down, get banged around, and renew any existing swellings and bumps. This taking to heights so as to fall down, and thus authenticate differences in altitude that nature so delicately provided, allows young people to always see these structures from below and to be up high, or falling, in every other circumstance. In this way they don't stoop to blows, since old age begins with neglecting such things.

WHAT DO YOU EXPECT: I MUST KEEP PROLOGUING

What do you expect: I must keep prologuing while avoiding the abuse of prologuing the prologues; and while I'm at that I have to make them prologues of something, that is, they must be followed by something (a novel); meanwhile I can't permit my novel the caprice of prologuing itself (which is the equivalent of making biographical allusions in histories or doctrinaire declarations in the text of a novel in progress); meanwhile I must assure you, as I do now, that I am well on the road to auto-prologuery, which should definitely dampen the prologues' hopes (they complained once) for autoexistence (autoexistence is the ultimate response to the mystery of the world, which involves eternity), meaning they would not have to subordinate their existence to whatever follows; the auto-prologue would be to a shaky literature, anticipatory of prologuing what the two most usual forms of reportage—auto-reportage (without a reporter) and reportage without anything to report, or antiquated reportage (which demands two people and a fixed appointment)—what the speed and expedition of our epoch have eradicated as too complicated, less than fiscally sound, and even informal in our obligated lives—what do you expect, until the novel comes, you'll have to make do with what comes before . . .

WHAT'S HAPPENING TO ME

I, who once upon a time imagined himself a man of complete good fortune, a man who elbowed his way through the multitude shouting, Make way for a happy man!—on the contrary, I must ask that you favor me with a show of compassion for all that's happening to me, because everything is. See for yourselves:

I yearn for the destruction of cities, and what happens? I end up with a cousin who toils, with extraordinary talent and vehement determination, on behalf of urban prosperity and growth and resolves transit problems.

I invent the best titles for novels and essays, and upon reflection discover that it is ridiculously unjustifiable to title a work of art.

I seek out the most dolorous and intense of affairs for a novel, poem, or play, and some time later my meditations on aesthetics impose upon me the obvious truth that affairs are utterly worthless in art, they are extra-artistic, and that moreover in art the invention of affairs is superlatively lazy, since life is full of affairs of all sorts.

I conceive and produce a few captivating, eloquent poems, and, as I'm always in search of truth, I later discover the truth of the artistic nullity of poems, in prose and especially in verse, in so many stories and personifications.

I deny death and spend my time researching a way to prolong life, and all I've managed is to avoid medication.

I go to a lot of trouble to cultivate elegance and talent in literary redaction, and I end up with a character, the President, who eclipses me with the grandiloquence and tear-jerking desperation of his letters, and another character, Maybegenius, who tries to woo me as a protagonist in the most counterproductive and boring system ever: short story writing.

I expect that a story that turns the corner will only turn up jokes.

I make friends with the reader, who makes me write better, and he confides that in me he found an author who gives his readers a bad reputation.

In the end, when I had assembled a complete cast of aesthetic experts, scientists, and philosophers in this novel (three grammaticians, a chemist, a historiographer, two inventors, two biologists, a man of genius, a painter with talent, three poets, an astronomer, two musicians, a mathematician, a psychiatrist); when my inventive plan was ripe, full of embryonic theories, and deciphered palimpsests, with the characters at the helm of scintillating dialogues about art and philosophy, just now I'm captivated by the simple, amiable, and generous conversation of friendship; and all my plans, to present the first novel to come complete with a lab and technicians, pathetically crumbled.

Now the only thing left for me is to make a proverb of my misfortune, saying:

> After wrongdoing
> The worst you can do
> Is to think it through

I won't start it, reader, because upon summary examination I understood that I already had "La Novela's" porch in place. I feel intimidated: it's just that I'm easily entertained by making prologues, and for the first time I realize that I've been promising all along to write a novel—that the moment will come when I have to conceive it, complete it, and give it form. I don't recall how the idea of authoring a novel—which to me signifies an attempt at Tragedy, otherwise I don't understand the point, at least as aspiration, of the novel and all art—I don't recall how this idea began and developed in me; and the composition of prologues has sheltered me from the arduous responsibility of what they are meant to precede.

I proposed to myself that we take a prologue to go over the results of something that I had taken care of previously: a general rehearsal of the characters' psyches (rather than one for the plot). It was a kind of test for the characters, or better, of their "good character," the resistance that comes from good humor and from selflessness that each shows in the face of adversity; an altruistic "armed forces," governed by camaraderie. It'll be necessary that some of them have altercations and even become enemies, as is obvious, considering the close quarters they share, living in the same novel: characters destined to be permanent rivals, or those who are so only for a moment, must both conduct themselves as people who nevertheless share the same death, at the same place and time: the end of the book.

I already have my Novel's porch, it's the first place you cross; you enter through the porch to get to the first chapter of the novel. It's already occurred to me that we're in the immediate fascination (I am fascinated with tragedy—of which I must conceive—and I don't have the words for it, just like in a recent dream that I had where there was a person, and I knew who it was, and that person directed everything that happened in the dream, but I couldn't manage to see who it was or remember a name; in a certain way, even if it's a vagary, I have the emotion of this person without an image or a name)—we're in the immediate fascination of the Novel, as if we had fallen into its fevered interior, so that it's more and more difficult to prologue it.

The novel for the present prologue fell in love with the Novel and aspired to be a prologue for it, which is why I've trapped it and put it in to the Novel, thus incurring another prologue. (I should say that all of the prologues and all of the characters are in love with the novel, and that even all possible topics for its prolongation have been besieged by love; there's nothing but totalove in the novel, there's not a pen, word, or idea that, if separated from the novel, does not seek her out, smitten: Voices, Gazes, Laughter, Sighs, Sobs, Diversion, all want to see Tragedy achieved and to be with her.)

This proximity to Tragedy that I'm experiencing now myself and which diverts me towards it, this is Life itself wherein all is post- or ante-Tragedy, since this isn't yet Life but its Mystery, the Mystery that brought this humble "Prologue" to me in its anxiety to be wherever the tragedy unfolds.

You won't want to believe, reader, that prologues just show up somewhere and fall in love; but I know that they do (and it's not an infatuation), and I must take care of this one, now that it's here; I need to attend to its topic. Because what I've got here is a prologue that's not even started, and it should be put wherever I need to say something unimportant about the Novel, out of anxiety, something that needs to be said somewhere but not IN the novel. There should be something roughly equivalent to a Chapter One, but it would be a crass confession, gratuitous and antiartistic, like, for example, if I were to show in the novel itself that it's a novel.

So I'll say it in this prologue: 1) That what is detailed in Chapter One, "The rowdy thirteen characters are home again at last, from the rehearsal of the novel," is a drill maneuver for the characters, something that has never before been done. 2) That everyone was excellently behaved, as if they knew that art itself were reviewing them; but I can assure you, with all of the inside knowledge of an author, that none of them thought about it, consciously, except that they didn't want to make anyone unhappy or to go against the novel in any way with a mistake, an absence, or breach of contract. They think of it as returning, not home, but to the novel, and they know that the novel is keen to achieve Tragedy, which is what all characters of Art in all times have longed to execute, witness, and suffer.

How did this inspiration happen in the *Quixote*, in the *Fifth Symphony*, in *Tristan and Isolde*? (Pardon, reader, I'm anxiously studying and examining the problem of Tragedy, looking for examples, my commitment to this undertaking frightens me and I forget myself, in these last, weak revisions, since now is the time not to study but to go to work.)

There are two useful exceptions that I'll add here, that will augment the pretexts for existence that we need for this prologue.

1. Let the record show that the rehearsal of my characters does not imply any doubt in the fundamentals with which each one of them came recommended. It's nothing more than an irrepressible nervousness on my part.
2. Let the record show that the good behavior that all the characters desired, and in fact achieved, was not that they came home on time but that they came back today at all costs, so as not to leave Sweetheart alone in the estancia. They all knew that because of the brevity of her appearance, Sweetheart would be the first to return. I'm not spoiling any part of the novel with this; I want to establish that in my novel there are neither schedules nor examinations in conduct.

Let the record also show that since there's a continuous Traveler among the characters, they can't all gather in the same house at once, that is, if the novel has to be true to life in all respects.

PROLOGUE OF THE KETTLE AND THE WARDROBE

The author of this novel is freshly renewed each time he takes up the pen; Eterna taught him this. He's like one of those kettles that learns to whistle all over again each time it's put on the fire; after a long interval of silence, some hesitant notes break from them, then a timid first whistle, and finally again the old refrain.

This is how I recently remembered to talk about the President's "little wardrobe," and his haste to hide himself in it whenever he was displeased, but only in his conversations and relations with Eterna, when, humble and sad, not angry, but more in love than ever, he would make his way to her corner. He is absolutely an eternal child, following Eterna and holding on to her skirts, or running away and shutting himself up in the wardrobe.

WITTY¹ LETTER THAT I WOULD LIKE ONE OF MY CHARACTERS, THE PRESIDENT, TO WRITE TO RICARDO NARDAL

I've said before that the most ridiculous situation for a novelist is to wind up taking on a character of genius, since an author must know how this genius will perform in terms of conduct and intellectual prowess. What ideas, deep thoughts, audacious doctrines, and discoveries can he attribute to his genius and will he describe these as concrete exhibitions of "brilliant ideas" if the author is not himself a genius? And if he is one and believes it, the fact of taking responsibility for a character who has said he is a genius from the beginning (and in the meantime it should be said that he's blonde, tall, moody, moneyed, and very fastidious with his ties, toilette, and shoeshine, though neglectful to shine it in the heel, as happens to soldiers when they are called to a sudden review); here let's add a brilliant exception, like this: "It occurs to us that there is an 'Ethic of Polished Uppers,' which is strictly applied only to what can be seen, but which isn't only limited to the President. Let's reassure him, despite his puerile ways and the fact that when he's wrapped up in a correspondence he's totally useless, left in the idiotic state of 'writing a letter in response,' wherein his talent in no way resembles genius. Why does correspondence, such an entertaining opportunity to show off one's inventiveness or avow one's passion, lead to such mental insipidity when writing 'a letter in response?' The 'Divine Postman' of our novel must have known that the thirty thousand letters that he burned out of laziness were correspondences whose destruction saved thirty thousand close friends from the perplexity of ('what should I answer?'). And what follows here? Since we've interrupted what we were saying about how undertaking to create a character of genius is to declare oneself a genius author, which one never is; it's better to take on only maybe-geniuses.

Very well. I would like the President to be capable of writing a "witty letter," because an author who is not amusing must have someone he can ask to rescue the situation when the public is clamoring

---

1. Awaiting a throng of readers.

incessantly for even a spoonful of wit, with no substitutions, just to be able to continue the novel. Once he's written the letter, I'd like for him to decide that it's for Ricardo Nardal. If I see later that it isn't for him and that the President didn't employ a shred of wit in the entire novel, I'll resort to a note at the end that says: "Warning to the reader that my genius protagonist, the President, appears in the novel during a brief personal interlude and that, unfortunately, this period coincided with an eclipse of his intelligence, a period in which a certain watering-down of his psyche prevailed; but his life has been much longer than this, so have no doubt that before and afterwards he will show himself to be what I would call witty." Thus it couldn't be proved that the author was lacking, despite the absence of any glimmer of wit in the President, or that the author was not himself personally a genius of novelistic execution of this category of character performance. With this, I give you the letter that I wanted the President to be capable of writing in order to demonstrate his genius.

Dear Ricardo Nardal:[2]

Before I was a protagonist in this novel, you will recall that I attended a banquet in your honor and that I dedicated my discovery of the four kinds of applause to you: applause for calling the 'waiter,' for shooing chickens in the yard, for hunting moths in flight, for opening the door, and for encouraging the first steps of a young son; but it happens that in the following ten years I have discovered two new kinds of applause that I cannot omit, and I don't know what one is for—what a mysterious ring in the phrasing—it seems to me that before I can submit them to a public that is likely eager to know of them, I must assemble them together in your name for a certain ranking or a ranking impulse that I cannot define: indefinable!

Kinds of applause are valuable because they are scarce: only two are discovered every ten years. I list them here: the first is for an author or orator who applauds himself using these kinds of phrases after a finished paragraph: '*Very good*, therefore, gentlemen, as you can see . . .'; '*Perfectly*, therefore . . .'; 'having *convinced* you of the proceeding'; 'And this, *clearly* . . .' The second kind of applause consists of the long musical finales of operas that themselves have a beginning, middle, and end

2. Originally Leopoldo Marechal.

and that can only be interpreted as applause that the opera attributes to itself. Those are all the applauses extant. You will say that there exists applause of approval, admiration. But this bears two errors: it comes at the end, and it could mean finally! that's over; moreover, the supposed recipient of the applause always doubts whether they're applauding where one is or it's only one that applauds.

You may now consider that I've brought you the complete list of the seven modes of applause, four for others and three for oneself; it's not a bad omen for humanity that there's more altruistic kinds than egotistical kinds of at least one thing.

> Happy labors, dear Nardal.
> *El Presidente.*

Of the seven applauses in the world, which one will be for me? Since in my case I've arrived late as an author—which is early, if no one's expecting you—I might, in my innocence of the grand psychological novel, undo myself in excuses to a public that might be better served by my not showing up at all.

DOES SIMPLY "COMING BEFORE" MAKE A PROLOGUE?

We want to present a good novel, even though the author does not promise never to write again, and as a guarantee of such an altruistic pact—a sacrifice of a thinker of such great power that he foregoes publication, or he already has, as he isn't known or even thought of for his books—he throws all four (pens)[1] to the bottom of the ocean (Does it have a depth worthy of these deep instruments with which some plumb and others pluck at mysteries?); or, as we know, when he retires the pens are given over to the adoration of one of the loveliest and most universal cities of the spirit, Buenos Aires, a city capable of understanding what it means to live on promises. There was absolute originality, if not in what they produced, then in their surrender; and in this act there were signs of the serious character of the writer, a suspicion that led to a justified mistrust and at the same time to the perspicacity of knowing where to find more pens: in the cabinet full of all things commercial (there's always at minimum one man of letters in there), where one can even find manuscripts of entire works of his. He shows this by coming out with a new book just after the spontaneous capitulation of the thinking pens and the editing pens. The new book appears to have been written with the same.

That a promise to Buenos Aires has not been kept is a remaining subtlety in this matter.

I don't know how it feels when promises aren't kept; I give the novel what I promised; the promise not to write has not yet been invented, and I lack the ingenuity. What internal drama for the person for whom writing constitutes a broken promise!

I think I've arrived just in time, a day before the genre of Novel becomes impossible. Art is possible but any question of Art's possibility is impossible; my novel has been possible and it contains only impossibilities.

---

1. It will be remembered now and again (to strike dead inexistence, Chapter IX) that a certain book of conventional literary success was displayed in public in a case alongside the quills with which it was written.

I can't boast of having discovered the region in this novel where nothing happens, which is known by another name, "Land of Lions." But all the impossible things happen in it: there's all of life for the possible, and for this and its equivalent besides, to what end realism? I only know that the reader complains when something Impossible is not achieved in my novel, and he knows that somewhere, in Art, to which he has recourse, there must be found something that you can't get by tossing about in bed or looking out the window: the Impossible, which isn't what's left out, since there's all of that in the world, but what is lacking when we want it, even if it existed before or after the desire.

This is how Eterna was an impossibility for me for many years, yet still she existed, perfect.

The only absolute impossibility is death. How limitless is Possibility: though now I can't conceive of it, it was possible for me to live long years without Eterna's love, even without knowing her.

Thus the President deliberates and resolves in his tormented spirit, he to whom Eterna says, "Let him love what he has believed, and not what is."

THE MODEL PROLOGUE

The model prologue is the best prologue, and I'm only abandoning it because I fear my originality *is not up to the task, since it's already worn out.*

Even Cervantes, Dante, and Manzoni begged the indulgence that their work be considered perfect, which it would have been if it weren't for "the miseries and privations of prison," or because with "long study and great love" they were poorly done, or because their contemporaries didn't know how to judge: "ai posteri l'ardua sentenza."

Under cover of reticence and disguises, therefore, the perfect prologue—that is, the prototype of the bad prologue—may claim:

1. Lack of stimulation, of ample time and accommodations for writing well.
2. Recommend itself to the indulgence of the reader of bad books, like the carpenter who builds an unbalanced chair, and then recommends it for the acrobats in the family.
3. That in my childhood nobody told me that I had talent, and nevertheless, after trying everything, with the present literary system I have here my book. Just as the advertisements for drugs and other longevity systems intone: "I was delicate, with poor appetite, irascible, pale, no one believed I would live, but I used the Kühne system (or vegetalism) and today I can withstand considerable tasks: I effortlessly read Dante's *Paradiso* and the wisdom of Baltasar Gracián without the slightest fatigue."

What pains me is to see Cervantes put forth excuses with the deep cunning of one who knows that he's written an immortal work. Nevertheless I'm recommending to everyone who wants to write a perfect book that moments before setting to work he should rob or kill someone, so that he can be in a dank jail with rats, humidity, hunger, and cold.

Now, I recommend for whoever wants to write a perfectly bad work a long treatment, if he can stand it, of Gracián reading, and the frequent recitation, while writing, of the entire poem (it's the only one of his that I know) that begins "¡Éstos, Fabio, ay dolor, que veis ahora!" Fabio, these, o sorrow, you see before you! Even better would be, following the counterexample of Cervantes, to live a long life of excess, luxury, liberties, strolls, and relaxation and to later sit oneself down one fine day to write. If in the most uncomfortable situation Cervantes wrote best, he who writes in complete comfort will produce a terrible book.

FOURFOLD PROLOGUE?

I hope that my numerous prologues—a kind of "Complete Works of Prologuery"—and my novel will be considered so good that it will be as if Posterity itself, which decides what is good, had commissioned them.

And I seriously believe that Literature is precisely the belarte of: artistically carrying out something that others have already discovered. This is the law for all belarte and it means that the "subject matter" of art lacks any intrinsic artistic value or that the whole value of art is in the execution. To classify subjects, deciding that some are better or more interesting than others, is to speak of ethics: aesthetics as such is the artistic rendering of any subject. Everyone can easily find subject matter, it's superabundant: artistic pages are extremely scarce, and manufactured with desperation, with Labor's tears and rages.

Maybe this suffering and constant failure annexes the artistic urge, it's the punishment for whoever prefers dreaming to living, art to life, when life has for us an Eterna in whom all beauty finds expression, heartbeat, breath; so that to look towards art is like using flashlights during the Day.

And if, having Eterna, we still pursue inventive art, we're all the more blind and we walk as though guided against our better selves, carried away by baseness, since persisting in invention despite having found a living Eterna is a horrible option contrary to our nature.

In Eterna's orbit invention is meaningless.

Observe that my novel is corpulent, and very mouthy; it has three outlets (the characters' training, the conquest of Buenos Aires, and the final separation), two resumptions of the beloved quotidian: life in "La Novela" (after the Training, after the Conquest); the presence of the Traveler at the end of each chapter; Sweetheart and Maybe-genius are in charge of the beginning of each chapter. There is also the entire prehistory of the novel's existence in two, very different forms: first, ten years of reiterated promises of its future publication, and second in the seventy prologues designed for it; it also features loose pages, a total novelty for novels, as well as a model page and an exhibition of a day in the estancia "La Novela," a cast of discarded characters, a sort of character internship, and an absent character; moreover, it expands to include the merit of never having been accomplished before.

Thanks to a flippancy, even a fraternity, with inexistence that permeates the novel's tone, this bodily robustness, this substance on which the novel prides itself, does not result in a suffocating excess of atmosphere for the Lover's slim figure, despite his aversion to existence.

Since I felt that there's a good Literature to come and that Literature, or Novelism, had been bad up until now, with all of the publicity that I got thanks to my friends at the newspapers, who repeatedly lobbied me to announce my projected, great, and genuine novel—"Eterna and the Child of Melancholy, the Sweetheart of an Undeclared Lover"—as an inauguration of Good Literature, I proposed an entertainment for the reading public, that they indulgently continue reading the bad literature, relieved by the knowledge that the good stuff was on its way, since I know that it's the virtue of dedicated readers to read while they wait; but if they don't read they might abdicate readership altogether, which is to say, for my novel too.

This is how the period of promising my novel began, and it soothed me to note that people kept reading the bad—for which I thank the bad authors—and awaiting the good—for which they should be thanking me: We've cooperated, you could say, but we parted ways decidedly when I began to write. The only explanation is that since the new novelism is so good, no one knows when it will be fully realized.

Thus I justify my repeated promises of the Good Novel and also the confection of my Bad but final Novel: to keep the reader waiting, and yet still in good condition.

We'll make a spiral so twisted that it will make even the wind tired winding inside it, and it will come out the other end dizzy, and forgetting which way to blow; we'll make a novel that for once isn't clear, isn't a faithful, realistic copy. Either Art has nothing to do with reality, or it's more than that; that's the only way it can be real, just as elements of Reality are not copies of one another.

All artistic realism seems to arise from the coincidence that there are reflective surfaces in the world; therefore Literature was invented by store clerks, which is to say, copyists. What is called Art looks more like the work of a mirror salesman driven to obsession, who insinuates himself into people's houses, pressuring them to put his mission into action with mirrors, not things. In so many moments of our lives there are scenes, plots, characters; the mirror-artwork calls itself realist and intercepts our gaze, imposing a copy between reality and ourselves.

Art begins only on the other side of truth-telling, which is itself science's justified hard work, but it's an ungainly intruder in art. Let our characters remain ignorant of whether we are bringing them to the estancia "La Novela" or to the novel itself. I want to know what it is that scenic actors are pretending to be. Are they pretending that they are people and not characters, which imitate men and aren't alive? But their personal lives still are happening to them; whatever they are on paper, they are not paper characters, that is, they are not written. I don't want my characters to resemble either people or "actors," I want the enchantment of being "characters" to be enough for them.

THE PRESIDENT AND DEATH

The President sought the happiness of his companions, but after he had achieved something of that in a deeply held Friendship and in a sustained and amenable Action, plus the most joyful of returns to the home of the novel with high hopes for regaining the happiness of the past, his sick impulse was to impose upon them a goodbye that, robbing them of speech, would only exempt them from the inevitable heartbreak of seeing each other die (only an earthly death, since to his credit the President had given them eternal serenity by inculcating them in his "Metaphysics without Death").

The author is only happy with this novel of mine because there's no Death in it, even though, to his great surprise, it's so sad in the end. (Not as sad as the *Quixote*, the most spontaneous, unpredictably pessimistic novel in all of literature, even for its author; the *Quixote* is much more sad than this fancy of mine; in the *Quixote* the failure of Living is sanctioned—involuntarily, I believe—and also its Fleetingness, and that of Innocence: justice; in mine only Happiness, not Personality or Eternity, meets with failure).

The President resists this adieu in the face of the Nothing, before the eternal concealment of existences. (Even though he knows that the presence of bodies in the absence of love is harder still: Oblivion). The President also believes, perhaps thinking of the Lover, that if something big and new doesn't happen after seeing the beloved, we'll always see her with the same feeling that we did when we saw her before she "died;" because without new things happening there's no forgetting, because there's no Time—which is nothing—outside of events, which weaken our images of the past. It could be a formula for unforgetfulness: to remove oneself from new important events when one is obliged to stop seeing the beloved.

In the end, the President believes in an eternity of Personal memory, individual memory, of all that once made up someone.

It's also known that, in addition to his general obligations in this novel, the author—who sometimes is and sometimes is not the President—has two different metaphysical obligations: one to Eterna; to show her the nothingness of the Nothing, that is, of Death, because for those who already have Love their entire concern is the future and the possibility of its ending; the other obligation is to Sweetheart: to show her the nothingness of the Past, where she had her greatest humiliation and sadness, thus liberating her from the tinge of reality that she gives to a certain tortuous scene. This image must be annihilated as such so as to convert it into an image without this tinge of reality, which is to say, a fantasy image of mere unreality.

But what is the President's *personal* metaphysical anguish? He doesn't believe in Death, but he can't love what he believes to be mortal, or what he does not know to be immortal; he describes this sentimentally as a disaster of destiny: "He who cannot love someone whom Death awaits." From which it follows that Eterna's misfortune (to believe herself mortal) is the immortalist President's misfortune as well (incapacity to love the mortal). Such is the President's metaphysics, which we found among his papers, finished, period.

FOR THE READER WHO SKIPS AROUND

I'm confident that I won't have a single orderly reader. An orderly reader could bring about my downfall and strip me of any celebrity I've more or less honestly managed to swipe for my characters. And failure is a dubious distinction at my age.

To the reader who skips around, however, I accommodate myself. You read my entire novel without knowing it, because I scattered the telling of the whole novel before I started, and so you turned into an unknowing orderly reader. With me, the reader who skips around is most likely to read in an orderly fashion.

I wanted to distract you, not correct you, because contrary to appearances you are a wise reader, since you practice inter-reading, which makes the most forceful impression, in keeping with my theory that characters and events that are only insinuated or skillfully truncated are the most memorable.

I dedicate my novel to you, Skip-Around Reader; you, in turn, should be grateful to me for a new sensation: reading in order. On the other hand, the orderly reader will experience a new way of skipping: the orderly reading of a skipping-around author.

A CURSE ON THE ORDERLY READER

I never believed in the existence of the Orderly Reader. And, for that matter, I am most often right when I don't believe in something than when I do. Yet I have stumbled in my novel across the only existing orderly reader. He's the one who will ruin and betray all my weak efforts as an author, getting them on the credit of his accumulated imcompletenesses and lack of attention. If he's anywhere around this novel, I already know that all hope is lost.

What would it cost you to just shut up, sir! Doesn't thwarting Eterna's serene and sorrowful talent bother you? Were you not conquered by tender Sweetheart's meekness and cruel destiny? Doesn't the Lover's inextricable entanglement, in what you cannot deny is the mysteriousness of having one's soul in one place and one's body in a novel where he waits his beloved's return from death—doesn't this mystery fill your artistic practice with rage and sorrow, as you string together a solid life, day after day, placidly dining each night with thoughts of the next day's lunch? Will your betrayer be Maybegenius, who has taught you previously unknown skills for the conquest of ladies? Perhaps, in the execution of these newly acquired skills, you will know success for the first time in touching a woman's soul! May you then throw away all your breakfasts and lunches, thus correcting your bile for this publisher of defects!

No, it's hopeless. A book could never make you so happy.[1]

1. Indicates a 68 reader drop.

PROLOGUE THAT STANDS UP ON ITS TIPTOES
TO SEE HOW FAR AWAY THE NOVEL BEGINS

The sun comes up in the quietude of the estancia "La Novela." A first window opens. A morning chill.[1] It's cold for the author, too, faced with what is for him the most uncertain part, the irreparable beginning.

I have a friend by my side cheering me on, saying:

"Everything will come out well, success is guaranteed. Don't make the characters wait any more! Don't you want them to be happy? They deserve it."

"But I'll disgrace them."

"No, 'characters' can't be disgraced. I envy them all, even in the times when they are clamoring for death."

"But mine are clamoring for life."

"I cannot believe that characters you invented would have such bad taste."

"I think they're still happy in the novel, and it'll be later on that they ask for life; but they will surely ask for it. This is a very sad novel. I can't look anymore. What I wanted to see by standing on tiptoe was whether Sweetheart had yet approached adequate happiness, leading her to beg for life and to get someone else to play the rest of her part."

But this prologue-character won't want to know anything ahead of time after this. It already senses that this will be a book almost as sad as the most vigorous tome of Pessimism: The *Quixote*. So much so that the author didn't have the strength to tell us how the sad, disgraced protagonists of his novel parted ways: the President and, even more so, the unfairly frustrated Eterna.

1. Sometimes I get confused in my simultaneous undertaking of both novels and in this, the good novel, I write something that belongs in the bad genre.

FIRST: POSTPROLOGUERY NOTE;
AND SECOND: PRENOVELISTIC OBSERVATIONS

Useful postprenotes here occupy four or five pages, replacing the same pages that, because they were blank, said nothing in this common tome of the "marked out–traditional–structure–of–literary–binding" which the Editors have imposed. I hope that my Editor will not rob me of what I'm owed in universal ridicule by inserting the five blank pages–which I am here replacing–and then inserting the present critique of said practice. If there is a Critique for the written, I'll write the critique of the blank; this way I get both the editors' publicity and their criticisms, which are all homage for the written. These blank pages, texts that disdain the literary, are the pages with which in every book the non-authors and the always-unedited editors disguise themselves as poligraphers.

I repudiate all the blank pages published here as forgeries, that is, originals bearing my signature; actually I don't know if they are authentic, although they do partially contain something ingenious or some thought, and some editor would even have you think that one of them sprang from my own pen in correlation with certain moments of mental "blankness."

Consider then that these are: four or five pages at the beginning of the novel–the Editor is about to start his own–four or five more after the End, as if the Novel had to continue, if only in blanks; there are various pages between chapters; there's another with the title of the book; another that bears a repetition of the cover; and all sorts of abuses of margins–about twenty pages, then, where the author isn't publishing a thing and the continuous reader has purchased nothing at the bookstore.

Editor's Observation: Permit me to assert the response that, in effect, the great novelist that I edit here, and whose talents of genius and facile extension of paragraphs the public has known from afar (with our marketing, he'll get closer), has necessitated (I'm not talking here of monies) at times, when I was fed up with his literature, the insertion of a few blank pages, bound in folio, from some short story, and we understood that this constituted an extra-contractual practice.

WERE THOSE PROLOGUES?
AND IS THIS THE NOVEL?

This page is for the reader to linger, in his well-deserved and serious indecision, before reading on.

AWAKENING. NOVEL-TIME BEGINS. MOVEMENT

Minute one: Evocation of Eterna's face

> *The kisses you denied me bite your lips*
> *Biting each other*
> *lips make each other bitter*

> *You write the manuscript of this your novel where*
> *I give you my spirit as you gave me yours*

> *And for what I could not be, I have your*
> *Gesture of divine sadness, of your I Cannot,*
> *In this denial my being made whole*

> *Whole persona, you raised me in the no "Living"*
> *And how much more in Loving.*

CHAPTER I

(TIME, THE CAUSE OF TEARS, FLOWS)

THE "CHARACTERS" ARE TAKEN OUT FOR MANEUVERS: THEY TRAIN TO STRENGTHEN THEIR
AFFECTION FOR ARTISTIC NON-BEING.
TEN GOOD-HUMORED RETURNS DESPITE STORM AND FATIGUE.

Moments before the present instant, the very present in which you, reader, are reading, the President abandoned his chair, which reclined against the back wall of the estancia "La Novela." He usually occupied this chair when, separated from the rest of the characters, he meditated on sadness or action. In leaving his chair, he opted for the latter.

The modest old white house on the estancia seemed quiet. It was said that its façade, doors, and windows murmured in much the same way as the spirit of dust on a wide road murders when there's no one walking there, only the noise of a dull footstep or the happy sound of a carriage's bells in the distance. What does the house say, what does the road say?

"Men pass through me, immortal men."

The house on "La Novela" has four windows: Time is the cracks in its plaster; the whisper of the wind in the kitchen chimney; the ever-present undulation of the brook next to the River Plate, its vibration making rivulets in the sand and waves like silk on the Plate's horizon; and like the little triangular flame of a candle, standing very straight in the distance: the eternal boat of weak human endeavor, which every gaze encounters on every sea, moving along the horizon wherever some small sail touches the sky.

Rays of light along the length of the little valley where "La Novela" stands, a single cloud wandering in the green light of the last calm moments of the afternoon, collected one by one in the last hour of the day. Nevertheless, one can still make out the inscriptions on both pillars at the entrance to the estancia: "Leave your past at the gates;" "Pass here and your past will not follow."

The subtle Watchman of the novel is at his post and he watches;

his delicate, slim silhouette (he's really a very small watchman) might be taken for a piece of fencing crowned with a motionless nest. He's always at his post, which is a little ways away from the entrance to the house garden (except when he thought up and pointed out "part" of the finished novel, which was a lot of work for him, concerned as he is with historical and artistic truth); his perpetual immobility makes one think—and indeed some have thought—that he is an inanimate post, but if you want to be convinced that he's watching, look at him when the last light of the day strikes his forehead with the additional luminosity of the lark's song, or when the dark owl alights there, mute but meaningful, or when Fantasy unites all the characters of this narrative, here in the novel and in the estancia, like travelers brought together by chance in the same runaway stagecoach—except Eterna, who recently arrived during the night, and is hidden from the others, who do not know that she joins them in the novel.

ETERNA ANSWERS THAT IT'S "STILL NO" AND THE PRESIDENT LEARNS TO LOVE.

"But you led me to believe that tomorrow you were really going to put all the characters through their paces, and I've come not only to watch this training and assure myself that you are armed with the lucidity and strength necessary for undertaking this action, but also to convince you that I should ally myself with your venture and be near to care for your spirit."

"That's how you should think of it and that's how it should be; I understood this when I saw you. You always think and do what each instant requires. But at the same time, seeing and hearing you close to me, I have suddenly lost confidence in my plans, even forgetting what it was that brought me to the idea of this action that now must absorb me, since I lack the talent of absorbing myself totally in the kind of passion that only you can bring me. I've suddenly forgotten why I didn't win your love, or my own love. How did you fail to elicit in me the absolute passion that would have been absolute happiness, as everything I think and undertake is nothing more than a miserable 'process' of passion's incapacity, a mimicry of thought and undertaking?"

"This does not move me, nor does it hurt you. As for what my presence here might bring you, leave it alone, think about it later. Don't waver: perhaps after the action you will want to speak with me again and possibly with different feelings."

"Yes, let's dedicate ourselves to the ultimate sorrow: action without purpose, without love; I sense there's salvation there, by which I mean I could thereby learn to love you."

"Let's not think about ourselves anymore. Tell me what I need to do."

"At dawn tomorrow we'll all go out with impurate purposes to return the same day. Eterna, you will be the one who changes Thought to Love, and I will be the pause or the anticipation during which time cannot change things."

"Goodnight."

"Goodnight. I will give each of the others his mission."

These are the missions the President gave each of the others, calling them separately while the rain began and a sudden wind moved in the trees surrounding the estancia, filling the house with the sounds of the foliage:

To Sweetheart, whom he called first and who, upon her arrival, looked at him with interest and melancholy: To seek out and find something "so good" that afterwards the only possible happiness and optimism is the determination to extinguish one's life, because this aspect of life or of art was "so good" that it is followed, in this case, with a silence like suicide.

To Father: Seek out and find the injury that would kill the unjust offender, whose fault came of a justified rage but killed us with desperation or left us unhappy forever afterwards.

(Father was nearing the President's office at just the same time as Sweetheart was leaving, after receiving her mission. They said:

"What, you're here, Father?"

"And you? Here's where you're hiding? I'm a friend of the President."

"You shouldn't have come. The moment I found out what you were thinking of doing with me, we should have each lived as if the other were dead, even though for others we are still alive."

"How did you find out?"

"Why talk about it."

"But I want to talk."

"No."

Sweetheart left, and Father went to receive his mission.)

To Maybegenius: Collect the secret that is told, but "in secret."

To the Lover: Bring back an imperturbable hope that lives in an unflagging memory.

To Simple: Find the only novel reader left who is moved when the novelist concedes that he doubts his own truthfulness or that something of what he narrates might not be possible.

So it was that the inhabitants of the estancia found out their tasks in the training maneuvers, by means of which the President invites them to change from living beings to "characters" in a novel, as if to say to them: "You can live and still be happy: I invite you to a training maneuver of 'characters' so that you can appear in a novel."

The next morning they all left, with scarcely a chance to see each other. It was very dark, and the wind and rain were beating on the house. Eterna left first of all. They all had to leave, walking alone, those who had felt so happy and comfortable in the house surrounded by peaceful eucalyptus trees whose music, in the storm, was so pleasant to listen to. Even a couple traveling in the same direction could not go together, nor could they remain in the shelter of the estancia. The basic routine was this: each one separates upon leaving, even spiritual things that had been commissioned by nothing in particular and did not necessarily have to leave.

Maybegenius and Sweetheart looked for each other in the scant light. They walked together to the gate, and there each one took a separate path.

The President also left without seeing anyone, absorbed. The Lover walked with a tranquil pace, ecstatic.

Father's pace was disheartened. He was always the only one to comment on the rain, but he did it with a certain verbal disdain: "Water is cheap."

The little valley filled up with the river. The Watchman saw them all leave, rubbing his eyes, though this did not help him tell if he were dreaming or awake.

Each one returned that evening, breathless with fatigue and haste (because they had to hurry to get home before Sweetheart, so she wouldn't have to be alone), soaked with rain and mud. Eterna, whom no one had yet seen, returned home first, and she said:

"It's done. Is it for the best?"

The President got there later.

"It's done. Will it work? I don't know. At least it's good for morale."

Sweetheart and Maybegenius were reunited at the gate where they had separated that morning. Each exclaimed as they arrived:

"How wonderful, today we only saw each other in the dark!"

"'Tomorrow we'll see each other all day long," added Maybegenius.

"After I talk to the President. But let me say this: I caught a glimpse, from a distance, of someone arriving who must now be at the estancia, a woman."

"I don't know who."

The Lover came in and said:

"What a sweet old house! How I would love to do my work of remembering here!"

Father came in and said:

"The day is done. May it always be so for me, as long as I forget."

Simple came in and said:

"If the President puts me in charge of bringing mud, I'll go and come back in five minutes, but finally I'm back in 'La Novela' once again, where it's nice and warm."

"Goodbye, then. I await your letters. I think I see it better, now."

"Yes, I understand better than I did last night. If you don't stay here, the happiness of today is ended. I will write to you many times, I have more hope now. Goodbye, Eterna."

Father and Sweetheart met again.

"I'm going. So tell me, how did you find out?"

"When the President lived with us he wrote something. I found it afterwards, unexpectedly; it was called 'Diary of Sweetheart, Writing to the President During His Residence In Her House.' Here I read what happened at our table the day you got so angry at me, because of the terrible upset that I had caused you that morning, like so many others, with my carelessness. At the table, to placate you and to exonerate me, he said that I didn't pay good enough attention or have a good memory. I said, "Yes, I'm not suited to jobs that demand memory, only for a continuing job or course of study." And you looked at me so terribly, with a menace that I didn't understand, and looking me up and down you said a few furious words. (Father remembered very well what he had told her: "I know what you're good for.")

Days after the horrifying instant we shared, I understood all of your punishments, injuries, and blows couldn't reach me, no matter how sorry you felt for them afterwards, and even if you and the entire family had been driven to this behavior by the extreme misery and eternal despair of my incredible carelessness. I understood that I hardly even remembered these undeserved punishments, and I sadly supposed that this is why you had proposed a model correction.

(Father recalled in horror the moment in which, it was true, he had thought about making a mark on his daughter that no one could erase. He thought: "Happily I cannot commit that act which is motivated by desire, and never hatred.") By then the President had guessed your purpose that afternoon and, thinking I was neurotic, he warned me that if we didn't separate either I would kill you or that, mad with rage at the calamities I caused at home, you would humiliate me; he also said: 'Your father is a very good man who loves his entire family selflessly; there is no one more generous and compassionate than he. But there's a trace of hysteria added to the growing burden of his bankruptcy, which has been accentuated with you. Avoid him until I return.'"

"It's true, I thought: Poor President!"

And yet in truth it was Sweetheart who was to be pitied, "perhaps for her shame," her form both innocent and sensual, her agreeable yet not meaningful face; with a beautiful voice lacking in musical sensibility, with a bit of a chip on her shoulder, blonde hair; very docile and kind and very intrepid regarding personal combat, to the point that when Father admonished her he had to be on the lookout for her combative, though not hateful, reaction.

In Sweetheart's innocent and sensual curves one could see Buenos Aires gleaming, that supreme city prowling through the shadows of the limitless land, living in the darkness without destiny, like an ocean liner, illuminated in the vast darkness of the sea whose heart it cleaves; both live directionless, in the fullness of the present. When one lives historically there's nowhere for Passion to go, there's this *progress* of humanity, which is the emphasis of History; once one has experienced the passion of the present, progress and the future become pointless; the depraved notion of progress exists only in historical writing, not in anyone's heart.

Passion does not think of situation, or time, comparatively; each lives the same present continuum; the insatiable notion of Progress is always empty, always nothing; everyone has the opportunity to "weigh anchor," everyone has the opportunity of the Quixote's two sallies towards Passion. Buenos Aires, Passion, Sweetheart . . .

Father finished his goodbyes, saying:

"Who knows when or whether we will see each other again. I'm glad you're staying with the President. Goodbye, Sweetheart, I think you will forget me. I didn't imagine that you were sick, and it even displeased me when the President told me his view of the situation, so that I wouldn't punish you. Now I'm convinced. Goodbye."

"I don't know how I've had the bravery to remember and explain, nor how you've managed to hear me. Goodbye."

As for Nicolasa, Federico, and Mountainclimber, upon whom the reader cannot rely—they aren't in the cast, but they asked to undergo the training maneuvers of the characters so as to be worthy of another novel—it will be remembered that they brought back what appeared to them to be good; and between the three of them they were able to procure only a single thing, which they triumphantly handed over:

"Here's what this day is worth (no one would have believed it)."

It was: the reason why gangster funerals are so well-attended, discovered after dedicating a day to attending such an event. Despite the rain, all of the people whom the deceased thug had threatened in life had attended his funeral without fail, out of gratefulness for the longevity he had conferred upon them by not carrying out his threats.

But Federico, who was bored because it seemed to him that the mud and the rain were scant, slept in and dreamed that the President said to him: "You who are light of foot, go all the way around the world in one day; humanity will forgive you for the long stick you carry if you dedicate some time this afternoon to putting a banana peel in front of every uneven patch, hump, or hole on every road in the world. This is the banana peel that every man who stumbles wishes had been there, just as common courtesy, to take the blame for his fall." And he dreamed he exceeded this task, bringing also the little banana peel of the mind that we wish everyone would see as the cause of the moral slip up we have when, in the heat of an argument and out of vanity, we make an unmeditated assertion and we stumble about, searching for the arguments we need to substantiate it.

Emboldened by his dream of twofold success in his mission, Federico dreamed that they let him be in the novel—be *real* in it. But he only dreamed it; this is why he once approached Eterna to ask if, with her gift for changing the past, she would divest him of the notion of having once been a part of the novel, since no one was ever going to let him live there.

"DIARY OF THE HUMILIATED CHILD SWEETHEART WHICH HER FRIEND THE PRESIDENT COMPOSES IN SECRET, HIMSELF ALSO UNHAPPY, WHILE LIVING IN HER HOUSE FOR TWO YEARS."

Sweetheart unexpectedly reads "her" Diary, which she finds in the

President's desk, believing that he's left it there on purpose so she'll be driven to reflect on her passion for him, and to give up loving him. It was actually only carelessness on the part of the President.

The most interesting chapter in the aforementioned Diary is the interruption that happens in the very moments when Sweetheart's unparalleled misfortune befalls her, and which will later be taken up again by its author, unaware of what he's been reading, until one day he finds a note from Sweetheart thanking him for the interest he shows in her with this manuscript.

There are three reflections of the President in Sweetheart's mind:

Enamored of him, she wants to meet him, when in one of the journeys of her uncertain life the President takes up residence in her house for a while and Sweetheart thinks he is unaware of her love.

One day, upon reading the Diary written by the President pretending to be her, she sees that he had avoided being the person to whom the love applied in the title the Sweet-Child-of-an-Undeclared-Lover that, although impossible, was now more undeclared than ever. And now she knows that the President is her "friend."

After a while, the President and Sweetheart meet as friends in "La Novela," a third reflection of one life in the other.

The Traveler appears, saying:

"I'm the only one who believes this is happening. Why don't the others believe that I travel? And why am I the one in charge of destroying the hallucinatory moment when the reader believes that it really happened?"

CHAPTER II

Sweetheart: "What do we have today in 'La Novela?'"
Maybegenius: "Pure time."

All week long they commented upon and enjoyed that day's events with the happy air of leisure.

Afternoons they got together with the President. When they separated early in the day it was with their minds fixed on these agreeable afternoons, as each one tended to his own tasks and preoccupations. Later they would tell him—his favorite pastime was to hear about it each night—what had happened to them or what they had thought during the day, when he wasn't there.

(It was at these times, when they were all united in friendship, their voices animated without any ill humor, that a little being liked to pass unnoticed among the characters: a little doll with the power of thought, to whom Eterna wanted to give life, because the doll once smiled at her; there is also a little plant that is so delicate and meek that any visitor who fails to caress it is denounced as perverse.)

Each one of them had determined on his own to live on the estancia with the President, having lived in various places and having occasionally seen him, and gradually, through casual dealings, having made friends with him. Each morning they all left together, except Father, who was only irregularly present, heading towards their studies or commissions in Buenos Aires in an old hack. The estancia was located twenty blocks from the station, on the bank of the River Plate; from there, it was ten minutes in the train to the Constitución station in the city.

The "estancia" was about ten hectares of perpetually disputed land, to which the President had a prominent claim. There were other interested parties whom he recognized, and from whom he had obtained permission to dwell on the property, in exchange for keeping an eye on it and settling its claims. The characters thus congregated haphazardly there, thrown together by the whim of an

135

artist in the pages of fantasy. They kept the President company for almost two years in that old estancia, on that land awaiting judicial decision.

All the inhabitants sensed the dream-like quality of finding themselves there all reunited, on this unstable settlement, due to a lucky encounter with the President, who was passing through just as they were, but who could have left them at any second. They associated this quality with great dreamers like themselves, living there together freely, finely, affectionately, changing, with numerous new sympathies, living their dreams, not being able, no matter how they opened their eyes, to convince themselves that they actually were where they had dreamed they were. They resigned themselves to the fact that it was a dream, which initially made them feel anxious, but later gave them the feeling of being real. Their suffering grew less as they renounced its realization, accepting it as a permanent dream that wouldn't carry over into reality—but not verisimilitude— as if dreaming alone were their vocation. This is why they felt real when they were in the streets of Buenos Aires, and became anxious to return to and thrive in the novel; they went to the city as if it were Reality, and they returned to the estancia as if it were dream; and each departure was a sallying forth by the characters into Reality.

Two years ago the President decided to make friendship the focus of his future life. And his reception with each new friend was characterized by open curiosity and sympathy. (Each one said to himself as he arrived at the estancia, moved by this double impression: "I entered 'La Novela,' and I entered the novel.") His last conquests, whom he had befriended and brought to that place of cohabitation, were The Lover and Sweetheart.

The Lover impressed everyone most of all. But everyone soon forgot that he was there with them—it even took the President a while to consider him a real inhabitant—until they happened to see him again. Only after some time did a certainty grow that the Gentleman Who Doesn't Exist was living among them, even though they saw him constantly.

Each one remembered the first day they arrived, how they felt the dark attraction that brought them there, as they saw everyone's face on that day when they looked around the house and let their bags and parcels drop at the front door. And then what future? How did they first move towards the novel? Was it the President's words when he met them, and afterwards invited them into his home, or was it the image they saw, in that instant, of the estancia where they were to dwell? And what about how each one left behind family, past, sorrow, or solitude?

All of those who are today present in "La Novela" were there when they were treated to an unexpected pleasure, the arrival of the Sweetheart—or so they later baptized her, the only female inhabitant there—so graceful, carrying flowers from the city for the President, as she walked across the garden. (What sweetness to see her like that, so absorbed that she didn't sense the charm of crossing a garden with flowers. But nobody saw her. How do we know about it? Magic.) Father was not a regular resident; he came and went from time to time, but that day he wasn't around. Sweetheart only knew that he was an acquaintance of the house, and only saw him there that night before the drilling maneuvers.

Maybegenius was the one who opened the door to this surprise. It was rather a cold, cloudy day; the waters of the River Plate separated, and rippled along the banks, and the stand of trees which bordered the estancia shook. Sweetheart was taken to the warm, whitewashed, thick-walled camp kitchen, with one of those campfires that are so loved in winter, and a constant sibilant wind in the rooms of the countryside home. This wind was like a voice that Sweetheart never knew and that we heard on our first vacation in the estancia and, a half century later, in an unexpected or longed for return to the country, we again heard this same timbre, the same word that the wind eternally whispers in crevices and which reappears in the ear, unequal to the flow of individual life.

Maybegenius, who regularly cooked for everyone, brought her some well-prepared hot food. Before they were reminded that anyone was in that silent house, or even realized that they themselves were there, Sweetheart and Maybegenius conversed for two hours in the kind of happy colloquium where each person talks more than the other. These two hours were the only truly happy ones in Maybegenius's love for Sweetheart, and in Sweetheart's friendship with Maybegenius. Both the friendship and the love affair were born out of this lively conversation, without either of them knowing it. Are not this relationship and this dialog, this friendship and love, always burgeoning in their souls? Why must we say it began, if they didn't sense it beginning, or didn't think of it afterwards as something that had begun? In those two hours both made themselves absurd by the sadness of mutual recognition, the absurd encounter between love and friendship.

The wind in the eaves always repeated a single word: there was always friendship and love in those poor souls, but those two words, out of the exchange of dialog, gave birth to sorrow.

A DAY IN THE LIFE OF THE INHABITANTS OF "LA NOVELA"

I'll randomly select a Thursday in August of 1927, the second winter that they had spent in the novel. Everyone—except the President, who didn't go out anymore—left together, early, in the old carriage. They passed the Watchman, who liked them and was curious about them, and they passed through the humid little green valley. They looked at the little snake that the river traced along the lower edge of the coastline; from the estancia, at any time of day, the undulation of the waters could be seen along the line of earth that it lapped . . . And so they went, in the chilly, windy morning, talking and making observations from time to time until a large newspaper from Buenos Aires absorbed their attention, as a gust of wind pulled it out of their hands and sent it flying along the road in front of them, rolling along in the same direction as this *pampero* wind. They couldn't occupy themselves with anything else, so transfixed were they by the flapping and tumbling of the broad, printed pages as they settled and rose, nervously shifting or running ahead of the group as it traveled, filling the carriage compartment with their exclamations, until, transported as it was by recurring gusts of wind, the paper came along with them for maybe fifteen blocks, almost all the way to the station where the carriage stopped. Sweetheart was most excited and intrigued of all, vacillating between hilarity and superstition when confronted with the capricious path of the periodical. This pleased the Lover entirely. It was enough for Maybegenius to watch Sweetheart's enchantment with what was happening, and the Andalusian didn't care about anything except that she might brush up against him; nevertheless, his comment was enigmatic: "Newspapers! Does anyone believe that what's going on with this periodical is newsworthy?" Nobody answered this, and they got on the train.

When they arrived at the Constitución station in Buenos Aires, some of them split up, and part of the group went on together. Downtown, Maybegenius accompanied Sweetheart to her office and, kissing her (this is true, but inexplicable), he went to the Palace of Justice—because he was a solicitor (inexplicable, and also true)! The truth is that he went through all the offices and files so sweetly and conscientiously, just as if he were at the pots and pans of his country kitchen, and it was rare that a judge had the heart to rule against him, just as his pots rarely boiled over and his pans rarely burned him. The Andalusian got lost in the bars of the city, fishing for news for the President. He played the lotto, read the palm of whomever would buy him a drink, and when the patron was generous, he predicted a happy future and separated in his fortune all the Fridays from their thirteenths, though how he arranged this we don't know.

They all met up again at nine in the bar at Constitución to get on the train, all tired and with the good humor that comes at labor's end, taking their tea with an end-of-the-day pleasure and zeal, as was their custom every day after their work was done. See how they live this moment of sympathy and pleasure at the end of each day, since besides their labors, deceptions, injuries, humiliating obligations, or indifference towards their anonymity in the crowd, they also have the sorrow of having to be far from the estancia every day, for long hours of forced privation; see their happiness, their innocence, and think: not one of them feels lifeless!

The President awaits their noisy arrival in his hammock chair under the vineyard loft, all twined with climbing wisteria. Later they disperse throughout the house and make themselves comfortable, while Maybegenius and Sweetheart, who assists him in the kitchen, light the fire under the pots and warm the meal prepared earlier that morning.

THE PRESIDENT TO ETERNA

"Profoundly, decisively: here is the formula for the fulfillment of my soul with which I call upon destiny in this unexpected moment, convulsed with uncertainty and sadness, with my intimate and contemptible humiliation, heavy with inferiority:

"If glorious love can be attained—it would only now have been given meaning, which would explain the apparition of one individuality more (that is, mine) among the innumerable traces of Being. In truth love would give me the individuality that I didn't have until today. Love makes the present eternal, it totally occupies the memory, and makes of the eternity that awaits us only an instant, or only the memory of an instant made eternal by perception, which is to say memory triumphs over Eternity, replaces it with the instantaneousness of Passion, of totalove, which happens at any stage of the totality of time, a totality that is ours since no life has a beginning; making not life but a single instant an eternity, the highest instant of perception. If, then, glorious love can be attained, it will only be after I have left off working on my soul and have made it as beautiful as yours, to return when my feelings have softened.

"Last night, contemplating expression of the happiness of love—that I took as my own when there was a moment, the first moment, and unknown to yourself, of love for me—of the happiness of love for another person (this same happiness of love, of pure and exalted and blessed sympathy, and your eyes searching this face for long hours, forgetting about all other humans) I lived two hours of your oblivion; I experienced "The Oblivion of Eterna," the unforgettable. This Oblivion also cures the past, using your unlimited powers of enchantment to substitute another past for the past of whomever was made unhappy, a dignified and graceful past, so overflowing is its single instant.

"Eterna, I often hear you say that a trip or fall due to distraction or clumsiness has no remedy; your ridicule has no remedy. I oppose this idea that to stumble is, better than the "game" and the "table," the opportunity to prove whether one's character is beautiful or ugly; and for a fully graceful soul (and a soul can only be so if it knows no other impulse than the one towards sympathy) there is nothing prosaic nor ridiculous . . ."

Eterna appears and reads the beginning of this letter.

When she gets to the place where it says that he would equally happily carry on a conversation with another visitor, she writes the following, wounded by the muddled President's lack of comprehension, pale, her eyes wet:

"Adios, President, no more for today. Nothing in my life could be crueler than to read these lines. I'm leaving, I think it's hopeless. Don't try to stop me. I can't imagine you will ever understand me."

She returned to her room with insufferable mortification, her face flushed with fever, and supporting herself, she repeated a prayer and truly took desperate refuge in a God who she had never defined for herself (since she didn't adhere to any religious practice) and to whom she addressed herself only when inundated with tears and desperation . . . Later, somewhat soothed, she exclaimed:

"And without prayers he suffers more than I do. Let him pray, I want him to pray. We are the miserable ones in this sinister life."

She took up the telephone and said only:

"Pray now, pray right now, and then try to sleep. I demand it: pray."

Then, feeling sorrier for him, the cause of it all, she hung up and sat on the side of her bed, sobbing.

"Poor thing, poor me, we used to read about Bovary, who destroyed her soul with each step of her existence, we looked at each other when reading about this unhappy destiny became intolerable, but always with this envy or juvenile jealousy to be a character in a novel. And now life runs roughshod over us with its enigmatic fury, and now maybe life will make us both piteous, we who were anxious to be characters who were read and to feel nothing, this character-being that every ingenuous reader finds enviable, no matter the misfortune and desperation which the novel afflicts upon it. We will go mad if we keep on like this, and we will want to escape from Life to a chapter of the Story. Who will show me that he never existed, that I only read about him, that I myself am nothing more than a shadow, a silhouette of pages!"

The President and Eterna could not realize totalove because he never wanted to rest his head on Eterna's breast, as a shelter, and she could not manage (this is her only imperfection) to liberate herself from this maternal inclination, which is wrong in love, and she couldn't live without this sensation in her bosom. For his part, the President was inept in that he couldn't love Eterna without thinking about her, that is, without representing her mystically. Thus it was impossible for him to see her as a being, because being cannot be intellectualized.

"Eterna: you are not perfect; your novelist must tell you this, since he is also your friend."

"Make me perfect, then, if you can, like God made Man."

"I can't: the image came to me inwardly; sometimes you go looking for a lover's head to Shelter on your bosom; and when, in this image, I evade you, you raise a sad, discontented face; I combat this expression and then this move, 'sheltering in yourself,' reappears. I am able to triumph over this mentally and again comes the soft gesture of sadness in your face."

Other times Eterna buys "outfits" for the President, who rebels against this maternalization of love, he refuses himself the attitude of shelter because it debases: he only concedes the identity of equals.

In the meantime, the Man Who Feigned To Live affects a perfect Absence.

CHAPTER III

Sweetheart: "What's coming up in the novel, Maybegenius?"
　　Maybegenius: "When I'm the author, I'll tell you."
　　Sweetheart: "And then what happens?"

The President approaches Maybegenius and tells him:
　　"Listen, Maybegenius, I have a job for you."
　　"If it's a really hard job, Mr. President, why not give it to the Lover, who has the talent of unflappability? Anyway my brains have been under the weather for a few weeks."
　　"Your eyes have been busy, though."
　　"I don't understand, Mr. President."
　　"I'll tell you another time."
　　"The Lover seems very bright and calm to me. It seems like he knows everything that I'm doing and thinking, and he smiles about it. I don't like him to look at me, even though he saved me from the dogs. As you know, Mr. President, the day I came it would have looked pretty bad for me if the Lover hadn't come to my aid so quickly. Frankly, Mr. President, I sometimes think I'm dreaming if I look at him."
　　"That's because you don't yet have faith in his eternity, which is the same thing as not having faith in him: a mortal is a non-being. If you must know, he seems real enough to me, but like everyone, sometimes he doesn't, when my faith is flagging."
　　"Regardless, when I have to do something, or talk, or instruct, I prefer him not to look, although sometimes he does anyway, and I perform badly. If it weren't for that I'd be with him all the time."
　　"Or perhaps you prefer other company?"
　　Maybegenius looks at him; he doesn't think the President really said it, he thinks he only imagined it, so he doesn't answer.
　　"Good. You will procure for us the support or discretion of Petrona. You must conquer her feelings in such a manner that, out of deference to you, she will abstain from talking about and disclosing matters concerning 'La Novela.'"

"Very well, Mr. President, I'll work on it."

"Just now Sweetheart was asking for you. She's lying down."

"I'll go see her. Also this gives me an idea about how to win Petrona's friendship. How much time do we have to start working on what you proposed?"

"Two months."

"Farewell."

"Farewell. Close the window if the light's coming in while she's asleep; you can talk to her later."

Sometimes Maybegenius thought about Sweetheart while he was with her; other times he dreamed about her; other times he thought about her without looking at her (Eterna would never forgive this in the President). But she was always Sweetheart.

(It hasn't yet been stated that Maybegenius truly had certain physiological traits . . . eyes . . . a nose . . . but *caramba*, that's a lot of work and now I remember that I have his photograph in my pocket, which, by the way, was taken at the renown studio of Generosius the Pole and is labeled: "Photography That Comes Out Well." I have it here, with the tremendous dedication that Maybegenius gave me: "Kind Author: even though I have been unable to detect any trace of the talent, sentimentality, caustic wit, and joviality that others attribute to your personality, I love and admire you profoundly, and I believe you to be the most sequential and clear of novelists because you helped me to entertain Sweetheart and to attract her attention, and you're on my side in working for her happiness. Your friend and humble colleague, Maybegenius.")

MOMENT OF ETERNA AND THE PRESIDENT, SCENES OF THEIR FIGURES, DANCING

The two pardons of Eterna.

Mischief in Eterna's fingers, isn't that forgiveness itself, the capitulation to love?

Today the President is at the mercy of Eterna's mischief.

Today he's at the mercy of her forgiveness.

Eterna is earthy of body, and yet no sign of desire shows on her face. She is just as exquisite as a headmistress, and no one can tell the difference between seeing her and thinking of her.

The President can't tell, either: he only knows that each time she comes to see him, Eterna covers his eyes with a little handkerchief that is embroidered with circles and diamonds, or sometimes just with her hands, pretending to put the handkerchief to his eyes: the

President can't manage to say whether he sees it or imagines it. If he says that he's seen it, Eterna asks him how many circles there are, and how many diamonds; he almost never gets it right. And she's crestfallen, because when the President sees her well, it's when his soul is at its most powerful.

Today the President is more immediately aware of both pardons: a powerful intellectual discovery reached in the last two days makes him directive and intellectual, seeking clarity in their love. Sometimes the President wastes the two pardons, the current one and the one from the past. When that happens, Eterna's sadness is complete; the President's fatal days are upon him; after which he has nights of dejection and later a tenderness of new delicacy. Today the President and Eterna are in a moment of clarity.

SPACE WHEREIN A DIALOGUE WITHOUT AUTHOR, OR NON-AUTHORED PROSE, TAKES PLACE: MAYBEGENIUS AND SWEETHEART ATTEMPT AN EXPERIENTIAL MERGER.

Maybegenius: "Sweetheart, don't ask me what we have in 'La Novela' today. This time we're not in character, we're going to speak for ourselves. This time we are, we *are* not characters; to understand what I mean, Sweetheart, look up there, at the heading for this page."

"But are you asleep, Sweetheart?"

"I was, but I heard you come in."

"So there's no point in tiptoeing?"

"Regardless you would have made noise to wake me up, so you wouldn't have to miss out on our conversation."

"It's true that I have here some great conversation, but I know how to tiptoe and what's more, I always walk around that way, because he who knows love does not seek out worldly ears."

"You know love?"

"See? Even you didn't notice! I tiptoe around with my love."

"You are provoking in me a great desire to converse. I'm going to get up."

"Should I go, then?"

"Stay, but don't look, and that way I can keep this conversation that you might otherwise have given to the Lover. The Reader shouldn't look, either, now and any time I undress. Read, but only over your shoulder."

"It's true, they are peeking."

"I can't even hear you breathe. Are you thinking?"

"It's strange—I'm not thinking. I'm waiting to see you, let me turn around now."

"You can. I'm preparing the *mate* and I forgot that you were turned around so you wouldn't see me; I thought you were entertaining yourself by looking out at the countryside."

"The *pampa* is peaceful, but I wouldn't take my eyes off of you for that; you wouldn't let me look, remember? But before I tell you what the President has ordered me to bring him, let me congratulate you on this insuperable *mate*."

"So the President is very active, then?"

"So much so that just now, with this last *mate*, I am on my way to get ready for my first interview with the lady Petrona."

"Nevertheless, the President also has his calm moments: sometimes he just watches his cigarette turn to ashes, and he burns himself."

"True. What an intense life the President leads, under his apparent placidity. I'm going now."

"What, already?"

"Not 'already' for me, certainly. Nor for you, since if the President finds your rooms in disarray he will be happy, deducing that you are placidly sleeping; he always recommends that we not wake you."

"He hasn't come to his office today, nor yesterday except for very late, when the lady came with her black dress."

"Just a moment ago I saw through the window that they had given her a room."

"Why?"

"Because she paces."

"What do you mean?"

"She paces her room; she passed in front of the window a few times and looked out through the curtains."

"What's she like?"

"You haven't seen her? I'm going to the patio; finish getting dressed and I'll come back and tell you a story; if you want, meanwhile, you can see her from where I'm standing now, she's tall and very beauteous in form. Better see for yourself, I won't say anything more. Don't forget to remind me to tell you this story, whose title is:

> "The lady at home
> At home without her.'"

Notice that by proposing this narrative, the crafty and sensitive Maybegenius found a way to change the conversation from the topic that would have made Sweetheart sad: the President's incognito visitor.

"Go get your story ready. I already looked, but I couldn't make out the person. I'm going to say good morning to the President, I'll go to his room and come back."

Maybegenius, to himself: "Pretexts, curiosity; she is mortified by the unexpected presence of this unknown lady"—then out loud:

"If it's just to give me time for the story, don't bother, stay. I already have it ready; I thought it up just now; I can tell it to you just as it was told to me."

"Wait five minutes, my friend."

"How it pleases me to do your bidding!"

"The President isn't there."

"So? Does that frustrate you? So often he's gone, but I am here now. And now I'm going too."

Sweetheart, to herself: "I know that you're here, good Maybegenius, but there's a reason for you to suffer these stupid allusions to the President." And then continuing the conversation:

"What are you doing here, Maybegenius, when you're walking through this chapter on your own errand?"

"I was looking for the part of the novel where I could have life of my own; I thought it was here at the window of 'La Novela,' where we could breathe, where life would come for us both."

"Why, Maybegenius? You know the President isn't interested in life."

"Is it possible, now that you have told me that I have your love? We don't know whether the President can love; he seems unhappy. Why live this unhappiness? But we ask for life for ourselves, we who have found this tenderness. For the President, who is down on his luck, to only 'exist as a character' seems a marvelous stroke of luck; he owes life to those of us who are happy in love."

"I can tell you . . . I don't know what to tell you, Maybegenius, you are making much of an instant of love that palpated in me for you; now what I feel is friendship; that instant was real, but fleeting."

She was telling the truth; in the spirit of their communal action, in the first hours of knowing each other, Sweetheart had fallen in love with Maybegenius for a day; Maybegenius knew it, and perceived that this love had faded by the second day. The Lover consoled him, saying: "Take this day of Sweetheart's love and make it your eternity." Maybegenius accepted this as his consolation forever.

"I don't like this conversation; I will ask you to start this dialogue over again. For example, I would come to your door and, opening it halfway, I would make my voice and my gait just as the President recommended:

"Sweetheart, are you awake? Because if you aren't, I'll shut this window that's letting in the light."

"Yes, Maybegenius, I'm asleep."

"For how long?"

"Since seven."

"It's two."

"Very well, I'll get up. What will Maybegenius do? (this is what you should have said)."

Sweetheart: "I don't understand you; and the poor reader!"

"I said that you said, 'I'm getting up.' You're right: 'without knowledge of my presence?' It's hard to think for somebody else. What's more, notice: I am the one doing the whole dialogue, but when it happens that you have to get out of bed, like now, you're the one who has to tell me what to do."

"Well then, stay here, and look away."

"Very well, I'll retire. Tell me something: I must conquer Lady Petrona. Sweetheart, what should I do?"

"Clean yourself up and tell her stories from the movies; I can't think of anything else. Do you need her help?"

"I'm afraid I do, she must not divulge the secrets of 'La Novela.' But I haven't cleaned myself up, as you suggested I do."

"Yes, but I agree. I steered you wrong. How will you do it? Your face looks nice."

"Now would be the moment in the dialogue when you again tell me: 'Today *I love you, Maybegenius*, character in *The Novel of Eterna and Sweetheart*.' But you say nothing."

"I keep silent so as not to tell you that great characters, characters worthy of Art, never say 'I love you' like any other character would; no one who truly loves would think of saying 'I love you.'"

"Oh, how I wish those were other words. But you do not have them for me . . . I'll press on in my preparations for my mission. Tonight I'll rehearse a little, and if this helps I'll tell you what I rehearsed. What's too bad is that reading Lombroso filled me with enthusiasm; it would appear that this man of genius is mentally ill. The President assures me otherwise, that Lombroso is very much a genius and not at all a lunatic."

"But how silly, to talk about genius! So much so that there's none to be found around here."

"Nevertheless. I am very sane."

"What luck! That's the important thing. But what makes you say that now?"

"It's just that I think a lot."

"And you don't get confused?"

"No, it's not that. When I'm confused, it's about something else."

"I hadn't thought."

"And how am I to resolve all the problems we have with the President, who is himself disquieted, if I don't think? If he weren't so preoccupied, he'd have had Petrona silent and compliant, all it would have taken is one enchanting visit."

"It's better if you go; don't tell him anything else about it. You'll have a good time on this mission, it will give you something to tell us about at night."

"If it comes out badly I won't want to tell you anything. But I'll do a lot of thinking."

"It seems like you're always thinking."

"I believe so; it's a facility I've got."

"And does the President really work so hard? Make me a sweet *mate* (I haven't had breakfast yet), and I'll ask you a few things."

"Fine. Where are the *mate* things?"

"There, you don't see?"

"Ah yes, I'll prepare it. Thinking it over, I realize that I, too, have time to take *mate*. I've already guessed what you want to ask me: the letter that he received, and the lady who arrived afterwards."

"Ah, there was a letter?"

"Here the dialogue would change, and I would beg you to relive what happened during those two hours in the kitchen, the day you arrived."

"It didn't even occur to you to ask my name, or why I had come. I thought the first words I pronounced here would be: 'My name is Maria Luisa.' Why didn't you let me say that, since I like to say my name and I had been practicing the whole way here? Though it's true it wasn't really my name, and I had forgotten to make up a last name."

"Your name was clear as day; I knew it the moment I saw you; your name is Welcome."

"You took my suitcase, and you said, 'Come with me.' But now

I'm going to get dressed, Maybegenius, there's barely time to tidy his office."

"It's a lot of work with all those glasses he wants shining when they're filled with water."

"And the paintings?"

"What paintings?"

"He calls those mounds and bunches of colored paper that you see scattered around his room paintings, since at first he had oils and watercolors, which he replaced later with chrome imitations, very well-chosen, but now all of that is supplanted by colored paper; it's his painting salon. He's a great admirer of painting."

"He's extravagant, and later he says that since Lombroso was a genius one must grant even less credence to the theory that geniuses are madmen."

"Again we speak of genius."

"It's just that I'm very level in my judgment (and as such, when I received you, although I relieved you of your load of boxes and packets, I didn't take the bouquet of flowers from your hands, even though it pained me to see you with it in your hands the whole duration of our long conversation, I never offered to take it from you, nor did I know whom it was for, nor did I ask)."

"Ah! It's true that you are anxious to clarify this problem with geniuses."

"All I know is that I'm very sane. It's been a while since we've heard you singing at the piano; the President says you should be studying music and that when a musician friend comes he'll have him evaluate your voice."

"So you're leaving?" Sweetheart says here, detaining Maybegenius as he gets up to go.

"I could stay here forever conversing with you."

"So stay in this 'dialogue,' that's what it is. Or go visit The Lover."

"He's not here now."

"How you love him! He's very delicate. If he had as much on his mind as the President, do you think he'd be as sweet?"

"I think so."

"Fine, since, as you're fond of telling me, you like it when I order you around, begin your visits to Petrona. You're just standing there staring, don't you like it when I tell you what to do?"

"I'm looking at you, Sweetheart, and I will go where you tell me."

"You will conquer her, Maybegenius; you know, I know nothing of conquest; you are good, intelligent, and free."

"Free? I was; I will never again be free because I cannot forget."

"You're in love, that's for sure, I can see it. How painful that must be! And she can't love you back?"

"No, she can't."

"So she's in love already."

"Yes, maybe she doesn't know it; and the person she loves is in the dark, too. I'm the only one who knows of her love, and I love her too, and she doesn't know it."

"How much suffering! That's life!"

"I'd rather you didn't sigh over it. I'm leaving."

"You're a good man, Maybegenius; you're good looking and elegant; she'll receive you well. But that tie . . ."

"It's bad, I know."

"Go get someone to fix it for you."

"Why don't you do it, put your hands on me for that. I'll only mess it up later."

"What!"

"You straighten it, and I'll mess it up a bit."[1]

"I don't understand a thing."

"Let me do it. I'll go. While I do encounter new impediments, I do have hope of winning her friendship."

"I understand even less."

"It's a great thought; In order to make Petrona love me, every day she must see something that needs fixing in my moral character."

"Moral character?"

"Yes, my moral character is how I comb my hair, arrange my tie, my watch fob, my hatband, everything that has a right side and a reverse side, that can be orderly or disorderly, put on the right way or twisted. I'm sure of it: for Petrona, this is my moral character. Don't worry about understanding it, don't think yourself unintelligent, since I wouldn't understand it either if someone said it to me."

"If you want I'll say I understand, but since you say I shouldn't worry, that it's a riddle . . ."

"You'll understand it better tonight when you listen to my communiqué informing of the result of my first visit. Goodbye, Sweetheart."

1. (Author: An unknown feeling pesters me. What if there's some bitter critic reading me right now, mocking me because, with my weak grammar, for "you" I sometimes use the Spanish familiar "tu" and sometimes the regional Argentine "vos"?)

"Wait, listen: I'm anxious about telling you what I have to say: why were you so good to me when I first came here?"

"Who knows . . . You seemed so sweet, and you looked frightened."

"I wasn't afraid; I knew the President well enough. Be that as it may, however, if I want to keep living I hope to encounter no more good people."

"How strange! That lends itself to confusion much more readily than my opinion about badly-knotted ties."

"Explain your incomprehensible seduction procedure to me one more time. I understand that it all happens naturally. Is Petrona not attractive?"

"She would be, except for her face."

"You also must explain why you feel no regret about making Petrona believe in your false love."

"Very well: The procedure—I'll shoo away the flies of regret—charms me to the extent that it absolves me of all morality, casting aside the fact that Petrona is a trollop. I don't think there's a single woman of her type, or even women much superior to her, who can resist the unsettling affect of a twisted hatband, or a badly-knotted tie, or a stain on a piece of clothing, wrinkled socks, or a loose button. It's an unease that, when prolonged by repeated presentations in the person of a single gentleman, drives women to such a state of desperation that they must take charge of the man entirely, to the point of using conjugal union to put an end to all the sartorial imperfections of this person who has so irritatingly crossed her path . . ."

"That's all fine and well but: Doesn't it seem undignified that you would push yourself up against a wall just to stain your back with whitewash—and on the way to see your beloved? What will the reader think of your plan? How rude, we never consulted him in this."

"Well then, why not tell us your plan, distinguished reader—or has he gotten distracted, and left us alone?"

Reader: "I am as interested in your ideas as I am discreet about them; you can be sure that I'll only distance myself when I suspect the fatality of a kiss, and I'll return once I've calculated that the friendly spectator would not be an indiscretion. Now, of course, I'm at your service, and I approve of your plan."

"Thank you very much, that's worth living."

Maybegenius went on his way and Sweetheart was left to recite her favorite quintet:

How good it would be
to be good and
Only with good people live.
To suffer with every pain,
And smile at every good fortune.

Simple: "Oh, Sweetheart, how have I not adorned my time here with your conversation, as I see you now free and happy."

Sweetheart: "It's true, I feel very happy. What delight to be a part of the camaraderie of 'La Novela.' I was doubtful when the President invited me to come, because at that time my life was so insignificant that any possible change terrified me."

"I also remember with emotion what he told us: 'I invite you to a "training of the characters," so that you may be happy in the novel.'"

"This change has been everything for me; I've forgotten my past, and I feel hopeful again."

"I already had some happiness in life. I had begun to understand happiness."

Actually, Simple is the most adept man when it comes to happiness: as an usher at the Teatro Colón, he knew to keep his place while the orchestra and the song of the great tenor and the great diva resonated together with an astonishing clamor of immense and powerful force, while the distinguished conductor waved and shook his coattails and hair, alternately calming and inciting operatic fury with his gestures. During all this devastating virtuosity, including the virtuosity of knowing how to absorb oneself in this opulence, Simple knew to keep to himself while the singer let out a string of "do re mi." He played a toccata on his guitar, docile and content and feeling satisfied with life, so much so that in some moments it was possible, amidst all that ruckus, to hear his instrument.

Sweetheart: "I, on the other hand, have had to learn everything here. Like everyone, I think."

Simple: "But for some of them it's difficult. It's difficult for Maybegenius, a man who couldn't learn to cough unless you put a conductor in front of him."

What joke of Maybegenius, told while they both painted the walls of the vestibule, had led Simple to try to poke fun at their mutual friend's difficulty with happiness? Sweetheart smiled broadly, and together they continued sunning themselves among the poplars, while Simple explained that he possessed a soul capable of procuring the "world on a string" for him. (It is not known whether, apart from the novel's time, there is also good or bad time that accounts for Simple's mood swings.)

Maybegenius makes his way to the conquest of Petrona, whistling. Is there something conceited about him, perhaps?

Maybe: a pinch of the seducer's infatuation, and two pinches of jealousy maybegenialize his character.

My perhaps frightening affirmation will perhaps come as a surprise, that besides Maybegenius's solid moral sense, that is, his general sympathy for the "other I," for the plurality of sensibilities or individuals which he displays in this motto: "In this life, at the very least everyone has to leave his seat warm; leaving his place, or the time and place in which he lived, a little more comfortable for the next man than it was before (or perhaps he meant: labor, and the warmth that disinterested labor yields, should be left for others, rather than taking recourse in the great egoism of one's own destiny); one must be the sort of man who did a little more good than harm;" very well, despite this motto and, what's more dissonant, despite his supreme elegance in egocentric and severe inspiration, Maybegenius is jealous of two things—and jealousy is the most durable indignity from which a personality can suffer, it's a fault in egocentrism (it must be, to be narrowly egocentric to the point where Passion cannot be realized as an absolutely selfless love): he envies the waiters in a bar their enviable muscular-tactile pleasure, as when they wipe down the marble counter when something has spilled there, and the consummate drying effect, almost not to be believed, so swiftly and softly has the rag run across the surface; but he is more envious of the grocer boys' delight as they sling glasses, teapots, and mugs down the length of the counter.

And so Petrona replies to Maybegenius:

"Your presence here strikes me as rather insolent, courteous and amiable though you may be."

"Truly, Señorita Petrona, I would love to be able to say to you in this moment what I expressed in a similar circumstance, in another novel, to a young woman who almost equaled you in charm. I remember what I told her: 'This mention of insolence is very cruel, Señorita Luciana. I am truly motivated to desist in this visitation.' This last part is what I cannot say to you, Señorita Petrona. Because today I do not feel the urge to desist in my visit, I will simply say: Your impressive and seductive presence alters my language and my bearing, and so I may seem insolent. I got out of this very well by desisting in my visits to Señorita Luciana in the aforementioned other novel. I cannot deprive myself of the exchange with you that circumstances offer me in this case."

Other honeyed words and a few improvised couplets made happy this day for Maybegenius (who wanted to tell Sweetheart everything) and the secret of "La Novela" is safe for now.

CHAPTER IV

LETTER TO THE DISTANT SHADOW OF ETERNA'S ADMIRER, THE YOUNG PORCIO DE LARRENAVE, AS IT LENGTHENS WITH THE PAST, AS HE FORGETS HER.

Fleeting gentleman, lord of Oblivion.

When, more than the sound of your steps—the silence that passes over your figure as you walk—the indifference of the steps before you empties your solitude and you stop for a rest, it may be that this letter reaches you, and then you might hear the distant rhythm of another's step as it starts down the path that you follow, beginning the lesson in sadness you have already suffered. Ah, you will say, it must be the one who shared Eterna's attentions, the one who came after I left, who innocently caused my departure with his arrival, and you won't realize that there's only room for one at a time alongside that sampler of souls, Eterna. You have my commiseration, then. Take it.

When I met her I said to myself: When she looks this way, her downcast eyes turned obliquely towards the ground in front of her or towards the table against which we are reclining, and in which our downhearted bosom casts its insignificant shadow, just as I saw Porcio de Larrenave four years ago, the night when I met Eterna, what is it that I saw?

Today I know what it is. I know that you see yourself like this: as a path away from Her, the path marked by oblivion, that you must tread from that night on, the path which from that night on is also mine.

How much sadness, Señor Larrenave, did this road bring you? Tell me how to take a little of the sadness away from this path. Your experience will help me to avoid suffering as you did. What do you think about while you travel it? It's best to think only of her, no? Think of her beauty, of Eterna forever, give Sorrow our life and body for sustenance.

You watched me that night, Larrenave, with piety and malice, and you were silent. Did you already guess, upon seeing her prefer me to you, that regardless there would come a day when I would travel the same path as you do now?

Take pity on me: the only compassion I want for myself in this terrible undertaking is yours.

Sorry for you also. Yours,

The President

With this, I tell the Reader how Eterna and the President first met, and how it was a boundless dazzlement both for him, an inexpert thinker, and for Eterna, though she is as majestic and profound in her feelings as she is suspicious and in control of the self-delusion and easy games of what men believe love to be. So it was that much time passed before the President sought her out again, having weighed and measured his passionate inclination, and understood that Eterna's attitude was not one of illusion, and he told himself that he would not be able to feel passion except passion for her.

That's how it is possible, thought the Reader, to travel Larrenave's road again, or else an Eterna will be lost to us forever—an insuperable, lifelong regret.

CHAPTER V

Sweetheart: "What do we have today in 'La Novela?'"
Maybegenius: "Whatever you like."
"Today we have each other."
"So we have Sweetheart's happiness."
"And the President's. Let him be happy for at least a day."

"But look, Sweetheart, here's the lady who's visiting."
"Black eyes; she's lovely; sad; she's serious, and attractive. How many of us are sad, Maybegenius! Of course she has black eyes. She is tilting ever so gently."
"What do you mean *of course* black eyes? No doctor could predict that a future newborn of course has black eyes. I predict that your blue eyes are the best and blackest, if that's what you'd like."
"If she sent a letter first, it's because they already knew each other."
"They might know each other, but as sure as there are good stories waiting to be told, if you ask him what color eyes she has, he won't know."
"You're wrong about everything, thinker; he's very interested in her."
"How preoccupied you are, Sweetheart! Your suffering is useless; he's not interested in her at all: it must have to do with his plans for the novel."
"And you're wrong about something else: the first thing he observes in people is the color of their eyes and . . ."
"So there is more than one first thing?"
"And their voice."
"So in these two first things you win."
"Don't criticize my grammar, Maybegenius."
"Your eyes are made for listening to a good story."
"You are such a joker, Maybegenius!"
"On the contrary, Sweetheart, I'm heartbroken. I feel the dizziness

157

of existing only in writing, when I could be here not in writing but in reality; this kind of engulfment is like what the film projector imposes on characters when it first of all projects the moment that they fall into a kiss, and then afterwards it has to withdraw them from sight. Tell our gentleman author, Sweetheart, that we should only exist in writing when we're in pain."

"Everyone's sad! . . . but I will say that you just complimented me for the first time."

"I'm in love, and I want life now, the life that is mechanically erased for cinema characters, when they should be given life in novels. In this, novels are sublimely superior to the cinema. I'm in love and I want life now that this love will make me happy; and so it's with fear that I think perhaps now the novelist will raise his pen from the paper and stop. Anyway, do you want me to keep complimenting you? Your mouth . . ."

"Your own mouth should admit that the first compliment was mine, since a minute ago I told you that you're an agreeable person, and good."

"Now I'm really leaving: here's Señorita Petrona's carriage, with the legitimate cargo of her personage."

And so they parted.

THE WATCH STOPS TICKING

Sweetheart: "Reader, I need you to breathe on this breathless page. Lean in more; all existence is so sad. Sweetheart is sad today."

Reader: "I'll trade my leaden earth for your levity! Why so pensive, Sweetheart?"

"Maybe because all feeling is sadness."

"Would that my life was worth lending you, was character-worthy!"

"It's enough that we each think of each other."

A SALUTE FROM THE CYPRESS

In the afternoon, while the foliage and the dusty ground make the initial music of a summer rain, the President, alone in the estancia, hears the desperate appeal of the Past interrupt his conscience: his soul clamors to recapture those nights at home spent in contemplation, aware of each respiration of the five beings in the filial home, all together under a single roof. Everyone was asleep, and leaving his desk in search of these beloved figures, bodies denounced for bedclothes, heads, hands. Could he be more gripped by the past?

ONE OF THE FIVE "LOOSE PAGES IN THE NOVEL"

The lady mentioned in the conversation between Sweetheart and Maybegenius was the august woman to whom the President directed himself for six years before the following letter, as careless in its redaction as it is ardent in tone, because of the agitation of those days of his life:

Buenos Aires, July 1923

To Eterna.

I can't go a single moment without thinking of you.

I can't quite grasp what impulses motivated your conduct towards me since the telephone call on Friday at two, which is to say Saturday morning, remember? Until today.

I have been tenderly but energetically chastised by the valiance and sensitivity of a great woman, peerless among those I have known, discreet, pious, active, pure—and my pride has not suffered. Before, yes, the rage I felt at losing everything, unsure of my attraction and calmed, in those days, waylaid by your constant kindness, not by infatuation but by the insidiousness of trust, of faith in the joy that possessed us and then suddenly went numb, I was humbled whenever I enjoyed your company; only fear ruled my conduct, faced with this first admonition of your lips; pride had nothing to do with it. From the moment I met you, the difference in worth and grace between us came to the fore, and I lived timidly, entirely submitting myself to the hour in which I would, in my inferiority, not win you, but lose you. I will consider nothing else now except what of you I might lose, perhaps even the sight of you; injury or flattery are now nothing to me.

Saturday night you showed me an evasiveness, a tormenting attitude in your constant clarity of tone and gesture, and your unfailing, inscrutable spontaneity. But I had already buried all my hopes, buried my heart, as the Spanish say, ever since the telephone communication of Saturday at dawn.

All the things you so cordially spoke about in the days we were together seem so different to me now. I enjoyed the profound goodness of our exchange for so many weeks and now those days are over! Perhaps there will never be another time like this for us.

I came again to your house on Sunday night, with the last day as an intimate illusion. The only thing I had, as I crossed your threshold, was this terror of even the most imperceptible shuttering of your manner. And you were waiting for me, and you confided in me and offered me again the precious consideration that enchants each daydream instant with you. I knew then that you had recently called my telephone; I was in constant agitation; I waited long moments in the vestibule before you received me, you received me with flowers, much more out of passion than charity, an unmerited abnegation given that, as you yourself said, no future can begin there.

What a dark hour we had, and what I couldn't grasp then was how you, too, were suffering. I was and am unjust, and I have been, in this ennobling attachment, the freer and happier of the two.

No rebellion was ever born of this memory, and nothing is left of my pride, nor do I want any pride to remain, where you or your memory reside. I only want holiness to reign in my thoughts and treatment of Eterna. One day I can hope that my spirit will be possessed of such powers that I will trade this phrase, which now and for a long time has defined the feeling of our sympathetic exchange, for something limitless.

But I will wait for so long, and so quietly, that maybe you'll disquiet yourself, be injured by my mute suffering, and, generous as always—or perhaps, as is my fervent desire, touched by passion—humble in your tenderness, not out of pity but out of delight, you'll venture to give yourself to the fullness of the immense feeling of identification, of love—and you, ardent woman, will be the first to speak.

You who suffered the most and toiled the hardest, who is more and gives more, who teaches yet has nothing to learn, nothing distant in your soul, ever

Eterna

And the truth is, Eterna, that in those days there was a world of things to discover in you. One word from you on the telephone in the last of Saturday's dawn was the first announcement—because of its tone, and when it was said, not because of its cold reception—of the flight of our happiness. How much more disillusionment must you have suffered by my errors and defects!

I think I know; and I am drawn, as in a nightmare, to name them all.

It had to be this way. No man can be great before you, nor can he ever hope to be, having come to you, unless he learns it from you. And even so: I wanted to learn, not invent, my holiness of passion. I hoped for everything from passion, I lived until today without it, and without wanting to prepare myself for it, only wanting to learn passion under torment, hopeless of any comparison with the beauty of spirit I would some day encounter. And even now, knowing passion, I live more for your pardon than for martyrdom, purification, faith in myself; I lived in the happiness of knowing a living Beauty, definite as a model of my virtue.

What a pious and august concern has been yours in these two days!

What depth of being you demonstrated, forgoing everything you cared about so as to spare me the pain you were bound to inflict.

I trusted in your forgiveness, before, and nothing more. And now: I believe it is I who suffers most. What a lightning bolt you were!

Forgive me.

Graces are reflected in your action: tenderness, energy, sensitivity, tact—even in these days, in the intricacy of such consternation, you have not abandoned them, nor your fantasy, nor the subtle mischief in your manner. These graces exceed everything I put in the little poem "You Went In The Night, Sad and Adorned," when I told you that I could not guess at you, could not reach you.

I didn't believe I knew so little of you, and that someone would teach me, and that I would grow in this way.

While you may believe that I'm tormented by love itself and have lost hope in any reciprocation of affection, I surprise myself alone, and I humiliate myself in measuring the delicate care for me that has so quickly been born in the heights of your sentiment. It shames me to think I didn't see the growth of your feeling: I condemn this coarseness in my own feelings, and betray that which I don't believe I deserve.

You'll understand, then, why I had lost hope when the first warning sounded, when, fighting against yourself, you resolved to shatter my illusion.

As little hope as I had when our involvement began, I have conducted myself as a common cad in my conception of the fullness of our destiny. And it wasn't caddishness but enchantment, and faith in the fortunes of Passion.

Something concrete must have intervened, not for you to change, since you've always managed to get me accustomed to the mobility of your sentiments towards me. But I'm already ashamed of analyzing these occurrences, what came out of our few exchanges.

You suffer no more, sensitive creature, if with such grateful happiness for my reappearance and, having retaken that lost path towards our existential communion in all its vicissitudes, the other day you showed yourself so jubilant and anxious for the reconciliation of our two lives. I return to you forever, and, impelled by the fear incurred by the grave risk I escaped, I accept these limits that you impose as inescapable.

Eterna!

The author: Here I have a letter that, it must be said, no great author of a great novel like this one would have written so poorly, with such excessive and sentimental language.

The President, apparently unconcerned, never thought it badly written, and in this I have the argument against novel characters writing private letters (since it's obvious that this is a private correspondence that's not intended for the reading public, since all the information needed to understand it and guess its outcome are missing, except for the person who already knows everything it's going to say and might even decline to read it, which is a very sensible abstinence, considering that the lover—it can't be concealed that the President is a lover, even though he expresses himself with a maximum of confusion in that regard—allows his letters to arrive at the beloved's house as if he hadn't really bothered himself to write them; he could have just burned them afterwards, telling his beloved when he sees her: "I wrote you a splendid letter that pleased me very much, but naturally I didn't send it to you because it was only an exercise in literary agility."

And then Eterna would ask the President every time she saw him, "Did you write me any letters?").

In the preceding letter, the President alludes for the first time (though doubtlessly he did so frequently in his secret conversations in the novel) to his telephonic communications with Eterna. (The way to achieve a purely oral conversation without vision or gesture is to talk on the telephone in the dark.)

It's true. They talked at length every evening, and Eterna always ended with a little song that sounded like the defiant, sobbing cry of a little girl who hasn't gotten her way, to which the President would respond: "I want to do what I want. Give me this, and pamper me a lot until I fall asleep, so that I can dream of how much I like you, and how the one I love thinks of me and dreams of me."

"I haven't learned how to do it yet; tomorrow I'll be better."

"But today makes yet another day without perfect love; one more irreparable day. No, the past is not irreversible, this is what you always say."

"Yes, there is every reason to Hope: when the days of perfect love number more than the days of turpitude, oblivion, laziness, and apprenticeship, the past is as nothing."

"And after that you change again?"

"No, perfect love lasts an eternity."

"No pity, no pity, President. No pity. The false lover is he who pities, or who asks for its recourse. Love is equality."

THE MOMENT WHEN, AS THEY GO TO BED AFTER THIS INTERESTING CHAT, EVERYONE IS TROUBLED BY PROBLEMS THAT PERHAPS SLEEP WILL RESOLVE

President: Hallucination of the past, with its culmination in the Novel; a situation and a scene has equal power over feelings that have changed, like tyranny, or confusion.

Eterna: Absolute oblivion; oblivion in favor of a great present; oblivion of the person with whom one speaks, whom one regards.

Sweetheart: We want different things, sometimes we put on the light, sometimes we put it out; to see and not to see; let them see us, let's see each other; let's not.

Maybegenius: A test of the novelist's art; to traverse the emotional state of a boxer at the ten count.

The Lover: The struggle between a present passion, a present beloved (her image), and the memory of a dead person.

Unlike his friends, Simple is not troubled by personal or imaginary—but more or less distant, idealized—problems; he has to honor the trust placed in him, his suitability to resolve this problem: with the perfumed smoke left over from forced smokers, cinema actors make an Illusion of Eterna, to cover up for their terrible gestures:

just as the Lover must weave his own Hopes.

Author: You, reader, since now you may enter my pages, lose yourself and liberate yourself from reality and from these problems, since it's just as worthwhile to stay in the real or to believe yourself real, if you're like me and half the rest of humanity (the whole other half is devoted to altruism, since it's just as easy to be good as it is to be evil, that's why, if you notice, you'll see that good people, even saints, don't even realize what they are. (If Leopardi had known this, how many tear-soaked rants over humanity's evils would we have been spared. (I'll speak parenthetically about parenthesis: I've ordered parentheses of two sizes to be made (I don't know why boring but emphatic literature, almost always written by grammarians, zealots, or artists, repudiates the emphatic parenthesis of the second order and yet makes use of two or three hundred adjectives; which is to say, organization of that instrument, the Word in lexicon and syntax as if they were steel workers forging palettes without thinking themselves artists by this action) you, reader, want the best for all humanity, and you tremble at the thought of its suffering. That's why you hope that each character will resolve his problems tonight and wake in the morning with his mind as easy as his heart.

Reader: That's so. Oh, if I could be a fly on the wall for your conversations, and in this way know for even an hour what it is to be a character! Who in "La Novela" does not breathe life?

Sweetheart, who seems to hear this echo of Life: To breathe, this rising and falling of the chest; ours don't respire, and this blanching and blushing of lovers' cheeks. Only think of the nothing that you and I both are, President.

Some want life, others want art. Only the Lover is happy the way he is. (Struggle between the author and the reader; the author wants to pull the reader towards the fading away of his being in character. The reader wants it, but he doesn't dare to renounce life forever, he's afraid to be spellbound by the novel. He doesn't know that he who enters "La Novela" never returns.)

Author: I shouldn't say to the reader, "Come into my novel," but rather save him from life indirectly. My quest is that every reader should enter my novel and lose himself in it; the novel will take him in, bewitch him, empty him out. The first reader who was exiled from himself and fell in the thin air of my novel (this happened while reading page 14) was a twenty-three-year-old student who fell softly into the pages, racking his brains to follow me and to identify himself. He smoked as he read, and sometimes I'd be concerned when some hot ash fell into my pages: but in time he too fell, relieved and thankfully not smoking, into languid oblivion. He very much loved, a bothersome coquette, fickle but affectionate. He was exhausted.

Reader: And I'm not?

Author: Maybe. I hear light steps; I sense a mischievous shadow on this page. You're here too, Welcome.

Simple: Let's make a pavilion at "La Novela" for spellbound readers.

New reader: I anxiously wait my turn to descend into the pages of the novel. Am I not there yet?

Maybegenius: Reader, are you truly the one reading, or does the author now read you, giving that he speaks to you, or at the representation of you that he has before him, and that he knows you like he knows a character?

Reader: I'm not interested in whoever I might be; this delicious dizziness is enough to bring me into the subtle orbit of the novel.

CHAPTER VI

Someone calls? . . . It's my beloved.

There's beauty: to soothe
The anxiety of a world,
To put to sleep in the laxity of success
The peregrination of this waylaid and prescient quest
That is the perception of reality
A quest that knows no road nor what it wants,
Let he who has it keep his appeasement
And trade his sorry thirst for delight
In all that is dream of the real
There's beauty: enough to hold back all Pain

Humans, breathers, those innumerables incessantly stirring the world's air, relentlessly ordering it into your chests, elevating your eternally open mouths to an eternal heaven, beings of the heartbeat and the voice that either brightens or breaks, which perhaps every day demands alternately an end or an eternity, there's beauty to give us all understanding of the Mystery, and to stop all pain. But where is it? Is it in Art, in Conduct, in Understanding, in Passion? In Cervantes, or Beethoven, or Wagner, or in some greater delirium: in adoring intonation, dazzled by Walt Whitman's Man?

Where is Beauty, which clarifies "being" and hypnotizes Pain? Where is Beauty? Where does she call?

Is she calling? Is she truly calling?

It's Eterna, the only one in whom our friend the Secret found security, who's coming so we can write this page, told only to ourselves, in which nothing of our secret will be revealed since words alone cannot tell it, if the whole secret were told nothing would have been risked, nobody would discover anything, neither what it is nor if it's secret in a dream or a secret in the real.

CHAPTER VII

(LIFE TRIES TO FORCE ITS WAY INTO THE NOVEL)

Sweetheart: "What do we have today in the novel?"
Maybegenius: "Today we have Suicide."[1]

Sweetheart: "Oh, tell me about it right away."
Maybegenius: "It's a story about 'novel characters,' not living persons, and it was conceived this way because in it I found a magical method for you and I to live and be people, because it seems to me

---

1. "Suicide" appeared in the journal *Columna* (1938) and reappeared in *A Novel Begins* (Santiago de Chile, 1941), as a preview of:

"The new, soon-to-be-published literary work whose cover will read:

Novel of Eterna
And the
Child of melancholy Sweetheart of an undeclared lover
Dedicated to the Skip-Around Reader

By
Macedonio Fernández

(Of the three existing types of applause—
the one for calling a 'waiter,'
the one for shooing chickens in the yard,
and the one for catching moths,
which will be the one for this Novel?)

The novel will contain the following 'short story' that the author has been kind enough to send us for insertion in *Columna*. A joke of a story in a joke of a novel, both are working at the extreme margins of Art, revising with a grave, desperate feeling and anxious but honorable investigation the limits of the aesthetic in the disinterested service of an Art most rigorous, stripped of all conventionality and sensuality. This is what Macedonio Fernández tells us of his aspirations, telling us also that he finds himself recently but assuredly rescued from artistic negation. Not so, however, for the 'natural aesthetic.'

We predict that his novel will provoke the most powerful impulse to the investigation and discussion of Art that has ever been felt in our rocky literary field, where trial and initiative are considered a pleasure." (*Editor's note*)

that the moment a character appears on a novel's page narrating another novel, he and all the characters listening to him assume a reality, and they only feel themselves to be characters that are narrated in the other novel: whether the reader likes it or not. There's another recourse that gives 'life' to 'characters,' and I'll ask the novelist that's writing us to use it with us if what we're going to do does not procure for us, Sweetheart, life, that will be happy for us both, since we love each other so. This other method (I hope our author is listening, that he learns it and uses it with us wisely) consists in the authors of novels (they aren't necessarily indifferent to their characters' suffering) depicting a novel bursting out in this sort of vehement exclamation (only in the last line of the novel, therefore, are there ungrateful 'characters' who take advantage of this instance of life they're given and go away to live it without staying for even a line longer in the novel) . . ."

Sweetheart: "I don't know that I wouldn't do the same, although our poor author inspires my sympathy . . ."

Author: "What's got my characters so piqued that I find them in conversation giving themselves alternate functions?"

Maybegenius: "Poor author!"

Sweetheart: "I don't know anything about him, but I sense him, vaguely, as a directionless soul, perhaps an unhappy one."

"I didn't hear anything good or bad and the only thing bothering me is that there's something envious about him, and now he's spying on me because of these two magnificent ideas that I've communicated to you. I've noticed that it doesn't make him happy to see the President set out to write a book and he criticizes his eloquent and moving letters. Who knows how he'd look upon the happiness that your love might give me in Life. As for me, I'm about to burst out with the exclamation that I've prepared. I'll take your hand and run away with you to Life, since I can assure you that this is a Life-giving elocution."

"Yes, let's flee, take me away this minute, say the word and I'll be yours."

"When I say, we'll both recite at the same time: 'Oh, unhappy me'—you'll use the feminine pronoun, of course—'with this Horror that we all must bear, sadness upon sadness for always, oh how it plagues us not to be alive, to only be a 'character' in whatever novel, when before we read, enchanted, believing that only in novels was there misfortune, desperation.'"

"Oh it's working, it's magic, each word lifts me up, takes me away from here, from this nothing; I feel . . . I am . . . Oh, Maybegenius, could it be true, could we . . . hold to this feeling. Repeat it, speak always, Maybegenius."

"I'm confused, I don't know . . . what a horrible pain . . . ay, Sweetheart! We could have done it! . . . I must weep! Please, Sweetheart, tell me again what you're feeling! What did you say, Sweetheart?'"

"Speak, for God's sake, say it again, say it quickly."

"Oh no, there it is again!"

The author:[2] "I've got goosebumps! I want to give them every word they ask for. What pain! Have these words ever given them what they hoped for? Luckily it's not Eterna who's asking me for life! If in her personal majesty and tones she had demanded, clamored as these poor young people do, if she had asked for a life that until today she has not seemed to desire, that in the frustration of her love's destiny she disdains! How could I reply? If this love is fulfilled and, in the privileged happiness that only souls' long suffering can give, she had begged to be made a living being, by means of the magic of the artist's words, would my talents be worthy of placating her?"

Maybegenius: "What's happened to us, Sweetheart? What dizziness did you feel?"

Sweetheart: "Nothing . . . nothing."

"Oh, these were birth pangs, but we're stillborn. Let me rest a bit, later I'll tell you that story."

"Better not to try anything more today; this suffocation is horrible. Better to know nothing of life!"

"Have faith in Maybegenius, don't despair so soon."

The author, rushed and curt in his speech: "How difficult is to write on one's own account something that one has thought so much about."

Maybegenius: "I'm a good man, Sweetheart—and maybe a genius—but, before all of my goodness, you must have patience with what you know to be my weakness, which is to appear not as a character but ruled by the author's formulas. I beg of you, consent that I present you with the story I promised, that's on its way now, as if the

2. It seems the author has had a fright; he thinks he's a character, trapped by his own invention. Will he recover? What if he stayed that way forever! This is the tenth time it's happened to him: for two years running, he's been thinking more or less every day about these characters, and sometimes he's known the sweat and suspension of feeling himself to be no more than a character! Is he really more real than they are? What is it to be real?

reader had sent it my way, and with these introductory parentheses, although the only thing that matters to me is to be with you, even when you listen to me only distractedly."

Sweetheart: "This is the first time, Maybegenius, that I've ever noticed even a drop of acrimony in you."

"Forgive me, I didn't even notice. Consider that I have accepted a life without hope; sometimes this gets to me."

(Pardon, if you will, a versifier who wants to switch to storytelling and, like all men of letters, will end up procuring for himself some theatrical failure—a ruinous finale, like the one met by musicians in the musical tonnage of "opera," punishing themselves with those clamorous denunciations of their little faith, for not having always been conscientious artists of powerful arts with instrumental purity like Prose or the Sonata, with their printed letters, modest and dis-colored, or with frugal octaves that any throat can muster—allow me to warn you that all of my stories lose their thread just as quickly as they brush up against some truth or scientific mystery, forcing the author, who cannot vanquish its scientific delicacy to—what did I tell you!—when, as you see here, the author bumps up against two prob-lems: Integral Automatism, or the development of the Consciousness by the Automatism of Longevity, the only imperative in life whose final outcome is to supplant the anarchic, fatiguing vital pluralism with a singular Cosmos-Personage, the monad-being at last liber-ated from its subjection to the perfidious relation of Externality, and, to come to the other problem, that of Longevity's return game which makes it the eternal anti-eternalizing Evasion Reflex (self-destruction), guessing each fault in longevity's plan, thus making it the Monad-Consciousness of Negative Affect, that is, the instant of a singular consciousness occupied by a single mental state which is pain, over which instance of monad-consciousness the Evasion Reflex reigns, omnipotent and instantaneous . . .

"If this is really about something so tremendous, the reader will surely say that he accepts the story's digression."

"Very well—here it is."

"Although Science appears to me ever more pedantic and sterile—since it reflects the horrible state of humanity—neither does the Story appear to me to be such a serious thing as a literary genre; it's juve-nile, and proscriptive. But here comes the story, come what may."

"You offend me, taking this as resignation."

"Then I won't wait any more, I'll go."

"No, no, it all goes at once. A reader's a reader. Although I once had a back-talker who was certainly unacquainted with a single form of applause.)

SUICIDE

Any state of pleasure or pain that occupies the whole consciousness at any given moment (to say it in turgid language) has at its disposition the full automatism of action (to again put it with little rigor, since the psyche does not casually determine automatism, rather it is at the disposition of the latter and of its sensory peripheralism or centripedalism).

This automatism is instantaneous and always the same: fleeing from pain, clinging to pleasure, conservationist with pleasure, destructivist with pain.

If this happens, therefore, in a child, who has lived enough to know from experience[3] that an organism is destructible, and by what means, that is, a pain that violently seizes the psyche—from here automatism must proceed instantaneously to bodily destruction. Or it's refuted that there can be moments of a singular state in the psyche, which I don't think has been alleged here, or that from the first bad headache a being will proceed to its self-destruction, with the same interior coercion that would lead him to flee a burning building. Would anyone be surprised by this frightened and immediate flight from the flames? Then no one should be surprised that at the first headache a human being with experience of corporeal destructibility, and the means by which it is obtained, would immediately eliminate himself. What's more, whoever affirms this does not believe that there's a hedonistic law in life, which is to say that life has a hedonistic value because of the mere fact of existence, which is of course more hedonistic than not-being. These pages are not made for conventionalisms: we've all known many moments and even long years of total misery, and we've done so because of our slavery to Automatic longevity without which Consciousness would have some power to tyrannize this automatism and order the act of annihilation. I must speak coarsely here, where I relate the death of Suicide.

3. Corporeal; sensory or psychic experience does not exhibit causality, and as a result shows nothing of itself in the Living Body's skills or purposes in carrying out its tasks.

Let's see. Life has no more value than not feeling. In life there's pain as well as pleasure. Consciousness or Sensibility has no power over the living body, but it senses, inevitably, certain changes in this body, although not all. And Consciousness experiences states coinciding with the beginnings of many actions, and their consequences. The physiological body has an ineluctable power over consciousness. The body dedicates itself exclusively to persisting in its corporeal organization; whether or not the consciousness that is annexed to it dies is of no concern. In any complicated series of actions, the body will never take the path towards its own destruction. Would it proceed towards its own destruction in the first moment of a series of actions corresponding to a pain in the consciousness, that is, the fundamental, congenital reflex to flee from pain would be the only possible *self-destructive* movement possible, under automatic longevity? What's the response to all this? That if Consciousness is susceptible for even an instant to being totally and exclusively occupied by pain, it's because there's a moment in the physiological processes of automatism in which its ultimate drive towards longevity fails. There is, therefore, salvation: to die with opportunistic hedonism, when life is worth nothing, despite Automatism's tyranny.

I think of all this when I evoke the details of the death of Suicide. It will already be supposed that I'm aware that 10% of all mortality is suicide-related, without counting the 50% of tentative suicides that failed, but which are, if viewed intelligently, clearly authentic expressions of a wish to not exist. But I believe, as many do, that a man doesn't succeed at suicide unless he's in a demented state, even if it's only a momentary, but total dementia. These successful suicides are not the result of an immediate pain, probably also not an adverse hedonic imbalance in the past. They are, undoubtedly, the result of a malfunction in longevity's empire, which we call life. How could Automatism consent to a mental illness such as suicidal mania? Automatism cannot wish for any death, neither of mutual extermination, illness, or suicide arising from mental chaos. The push towards longevity operates out of certain congenital appetites, which are never mistaken, and by means of action which is always automatic, whether or not the consciousness is aware of it. If the individual dies, it's never because of a mistake in appetites but because the Cosmos, Externality, allows or disallows the satisfaction of that appetite. So it is that Automatism must resign itself to the fact of death, and demented longing for death. These dementias and devastating instants of monad-consciousness of negative affect are, in a certain way, triumphs of hedonism over automatism, of the desire for happiness (even the negative happiness of not suffering) over mere, irrational longevity, which is the business of automatism, and which does not profit the consciousness.

But what is it that automatism mysteriously proposes that obligates us to live even when it isn't to our advantage? I ask again: Is it that automatism cannot discount even a single life among billions, that it cannot allow a single one to be truncated because in each one of these is potentially encrypted the hope of achieving the Immortal Organism? This must be why every life matters to automatism.

I return to Suicide, and I remember that in her there was not even the slightest trace of mental instability. Thus I must ask whether the total occupation, however brief, of the Consciousness by a single, painful state was even possible in the "psychic person." Her destiny kept this lapse in Automatism secret: it was victim of her consciousness's aptitude for total occupation, at least for a moment, by a mental state. And when this mental state was one of pain, the reflex to avoid pain was cleverly triggered, and with it her life ended.

What one deplores is that she seemed to be a person who, apart from her many charms, seemed predestined for all possible human happiness. Life's universal Automatism blew the life of her being through this blind alley, which was constituted by the combination of the evasive reflex to Pain and her Consciousness's rare aptitude for being occupied exclusively by one mental state in the briefest of instants.

Bride, wife, mother, grandmother, four chapters of life both ancient and regulated; these will not live on in her: she was eighteen when the aforementioned congenital reflex and the Monad-Consciousness of a few seconds . . . it's true she was named Suicide, but it's also the case that she was happy, a contented person.

It's certain that I've not made myself understood, and that I've failed to convince. But the reader must put himself in the position of this psychological case so as to conceive or represent to himself the moment in which a consciousness is nothing more than pain. If this consciousness in pain is intelligent, if it's true that we are rational beings, then it should opt at once for the act of destruction.

This is axiomatic: to allege that there are future pleasures is futile, not only because it's not certain nor even proximate most of the time, but also because the tyranny of the evasive reflex operates without reason. Moreover, the notion of a past pain must be at work in the future pleasures, if the claim is that in a present pain the notion of a future pleasure is at work. So it is that suicide occurs in the moment of pleasure. This could be a mistake, my only one: I could be wrong in affirming that when the personal, psycho-physical world, when the "person" is only two things—a Pain and a base automatism of pain evasion—the notion of a possible future Pleasure has no purchase, and thus there is no possibility to interpose between the instant of this painful monad-consciousness and the flaring of this Evasion Reflex. If this imposition were possible, we would already have another hypothesis; but since experience is not influenced by hypotheses, and my decency and passion for clarity make the notion of first principles repugnant—which fool no one but which confer celebrity and populate universities—I submit myself to the totalpossibility of Experience and I accept its petition for inclusion. In this case, suicide would occur in a moment of Pleasure, but this doesn't make a difference: since what I'm claiming is that the base reflex only triumphs, inflexibly, over an affective monad-consciousness.

It appears I won't find my way out of this thicket. But I know that I'm right in essence; only I won't stray too far from the point because another theory of mine, Integral Automatism, which includes automatism of the intelligence, strips all interest from my clarifications about Suicide's last earthly psychic state. In keeping with my systemization of Automatism, it is very likely that Suicide *felt* nothing, not before nor during this moment in which my narrative lingers, the moment of her self-destruction.

I believe that Hodgson's perception, his investigation of automatism was one of the most lucid moments in human thought. But under the stimulus of this formidable lesson, I believe I was able to integrate its truth and the problem of an automatism that fully and independently dominates all of life's action; the difficulty is: how can Activity have a longevistic *orientation*, without perception, which is the mental accumulation and selection of causal sequences (purified by Accident, that is, by non-causal immediate sequences that are masked by the apparent "accidental" quality of causal sequences once they are purified, and thus fixed). It's certain that congenital appetites are not in error, but how and where they can be satisfied is a matter of totally experiential, phenotypical knowledge. How, without having seen the cat that scratched us, can we elude, again unseen, the scratch of another? Very well, we need not *see* nor *hear* psychic states; we only require that the neural trajectory of the auditory or visual signal to transmit the vibration of light or sound properly and that there has been an anterior association with pain (that is, physiological harm, not the pain of this harm, since we supposed that Consciousness, the psychic Sensorium, is abolished or not yet established) with the presence and attack of a howling cat (a present attack, and physical, not psychic howling). The alteration introduced in the optic and phonic field by the presence of a new but identical cat will provoke physical evasion, connecting the earlier harm with its associated cerebral imprint.

The difficulty was therefore nonexistent and the rigor and comprehensiveness of Longevistic Automatism is achieved. There's no recourse to the alternative, declaring Consciousness a mere witness to all perceptive phenomena, since consciousness is affected only insofar as it's not a cause of anything, no matter what life brings.

If I've finally convinced you by now, it won't take much to add that each seed among a billion seeds is capable of absorbing the entire Cosmos, all Materiality, in the individual form that belongs to it alone, to the point of constituting the Cosmos-Persona. Like me, like a grape seed or a grain of wheat, suicide may be that seed which takes root and grows, which makes the cosmos of a person and overcomes odious plurality, externality—and with it, death—Automatism—that requires that neither I nor the seed dies—and which uses us to give itself some measure of Rest.

But even as Automatism is Total Truth, we can never know if the person we see living is also feeling. I saw Suicide live happily, but I don't know if she felt anything.

If she felt anything, we don't know it. And since the reader doesn't like us to exhibit her as an "example," wasting the well-known "readerly compassion," on an unfeeling character, we won't go on to find out, thus guaranteeing that Suicide suffers as much as the reader and author, since we're all now living with the shame of having conceived of the hypothesis of her unfeeling nature.

Hodgson, who knew that all knowledge is phenotypic, was baffled, perhaps by a residual survival of the *impression* of Intelligence's spirituality, which "remained" in his mind, resisting his radical "critique of consciousness," perhaps because of a moment of confused synonymy in his mind between the words "automatic" and "unconscious;" in summary, our dear Hodgson felt it would be too much to affirm the total automatism of Knowledge or Understanding, which, nevertheless, is merely the automatic purgation of the accidental quality of invariable sequences, a purge that takes place for itself alone, only because what is frequently repeated leaves a deeper impression than mere coincidences of contiguity or succession. This unnecessary purge of the miraculous "reasoning" suffices . . .

But Maybegenius is unfazed when he notices Sweetheart sleeping, and carefully wakes her.

Sweetheart: "It seems like this Hodgson you mentioned is a bad friend. You shouldn't go around with him if he's the one who betrayed Suicide."

Maybegenius: "Oh, if I had thought you were listening, I would have talked about 'ablation of the consciousness,' and I would have emphasized that in clarifying what remains of the integral automatism I profess, I have clarified nothing of the essential Mystery of the All; no explanation, either Mechanical or Psychological, can ever be reduced to the Mystery."

But since one never knows if the reader is sleeping . . . and it should be known that Sweetheart is not someone to feign sleep while listening to a story. She's so charming in her innocence that she's made me a non-irritable author who, on the contrary, sympathizes with the reader when he falls asleep on him; consequently the reader gives no thought to correcting his own behavior.

Once Sweetheart sympathizes with Suicide, she won't rest until someone finds her, consoles her, and ends her story, since Sweetheart so identifies with sadness and a "character abandoned in the telling" is the misfortune she most fears for herself and others.

I will rectify the situation (as the author or as Maybegenius) by saying that I don't admit a difference between suicide under conditions of mono-consciousness in the demented instant of pain and suicidal dementia: the first is a chronic state, a hunger for suicide, and it comes with a constant pre-representation of the pleasure of the destructive act itself. Demented is the same as anti-vital, not the same as anti-hedonic.

CHAPTER VIII

(NO.)

One day was not like the others. Returning from Buenos Aires they found the President lost in thought. Later in the evening he gathered them all together, telling them:

"I have bad news.

"I stretched this test of friendship over two years, and although you all have given me a life that is worth more than not living, it hasn't given me consciousness of finality, of dignity. Only Passion can give me this. And passion's cure for my soul, which I couldn't achieve through friendship, I now hope—my new, and final hope—will be achieved through Action.

"Tell me if you will join with me in this Action, whose object will be something we once considered: the conquest, through Beauty, of Buenos Aires."

It's true; the President's old hobbyhorse was to rescue that great city with whose destiny he so strongly identified, to save her. He observed the meaning of her history, the truth of her grandeur like no one else had. But she needed to be purged of a certain crassness and enervation of conduct.

The President had also exhorted the characters at other times, in what Maybegenius called his lucid meditations, like this:

"If solemnity, a prudent posture, statues, and streets with names were proportional to virtue and profound thought, how few they would be; this life does not need so much patience, nor does it abound in so much temptation to vileness in exchange for celebrity.

"For now, the profusion of statues, birthdays, historical volumes, named streets, and writings of secure virtue have made this society very suspicious of us poor, pardonable people; it runs in circles to recognize men's labors to appear good, in a civilization so enamored of Yale locks and pleasant tones, which are a trick to put victims to sleep.

"The best cities have streets named for Rain, for Waking, for Mother and Brother, for He who is Called, and who Goes Without, streets named You'll Come Back, and Goodbye, and Wait For Me, and Return, and Loving Family, Kiss, Friend, Hello, Dream, Again, Sleeplessness, Maybe, Remake Yourself, Forgetfulness, Undertaking, Come Back To Me, Literary Salon, Live in Fantasy, Home, Smile, Call Me, and the great avenue Later He Dreams the Day, which is crossed by the avenue Unidentified Man.

"It gives light, not ashes, to the day."

His gaze was distant, his eyes open wide, searching, and seeing the phantasm of the future and the vacillations of the route between a doubtful future and a happy present.

"One day," the President concluded, "friendship won't be enough for you, either—and you, too, will sit with your gaze fixed on the empty air in the hours before dawn, looking to the future and yet not wanting to look at it, feeling pained to look at the floor, the house, the present which you used to regard so cherishingly."

The long gaze that the President held that dawn was such that Sweetheart, asleep in her bed, became agitated with the anguish of friendship's farewell that she, along with the others, had heard of in the hours before. Her caring nature was able to discern the defeated sorrow in the President's decision. And she dreamed and mourned the now-truncated present, moments in the pleasurable length of their days which would see no more mornings when everyone was happy together in the kitchen or the garden, no more nights of every-one gathered together, animated, unconcerned—or even when each was troubled by his own pain but lighthearted in the harmony of communal life.

Such was his gaze, charged with sadness for Sweetheart's future, for himself and Eterna, with thoughts about everything that lay at Eterna's feet. He rested his elbow on the headboard of Sweetheart's modest bed and inclined himself towards her, his hand supporting his forehead and his gaze a screen, with his face at an angle to the bed and his gaze at an angle to his face.

Friendship opened windows on to phantasms; it filled the friends' eyes with phantasms; the gaze became empty again at the President's proposition: "But President, is it possible that friendship is not enough?"

But faced with the President's confidence in the project to abolish Buenos Aires's ugliness, they all longed to conquer in the name of beauty and the mystery.

"It's over, it's broken!"

"There's another one just the same, don't cry!"

"But Life isn't like that! That limpid, content friendship we once had will never be the same."

President: "And a love that once was impossible now will never be . . ."

Maybegenius: "But it was my first time in love, and I'll keep it forever, even if she doesn't return it. What is the 'beloved self?' Only a word; I'll have her love for him for myself."

The Lover: "In life. But in personal eternity? Eternal, individual time exists for every Possibility; impossibility only exists in terms of space and time: to be and not to be at the same time in a single point; for something to occur and not occur at the same time, this is the only impossibility. In truth there's no impossibility except contradiction, which is to say, senselessness. To love and not to love is contradictory, but to love today and not tomorrow is not."

President: "You give me eternity and, in her, total possibility; in her my invariable identity. But this identity is not that of one who cannot love a perfect lover today, but can tomorrow. Perhaps I'm not someone else when I feel what before I did not feel?"

But the Lover was silent, as far as anyone could tell: what I like most in "La Novela" is nonexistence's discretion, invisible and impossible dealings with the Gentleman Who Doesn't Exist.

CHAPTER IX

THE CONQUEST OF BUENOS AIRES

For some time, the President had followed the news of the fierce discord stewing in Buenos Aires, because of the antagonism between two gangs into which the population had divided itself: The Romantics and the Jubilants.

Each one of these gangs sought dominance; one by means of ultra-tender poems and the invention of impassioned tales, the other by means of literature and a multiplicity of other ingenious devices dispersed throughout the city to provoke the grotesque.

One of the recourses of the Jubilant Gang, it will be remembered, was that they used military force to pinch and distort the city's mirrors, a plan that was ordered and executed within twenty-four hours and by means of which they created a veritable hysterical crisis that put an end to all transit and business (official and otherwise) in Buenos Aires for an entire week. (The President himself was wrongly suspected of being the source of this measure, which would have explained his frequent excursions to the capital, and sojourns there.)

The next week the Romantics dominated. Bolstered by all of the loudspeakers in the city, they repeated in unison, for an entire day, a lacerating poem about a woman of advanced age and very plain features who had caused a young blind man to fall in love with her beautiful, youthful voice; this woman, the afternoon on which her lover was expected to arrive, and whose eyesight had been restored by a helpful surgeon, kills herself by burning herself in a pyre so immense that it instantly reduced her face and body to ashes, so that the young lover, believing that she anxiously prepared herself to receive him in her best clothes and that the fire in which she perished was an accident, was driven mad with sorrow and threw himself from the balcony. This story in verse was repeated to the population as if it were breakfast, lunch, tea, and dinner, with the result that by the end of that Romantic Week a mere boy was able to appoint himself to the governorship of Buenos Aires. And in truth, the story was doubly tragic: a woman who could not stand her lover's horror at seeing her, though he believed in her and he imagined her to be so beautiful: but he never felt this horror, not even at first, because someone who is born blind has no visual imagination and, once the power of sight is granted to him, he is almost never able to tell beauty from ugliness, because these are matters of custom.

(This civil war also reached the metaphysicians: between the Soulists, who wanted Human Consciousness to reach to the Third Reflection, and the Automatists, who believed that supreme wisdom is found by returning to the Zoological Psyche.)

The President meditated on this civil discord, and knowing that a certain inclination to tolerance, to civil coexistence, characterized Argentine society, outside of the bull-headed, had thought on it for a long time, finally deciding that this unusual *porteño* (as the inhabitants of Buenos Aires are called) exasperation must have a psychological, but non-reflexive origin, indicated by the city's various errors incurred in the course of the last thirty years, and maybe a few more to come, since it was particularly careless in the regulation of the tastes and aesthetic practices of civil cohabitation.

The President also attributed part of the disenchantment of *porteño* life to the failure to achieve a particular historic fact that had been featured, but frustrated, in the past.

Once Ugliness was eliminated from its history or its streets, once that historic injustice or excess of civic enthusiasm was rectified, the gang war would disappear and Buenos Aires would be forever ruled by Beauty and Mystery.

So it was that the President arrived in Buenos Aires with his diminutive but devastating army of characters, with the plan to meet with the leaders of both gangs and to convince them that their behavior, so dissonant with Buenos Aires's usual mode of being, could only be the fruit of an impulse, suggestion, or cause of which they themselves were ignorant.

And the Romantics and the Jubilants understood the sterility of their dispute, and the fecundity of beautiful work that common effort offered.

How did it happen? A novelistic miracle! (The most abstruse miracles, like immaculate conception, have brought the incomprehensible to life for humanity for centuries. The pinnacle of universal incomprehensibility is often fame, just as the praise of those who do not understand them has made certain philosophers famous. What's more miraculous than these glories is those modest, useful miracles of which the novel avails itself.) And, this miracle happened by means of diverse and subtle recourses most amenable to desperation or the bewitching of the Buenos Aires population, so that they became docile towards the President's forces. For example: in the bars, among the odors of alcohol and tobacco, rolled a boiling wave of savory stew whose vapors emitted a homey, charming perfume and which dismantled the incipient orgy; it also put an end to the imperfect irrigation of the trees in the plazas and sidewalks, some of which had been left unwatered, something that leads to the desperation of those who enjoy watching trees be watered; it put an end to that woman who walks around asking everyone if her face is wider than it is long; it dispatched all hanging mirrors that are so thin that they only show half your face; all falsely distributed automatic photography machines; the subsidized circulation of the fat and the deaf that was everywhere nothing but an obstruction, everyone yelling at the deaf people and watching the fat ones argue with the bus conductor: "Yes sir, I'm over 90 kilos, bring the scale if you like!," so as to take advantage of the free fare that was municipally mandated for those whose previous weigh-in was over 90 kilos; it got rid of the sound of corks squeaking in bottles (Maybegenius's favorite pastime); it dispatched with the backwards hat, and the poorly-knotted tie . . .

Among so many measures, which were indiscriminately employed by the President's whole company, Eterna thought of and used only one: to make a messenger with a lighted lamp run from one end of the city to the other, so he could give the lamp to an artist who was at that moment seated at his desk, filled with inspiration, but without a light.

Perhaps this messenger crossed paths with another that that joker Maybegenius also unleashed on the city: a trombonist with paralyzed respiration who carried a candle in the fingers of a equally paralytic hand, so that he could neither blow out the candle or let go of it; and gesturing for somebody to please put it out so he wouldn't burn himself, he ran for many blocks and ended up charring his fingers, just as Maybegenius had foretold, as he wanted to make him believe in the shocking egotism of the population, which prevented anyone from offering to blow out his candle; with this he proposed to play a joke on the vaunted fraternity or benevolence of the population, when in reality this negative attitude owed itself to a general distrust of transients, as well as the *porteño* fear of practical jokes.

Sweetheart competed with Maybegenius in the deployment of jokes as conquest. She found Buenos Aires's the most mechanically incompetent man, and also it's most myopic, and she sent him a very high-end radio as a gift, complete with a tiny, complicated closure, which made of this radio the first obsequity of a final calamity, since this poor man could not rid himself of the apparatus when he wanted to sleep or rest, because although he was slow and nearsighted, he was also grateful and kind, and he couldn't bring himself to shut the radio up with a hammer; what's more, he endured the complaints by those in the pension house where he lived.

I still remember the apoplectic accounts that circulated each night; electric telephone calls; powerful magnets surreptitiously distributed throughout the city, that invincibly attracted any bit of metal men or women carried on them; and the envelope-letters, letters written on envelopes and dispersed among all the tramway and bus seats, with a prize to whomever could tell if it was an envelope with a letter or a letter without an envelope. (The envelope-letter brought back one of the author's own advertisements from eight or ten years back, in which the same intent of the conquest of Buenos Aires was proposed: to give Buenos Aires a certain mystery that it never had.)

How was it that the population never took to the streets, demanding a President Painkiller to rid them of these many exasperations?

One can easily imagine the idealism of the Conquest by thinking of what few truly memorable actions there are, and so it was that the city of Buenos Aires opened itself to beauty, erasing all the facets and vestiges of *porteño* life's former ugliness.

It happened that certain past events were struck with nonexistence, making use of Eterna's talent for undoing the past and tying on new, substitute pasts. (This is why you'll sometimes see Eterna looking pale, and you'll notice that she can't pronounce the "n" in syllables ending with "on." When she says "passiom" for "passion" or "salom" for "salon," which are the only known signs of this fatigue, it's because she's spent the night in the immense mental effort of nullifying a past and, harder still, of inventing another that will content the owner of this sad story.)

Some of these past events are: Dorrego's execution; Camila O'Gorman's martyrdom; Irma Avegno's destiny;[1] the exhibition of a certain

---

1. All traces of this woman's path were erased—she who irrevocably disillusioned human piety—the path that sought a voluntary death in the streets of Buenos Aires and its suburbs.

writer's pens to the adoration of the intelligent and modest Buenos Aires public; and the publication of the letters of a certain empress, which were of such lovely sentiment that it would have been a shame to violate their intimacy.

One thing that never happened came into existence by virtue of novel-magic: Carlos Pellegrini's presidency over the Argentine people, the most interesting kind of presidency, since it seems we can't even breathe without the president. It's interesting because at least he was a humorless man, and now we know whether it's possible to govern without comedy.

The beauty of non-History came about; all homage to captains, generals, litigators, and governors was abolished—not a single recollection of a mother's magnificent act, nor a childhood grace, nor the dark suicide of a youth overwhelmed by life; death was left to the dead and people spoke only of the living: soup, the tablecloth, the sofa, the hearth, nasty medicine, little shoes, the steps, the nest, the fig tree, the pine tree, gold, a cloud, the dog, Soon!, roses, a hat, laughter, violets, the teruteru bird (there's nothing sweeter than to use children's nonsense to speak of Happiness); plazas and parks that bear the names of superlative human lives, but with no last names; streets named The Bride, Remembrance, the Prince, Retirement, Hope, Silence, Peace, Life and Death, Miracles, Hours, Night, Thought, Youth, Rumor, Breasts, Happiness, Shadow, Eyes, Patience, Love, Mystery, Maternity, Soul.

All the statues that saddened the plazas were evicted, and in their place grew the best roses; the only exception was that the statue of José de San Martín was replaced by another statue symbolizing "Giving, and Leaving." In the end, something happened to non-flowing time, like history, and there was only a fluid Present, whose only memory was of what returns to being daily, and not what simply repeats, like birthdays. That's why the city almanac has 365 days with only one name: "Today," and the city's main street is also named "Today."

Many other small things were also accomplished, whose tiny sorrows might fill a life with horror, like what was spared, for example: the half-full glass, or the little lamp with hoarded light, or the twisted tie, or artificial flowers on tombs.

When the neighboring areas of Buenos Aires saw that this plan to purge the culture of its recent past had been accomplished, public health restored itself. Everyone affiliated with the Jubilant-Romantic feud woke one morning wondering how they had ever lived by such a fixed, banal, and batty ideal.

Once the Conquest was concluded, it was left to the Mystery to reveal to the President the most singular fact of any city, of which he was the only witness. I have it on good authority that on a certain day of the year 1938, and during a period of mere living, of frivolity, when it happened that the body of Alfonsina Storni reached death's waters, the city displaced itself, spinning instead on her axis by moving a few centimeters. The President, still perplexed as to whether this urban gyration was a plea—"Don't die!"—or a sorrowful approval of a dreaded and sad refusal of life, knows that thanks to this occurrence in the sensibility of the heart of a city at the instant of the death of this dreamer's soul, Buenos Aires entered the Mystery.

When the President and his character army returned to the estancia "La Novela" at the same time the next morning, they greeted each other with "Good morning"s. But the President returned to Buenos Aires that night, and I know why. To assign to the two central Plazas the names "City that knows no Death" and "For Non-Identical Men;" these denominations took place at the intersection of the two Plazas (the non-identical is exempt from death).[2]

Thanks to these remedies and hopes, along with the Death-Concealer that Eterna invented, and the Joke-Laughter-Reviver that the Humorist made, Buenos Aires was blessed.

---

2. Perhaps some readers will find the much-vaunted Conquest of Buenos Aires by Beauty and the Mystery to be less than lucid. It's inevitable: the imperfection, truncation, and even insipidness of a novel that was only conceived as a cure, as Action without Object, as a state of depression and disorientation. If the author had made this chapter robust and gracious, he would have misrepresented the psychology of this Action. For the rest, I will satisfy my incredulous and clever reader by confessing that the chapter is simply the work of a dried-up writer, who can do no more.

Despite this confession, I must acknowledge a reduction of sixty-three readers, who demand impeccable style.

CHAPTER X

A MEETING BACK AT "LA NOVELA"

Sweetheart: "Listen, Maybegenius: I'll tell you now what I'm sched-uled to say—this novel is so well-organized—later on, in a chapter that has not yet begun. I can't hold it in; in my spirit today there is sadness and aspiration, longing, a discomfort in my whole being, discontent, and tears swarm. Have you seen the Respiration of the living? What a mystery! What a worry it must be that we never will feel *respiration*! What dignity, what communion with the cosmos!"

Maybegenius: "That does bother me."

"I love you, Maybegenius, sad friend; right now, I love you. We suffer from all we deserve, so give me everything you want to say."

"The pain we feel is character pain: tears that won't fall, that don't wet our cheeks. To breathe!"

"Yes, to breathe. Just as the author of this novel once said:

> Neither pleasant nor complaining
> I breathe the air of Life.

(The author adds a correction: Air should also be upper case! So yes, sir, my characters are citing me—of course it's Sweetheart!— they're making me famous. And it'll be a painful fall, to see how they long to live and I've no power to give them a life. It's only possible and polite for me to pardon her, to let her unburden herself here, saying what she's supposed to say in the twelfth chapter. I'll confess it, I feel myself falling in love, little by little: and if this feeling grows, if I fall in love (it could certainly happen), then I'll know the pain and humiliation of impotence, finding what is impossible in my own creation; such an intense daydream will hardly change for tenuous reality. Even though it's not in my best interests as an artist—the continuity of falsehood is at the core of novelistic Art's dignity—I will say that Sweetheart exists; I wouldn't say it if it weren't for the fact that while I wrote this note I effectively stumbled upon a principle of love for her, though I was saddened by its impossibility for an instant, since I forgot that she existed and that I could hear her admirable voice just by picking up the telephone; now that I've felt the nullity of my power to give her life, I understand the torture it is to desire an unreal life for another, just as I insinuated that Sweetheart desires it for herself. The thing I created desires its reality and also its author, thus finding its author himself impossible; how easily the mind forgets, confuses, knots itself up, and the feeling is torn between seeing its object in a space of reality or fantasy. I still don't know if my novel sprang from an impulse to the highest femininity, if it lived before or if a character, Eterna, has or has not been born; none of this implies realism, since I've copied nothing of Eterna; no artistic mind would have attempted or achieved it, nor have I even wanted to call this "Eterna's Novel," although it is she who has inspired me, refining my torpid perceptions and enriching my life with mysticism and passion daily.)

Maybegenius: "We've seen each other today more than ever and we spent a lot of time together in the months when you came along and helped me with my chores. I feel the sadness of this short existence that we have in the novel, I want to leave home, to be in truth."

Sweetheart: "What you say frightens and worries me. You really think yourself so bereft of life?"

"No, Sweetheart, I exist and I love it, because I've met you. Do we suffer from the desperation that there's nothing that can give us life? After I so graciously, so sweetly encountered you here, you who arrived so unexpectedly where I was, you whose arrival was so directly for me, when we met at the gate, and now we've spent so much time in each other's company . . ."

"You're such a friend, so courteous."

"And you?"

"I wish we had experienced something of life!"

"Sweetheart, we're not unreal. If we were, we'd be smoking, like characters in movies. We will have life, we'll keep asking for it; and we're the same as all of those with life who find themselves facing death, this slim, moribund being who begs for life in gestures and words and in reality doesn't feel pain from losing it, nor does he even believe that he has stopped living."

Author: "You're making me uncomfortable. What an itch you've got to exist! Who would have thought that characters of mine—this has never happened to another author; lots of them write contented characters, like Hamlet, Segismundo, characters who incline towards not being—I, on the other hand, am confronted with this vital craving."

Reader: "What an inconvenience, where will I read you if you go to life instead? Please leave a forwarding address. Also, what more do you want, then to be agreeable to life? Also, I object that the title of the chapter bore no warning: 'In which my appalling desperation, which no one imagined, is revealed.'"

Author: "You flatter me, Sir; if it weren't for my characters' cravings, I'd be so happy to have readers like you. What a beautiful, most complete desperation I've thought up, don't you think?"

Reader: "The characters pain me. But I exist. Is there another chapter that wants to live? If there is I'm not reading anymore; there's no spectacle so uncomfortable."

(Just then, the happy man who still seeks a country where being good is also being happy, passes by. He looks like the President: he has all of his happiness, without his penchant for literary theory.)

Author: "How can I expect you to grasp my Great Idea. Nevertheless, I can't predict what my characters crave; I only know what they're going to say and do. You yourself, Reader, are here a part of my work and yet . . ."

Reader: "Here, yes, but for myself?"

Author: "I see that you like to live, and for this reason I must not bring you up or let you talk here anymore, unless it's to fall in love with Sweetheart for yourself. I have the power to create appearance and death, to reign over all of this and yet there's someone on the earth whose soul wants to be sounded—and I can't do it!"

Metaphysician: "This is a lot of tangling, phantasmagoric tangling between characters, reader, and author. And it's not that they pretend to get tangled up; they themselves don't know what they are. This won't resolve everything: they're all real; any image in a mind is reality, and lives; the world, reality is all just an image of the mind. Affection is not an image; pleasure, pain. Existence is not pre-desireable; in the pre-desire to be there is already a being; what there isn't is a beginning, the not having been, from which situation we began desiring existence.

Author: "I don't doubt it: just try and extinguish it! Now you cease in my mind, and in the novel, so it can go on. Begone, Professor of Being! Exist no more!"

Metaphysician: "Wait, don't rub me out just yet: we can't be more than one image in a mind, in form and body; to appear in a mind is to be born."

Author: "Flee, Metaphysician, you are ruined by frustration, like everything here."

Metaphysician: "Call me at your eleventh hour, when you need an illusion."

Author: "I've got your eleventh hour right here! I won't write you anymore. Stop it!"

(And, effectively, the author stopped writing him; but it's such an incredible thing, resolving to stop being without an ontologist present, that the only effect is that the reader is convinced that they're not talking about him any more here as he reads the rest of the novel.)

Author (*to the Reader*): "But so that nobody thinks that the novel remains in the dark because the Metaphysician has been exiled, I'll tell you that I don't have the privilege of immortality, because this property is his, mine, and everyone's; my privilege is that, although you don't know a thing, you don't remember your glorious existence, which merely coincides with what happened earlier, I, exhausting and mortifying myself for many years, was able to bring to mind all I wanted to remember about my conscious pre-existence. This helps me to conceive of a conscious post-existence, which is personal eternity. And I can give a transcript of what's most pleasant for me to recall . . ."

CHAPTER XI

(A PARENTHESIS IN THE NOVEL WHEREIN A FRAGMENT OF AN ESSAY IS INSERTED THAT TREATS OF THE FOLLOWING: A THEORY OF THE "READ BY CHARACTERS FROM ANOTHER NOVEL" NOVEL)

Maybegenius: "Last night, since I couldn't sleep, I read a novel. It was full of love affairs and coincidences, the most extraordinary things happened in it. I will say that if it were a matter of fantasy, I wouldn't be left behind. What do you think about the Lover's idea of us all writing a novel together?"

Sweetheart: "It sounds very good to me. So many interesting things happen at the estancia. We'd have a story even if we didn't tell anything more than the Saturday afternoon when we all walked together among the trees on the riverbank. Should we give this surprise to the President?"

"But surely the Lover has thought of some subtle plot."

"And one as simple as he is."

"But now I want to read you a chapter of the novel I read last night. It's called *Adriana Buenos Aires*.[1] Would you like that?"

"Go ahead, I'm dying of curiosity, I must know these characters."

"I'll read you some scenes. 'Impassioned young sleeping woman: What heartbeat of the tragic soul makes you, so innocent, a mistress of temptation, so that everything miserable in me, the sorrows I have burned in my life, so that the bitter, fatuous ash of my sadness chokes me, so that trembling with guilt and mystery I approach, sweating and sobbing, pale in the pale light of this dawn . . . ! I'd do anything with you, Adriana, here and now is the only non-Impossible, the mandate of Tragedy. I don't know why I arise from my dark place and find myself, tremulous in the tremulous light of dawn, before my door, reaching towards your bed, which is my bed. Solitude pushes at my back in this corner of the sleeping house, I tread with rage on the past and the future alike. Everything is a stain on the world.'"

"How sad that is."

1. A novel at that time still unedited, which now constitutes Volume V of the *Complete Works* (of MF). (*Editor's Note—Adolfo de Obieta*).

"Does it seem to you, or do you feel like you're in a similar situation to the one this character finds himself in, or even if there's no similar situation, do you experience this intense suffering?"

"I would like to be this character. It's no longer about pleasantly reading a novel. I can't see an end to the desperation of this life."

"Make an effort not to return to this thought of desperation. I think that life is preferable when you and I are together. It's not true that our current existence is appetizing."

"Keep reading."

"But what's pathetic is that the poor girl, who's asleep, believes that the person speaking is her lover Adolfo, but it's actually a mutual friend who's in love with her. And he doesn't know whether or not to kiss her."

"Read me that page; let our pain keep company with the pain of these characters."

"'Blessed creature, soul of love, a maiden already maternal, I say to myself as I bend over her sleeping form. If I kiss you and you never know it, you won't call my name in your dreams and you'll believe that it's me, here, who you name and you'll call me by the name of the one who loves you, and made you a mother, and you'll receive me with open arms into your bed . . . I won't kiss you because you're sleeping and this painful reality will wake you; I won't kiss you because I don't know what to make of my impulse to kiss you: Tenderness? Desire? To take revenge on him? The vanity of knowing that I had kissed you?'"

"These are the passions of the living."

"Isn't it better to be as we are, darling Sweetpassion, I mean Sweetheart? What do you think about what befalls these beings?"

"Are they like us? Happier than we are? Are they like the reader and the author?"

"I wish I could explain to you what they are, to what realm they pertain, what their destiny is, and what they believe."

"I'd rather you tell me the story of that kiss."

"Well, it says here that he hesitates a while longer, then kisses her. 'No, I'll kiss you, Adriana, on the mouth, because I am seeking love's kiss, for you to respond to me. I understand that what moves me is love alone. After this desperate night I'll have neither the strength nor clarity to deny myself this quenching of thirst, this pacification.'"

"This 'life' is terrible. I tremble at it, it frightens me. But you know, for a few moments, faced with the vehemence of what you read, I felt as though Life brushed up against me?"

"That's possible. Last night, as I witnessed—as a reader—one of the most dramatic scenes, I felt my breath quicken, but it was so brief that I only dreamed, perhaps, that I was able to do what the living call breathing. I don't know how to tell you about the sensation, we don't have the words for it."

"And how does this scene end?"

"As he bends over to kiss her, whispering, 'Adriana, where is your mouth, let's kiss,' a shadow moves in the half-light of the doorway."

"I want life! I want these upsets and shadows, I want life!"

Reader: "I'm the one who's about to lose it. I feel like I don't exist right now. Who took my life?"

Author: "Pinch yourself, you need to get rid of this ringing of reality, of being. In dreams nobody pinches himself."

Maybegenius: "Do you think the reader is listening?"

Reader: "I don't understand."

Author: "Then you haven't been a good skip-around reader, Reader. You've succumbed to the vice of reading in order. My novel isn't an epic. It's not its genre that is irreproachable, impeccable; there's no recipe for this kind of artwork. Forgive this novel for being a novice."

Reader: "Ah."

Author: "As for me, I'm not the President; I'm about to find out who I am now. If I'm wrong, I'll be a finalist, but I will have had, by mistake, an exalted hallucination that I might call adventurous. The President pains me; I wanted life for him, and for him to have totalove. But I don't think he's headed in the right direction; his intelligence consumes him, he vacillates between passion and the mystery of being. He's missing a word, only one, a single perception that will save him. He says to himself: There are four options: The Mystery of Being, Passion, Science, and Action. That's not how it is. Science and Action are entertainments, they're life for its own sake, longevity. There's no excuse for entertainments, they're all abasements (of power, erudition, glory, riches), fleeting pleasures; the abasements of the second and third part of *Faust*, the toy store full of petty pleasures, which is only excusable in childhood. The answer is: within the mystery there is full clarity, a singular Certainty: Passion. Certainty is essential to a mystic state, but the only mystic state is not religious, it's Passion. It isn't religion, with its diseased negation of being, its subordination, that turn us into unreal appearances, but Passion, a consciousness of fullness and eternity, with nothing subordinated. I wrote a novel to make Eterna happy, and she wants it to end, and believes that she'll find it impassioned. In this way I'm the author of a fantasized metaphysics and of a metaphysical novel. It's my luck that Eterna won't be disillusioned in this, and I won't attempt anything more in art so as to never again risk the fears and discouragements I risk by writing this. I even felt terror just a while ago, writing; I had to say, strongly, 'I'm not the President.' This is fearful pressure: I trembled for a moment, I worried, I believed I was a lifeless character in my novel, creating the President, creating him so similar to myself. And already all my characters want to live. It will be sad when I stop, when saying goodbye I say: 'For those who want to live, I salute you.'"

CHAPTER XII

A definition of the pain of the past, a sentimental jewel that Eterna fastened to her breast; better to call it the pain of a most subtle Impossibility, ensconced in Eterna's soul, since neither in Being nor in the World does this impossibility created in Eterna's mind exist, nor in any other soul.

This impossibility is founded in irreversibility, the unassailability of any given segment of any given person's past, that which does not present itself as sentiment, but as when this person makes the always accidental discovery that it might or might not have happened, of the beloved or the person whom one loves more than oneself. Eterna, who is the only human (individual, not ideal) who has the power of changing another's past, even her lover's, cannot change her own. Moreover, her soul can't accept that her lover not love her for always, but after the inferior, insignificant action of "seeing her," it might happen that he never again sees her by his side, that he's indifferent, ignoring her and even displeased that she lightly crossed his path, she whom he didn't look at, so absorbed was he in his own egocentric affairs.

When they met, she changed the President's past, so that he already couldn't recall a moment in which he didn't know her and love her, yet in practically all of her history Eterna sees herself without him and without his love. And even when the President has made her understand—and not everything, but to believe in eternity and eternal personal memory—and even when she believes in herself and in him that yes, they are eternal after death (but not after forgetting), even then, Eterna fears the future. Maybe she believes that totalove can exist one day, but nevertheless she always has this weakness about mutual not-loving and not-recognizing, in this past without vision or passion that they share, even so Eterna fears for the future of love.

Such tears, Eterna . . . !

These tears only say "never" in your eyes, they are the highest point of a wave that has washed over Being or Reality, they are the World's supreme handiwork, as beautiful as a realized Reason For Being, after which even the cessation of Reality is possible and justifiable. Your tears over the mystical impossibility of a love that has no non-loving past, this pain hidden from the totalove that many women barely experience but which in you is constant, these tears are a clamoring demand that I fold myself into a meditation that will not manage to equal your Sentiment, since my certainty in thought, of the future, has no response for your demand that our past not exist, for your request that before our love you not exist. Your tears are the Tears of terror and longing for a boundless existence, for an impossible cessation.

The problem is as difficult as it is serious for me and for your welfare, Eterna; I need to consult with men of magnificent intelligence and nobility: pages from William James, Schopenhauer, Hegel, Fechner; making the problem less difficult as I seek aid in my quest for totalknowledge. I've read, I've meditated, I ask myself and I respond: In any present mind, the destruction of a past may be decreed and carried out, since in this present a personal past strikes the two notes of the personal and the past, and the operation of the psyche may, in that moment, with labor and insistence, disassociate the scene of a past event from a current image, from its two notes, or threads: the thread of the selfsame, and of the past, and make the image into a far-off occurrence of mere fantasy, not a real occurrence of the personal past.

What is indifferent, and cannot be destroyed, are the effects of the past event. These effects are felt, but they are indifferent to memory and the discrimination between "real" and "imaginary" and the designation of "far off" and "self-same;" these effects would be felt, but not as such, with a cause in our past. And what's important is that the only fearful effect of a past without love over a present love does not come: if one day we reach a fullness of love as we think we have, its proof is that the past can do nothing to harm it.

Thus it seems to me, Eterna. that it's specious to define the burning you feel as the bitter sentiment of having had a past before our love began. There's a bitterness there, it's true, but it doesn't come from the notion of a simple past without our mutual vision but rather, as I suspect, from an insecurity about whether our love today has reached its fullness. And so I pass from one pain to the next, suspecting that you are not certain of the fullness of your love or of mine, and that this is what pains you, not the past.

Here an elegant praying mantis has paused in front of my manuscript, undecided as to whether he would like to enter the novel.

CHAPTER XIII

As Sweetheart and Maybegenius know from listening to conversations in the estancia (long Saturday conversations about art and science, with the President as friendly mediator), that he (the President) is preparing a novel. This is why they want to give him the argument about life in "La Novela," since any day of this existence would make a charming tale.

The novel that the President is thinking of writing—and which, according to him, he'll never write—would entail an original conception of "novelism of the consciousness" or "the worldless novel." (So his passion for thinking alternates with his passion for creation.) Sweetheart and Maybegenius found these notes in his notebook:

The characters, who are not physical persons but consciousnesses, were living people, they lived in the World, or in the Dualism; they now inhabit the universe of events of consciousness, which is absolutely indeterminate (with inter-consciousness determinism: each time that someone experiences an intense mental state, it passes to the others; why does an intense mental state happen? Why does it work on the others? These "whys" do not exist: this is how it happens, and that's all).

They live as consciousnesses operating causally among themselves; each one with its conscious phenomenology; they conserve the memory of their corporeal existences; but they are not only memory, they are actuality. (Except for Mnemonia, she's only Memory.) Someone has a problem or forgets, has a fear or a confusion; the most powerful feeling sets the tone for the whole group of consciousnesses. The unfolding of consciousness is absolutely free; it is eventfulness, nothing more or less than how we can become dizzy without wanting to; in each consciousness the states come without reason; it's ridiculous to say that some whirlwind of dust would cause fear or anger, because why was the whirlwind there? It is continuous spontaneity, which is to say: we are truly inhabiting the mystery.

Therefore the characters in this novel do not have physical bodies, sense organs, or cosmos. Their communications are direct, without words (which the author will have to invent and attribute); they are nothing but direct psychism operating from consciousness to consciousness; the nearness that one consciousness might feel to another is not distance but consciousness; causation between consciousnesses, which are connected among themselves but individually disconnected from the cosmos; a plurality of consciousness with immediate inter-causality.

The characters must live on ideas and psychic states; they are psychic individuals. This "worldless novel" seeks to dissolve the supposed causality that the cosmos exercises over consciousness; that if without tigers we can feel that a tiger wounds and mauls us, we could feel what we feel without a cosmos: colors, sounds, odors. There is an original series of phenomena in conscious phenomenology: the first time they appear contiguously, and later they are voluntarily reproduced, they are copies; but an infinity of them are not—especially the ones that are truly the most important in themselves, like appetites, desires, affective phenomenology—the first ones are extrinsically important because of their supposed causality; the tiger appears as the cause of many destructive pains, but in themselves they are ineffective: colors, sounds, lines, noises—even though they cause subsequent events of a given intensity of pain or pleasure.

Put another way: The conscious effect that this novelism seeks is to delineate in the mind of the reader the mere conscious being, without a world, as an intelligible possibility. Now is not the time to discredit the entire library of novels, those that narrate gossip, of men acting on the world and acting in the world; consciousness without cause, with its own operability.

The current century isn't apt for tales of events in the relation Cosmos-Person, but for the dream of consciousness, for the merely psychic Individual, liberated from the Cosmos.

The novel should take place in a climate without disturbances, brawls, jealousies—although the sorrows of life exist, as direct but nonspatial intercausal groupings (the other consciousnesses are the external "world" of each consciousness). These are beings who do not draw or write castles in the air; I play with a death that takes place, yet never kills: Where Everything Comes Back From Death. The characters are all returned from death a thousand times, from a self-death, from mere desire, without poison, or stabbing; they take death as sleep, without a schedule, not nocturnal. (Death is not the policing that we know, but a table always crowded with guests, from which one rises and says: I'm going to bed. This is death.)

The characters that the President has sketched for his novel up until now are:

Posthumia: She wants to be a dead beloved, to only be loved when dead.

Suicidia: She's always dying "by her own hand" by a resort or conscious call to non-being that is instantaneous, which happens because of a lack of conscious simultaneity: when she's in pain, there's nothing else for her, and the automatisic evasion of pain executes the suicidal gesture.

Forgetful: The man who knows that woman's secret is intolerance for the idea of being forgotten by man: he feigns forgetting, because he knows that this conquers feminine nature. And among his adventures, always triumphant, he meets Notawoman (you must not be a woman to stand being forgotten) and Forgetful instantly loses himself; she makes forgetting both absent and present. Forgetful despairs each time she sees him, and he falls in love; he falls in love with someone he can't remember for more than a quarter of an hour; this is his punishment.

Bellamorticia: Beautiful because she exalts love, because of so much love lost.

Unforgettable: She never knows she is forgotten, not even in death of consciousness. (This death of consciousness, the only death that exists in the novel and which is procured by one's own wish or by means of certain defensive reflexes, only signifies a suspension in consciousness. So it is that via mental exertion, on earth, we call existence in the mental present a memory that escapes us, so mere consciousnesses possess the means to self-paralysis. And these solutions of continuity in Unforgettable, obtained by the consciousness's own impetus, are not capable of doing away with one feeling, the feeling of being unforgettable. In all of the psychic characters in the novel, the solution of conscious continuity which is death, leaves a conscious pulsation latent, a thread of conscious reality that never fails: in Unforgettable it is the inability to be forgotten; in Posthumia it's the desire to be a dead beloved, and so on, with the others.)

Lost: She doesn't know where she is; who she was; why she came; where she was going before; what she'll be; if what she's feeling is herself, or someone else. When she's oppressed by sadness she exclaims: How sad Unforgettable is! Or How sad Retrograde is (her friends).

Volupta: Aspires to one kiss in a year, and to die.

Indifferent: Eternal consciousness or eternal death interest him equally. He makes everyone tremble with this sainted indifference.

Presentless: He feels everything on the *border* of the Past, as a species of past occurrence: "I was hungry" is "I am hungry." His memory displaces his present: "I loved you" is "I love you." He lives in the past, but with a present sensibility, and actually lacks both a present and past.

Aspires to Life: Wants to return to corporeal life, in which he must have been very happy—a rare exception.

Amnesia: Has no past. Yesterday never happened.

Sweetie: Hates to be deprived of affection: Material. She seeks tenderness, caresses.

Retrograde: Changes pasts. Someone asks for a happy past. Others, that their past be changed so that they are convinced they lived a different life than the one they actually lived.

Mnemonia: She only has memory, she has no current life or being. But she has a perfect memory: there's no fact, no matter how fleeting or insignificant, that she can't recall.

For Herself: She only loves the dead. She doesn't want to be loved. She's alarmed or repulsed by any care or interest shown her. She tells everyone: "I found Mydeath. How happy I am. But sometimes I'm not. Poor me, what would it be like if I died." (She's looking for a man whose expression shows that he's lucky enough to die soon, the better to be happy beforehand; she doesn't want anybody to die, but she's looking for someone who will.)

Eterna: She knows no death; her consciousness is not suspended for an instant. She's the maximum intensity of consciousness.

The Lover: Awaits Bellamuerte. He must obtain the resurrection of her consciousness, and prove to her that there is no happiness superior to the fullness of consciousness in his actual, which is to say eternal, passion.

No Return: Without personal eternity; does not return. Everyone knows that she only has one life and one death, and so she has earned the obsessive care of those who know that one fine day she'll escape them. She must die for a reason, though; she can't die without one. And since it isn't known what the reason might be, they shower her with exquisite love and concern. But might it not be good fortune that kills her?

It's not believed that in any of his conscious planes the President works on his novel for any reason other than to distract himself with the aforementioned annotations. If someone knew better than Sweetheart or Maybegenius how to spy on his consciousness, or maybe even his papers, they would find phrases dropped from who knows where, ideas to elaborate, names, situations, charged words. For example:

"While the author has a body and writes for readers with a body, writing the novel of this group of consciousnesses he uses the words that this group does not use for anything but which the readers need."

"To exploit words in their excepted elements, in their irregular associations. To actualize or utilize words or nuclei of associations such as: The tick-tock of the clock on the night-stand—the whistle of the wind—thresholds—a glove—a small comb—distant thunder—a fresh gust of wind—a cat's tread as it draws back its paw—the first whistle of a kettle on the fire—a head tossing on a pillow—the anger of a rose—a closed piano—a loose button—the carnation's defiance—a suppressor of profiles—the gaze returned to its eyes—will there be another time?

To exploit the great ruptures and sweetness of family life.

The mnemonic context of the present: What position does any given present hold? I get up today, I think yesterday.

Within the generic matter of consciousness, to say for example: "It was sweetness that said yes;" "He spoke, and was sleeping;" "He felt that somebody was dying," "Through the door by which the incorporeal, forgotten gentleman was not entering."

Scenes: With the rose's laughter—with the tick-tock sound of the little clock under the pillow—with a sleeper's breath—on glances exchanged.

(Towards a metaphysics of inter- or intra-conscious novelism.)

Consciousness without a living person, not obligated to a "body."

Plurality of all those who were not "existences" but "lives," which is to say consciousnesses connected to material instruments.

The individual consists of memory: each one, in his differing mnemonic path; while still living at home, the feeling of he who feels the most is transmitted to the others, so that there's no more than a single sentiment; the strongest state is like a tonic and it invades the other consciousnesses, to the point of weakening whoever feels it the most and unifying the surrounding field of consciousness. The individual sustains himself in these multiple memories of corporeal existence that each one has; plurality is only in the conscious existence in which they find themselves now.

The spontaneous apparition of conscious states in me, I attribute to their apparition in others. Now, I don't know why these conscious intercommunications are established, their point of departure being the mind in which they first appear. Because I can conceive of being the only consciousness, and in this case nothing and no one else will be the cause of my states, neither other people, nor material existence. Why this plural world of consciousnesses? I don't know where the series of states began, what person began this contagion to all other incorporeal consciousnesses, without obvious or direct communication. I truly believe that the only feeling in this life is that consciousness operates on bodies and never directly, never without these bodies' mediation, which includes objects as well as bodies, which the World constitutes as temporal and spatial, and from which spatio-temporal constitution arises the illusion that we call Memory and the illusion of individual Identity, out of this memory, which seizes upon the external. Pure consciousness that has neither time nor space nor memory.

Are these beings equivalent to dreams, then? Is the dream-state equivalent to this state of pure consciousness? Is there nothing left over for daydreams? I think there is: a dream of the nearness of another consciousness.

An endearing insinuation: a pot of boiling milk (an earthly event) that makes these worldless beings shudder.

Francisco began to despair of his valet duties. Not even the unhinging of delirium saved him. "No," he said to himself, pondering, "I am not made to be a valet in such a rowdy house full of people with bodies; I'm going to offer my services to a house of people who are only consciousness." So he went looking for a Mystic who would assist him with a voluntary death. After an intermission in which this was effected, we have him here. "Someone's coming, Francisco, answer the door," he thinks, for example, now. Or: "Francisco, you must understand that things aren't exactly like they were before." And he goes for the door. He opens Nothing with a nothing key, and in an instant of immobile time later, he's chatting with the Forgetter.

This is the climate of dreams in which the President operates. Will Art save him?

(The President goes off a ways, arguing with the Author, saying it's in poor taste to talk so much about his projects and so little about

Eterna. And they come to a compromise, which is that her name should appear on every page.)

And Sweetheart, who went away in the night accompanied only by her dog and a willow cane that Maybegenius has peeled for her today, thinks gently of the light of the little house during the moonlit night, just as at other times she had liked to contemplate the lighted house from the dark fields.

She remembers that in the afternoon, when she was walking in the garden, the President had made up a story for her about the gardener's madness before the spectacle of the flowers, which presented to him an unlimited succession, each flower surpassing the last in beauty. Everything is possible in creation, there's nothing that can't be dreamed, that can't come to pass. Being does not understand no. The President told her this in his favorite formula: the totalpossibility of occurrence, the liberty of Reality.

INSTANT IN WHICH THE DENIZENS OF "LA NOVELA" APPEAR

Maybegenius and Simple suspended their chores of cutting the grass around Sweetheart's lodgings, an isolated, circular room with windows facing all four directions. Instead, they amused themselves with shared knowledge: Maybegenius says, "Signs kill things: widow's weeds kill sorrow; going to mass kills faith; theology creates atheists." Or "God made the world and I give it to you for study." (He notices the influence of the President-in-diminishment, and he fights against it: Since Progress sticks to the Present like a shadow, God is in Being and in Passion; the Present takes nothing away from Passion.) Or he even goes deeper with his meditation on human conduct: "Humans close their eyes thousands of times without a thought of death." Simple answers with his own thoughts, like "There are two truths that ugly women don't want to know, two fidelities they hate: one is the mirror, and the other is the photograph." Or: "Selflessness is possible, but not by throwing himself into the water to save a drowning fish."

The Lover dreams, because meanwhile he dreams that he exists; and meanwhile his beloved smiles at him, since they are sure of a venturesome encounter via a love made beautiful by death. Or he says these enigmatic words aloud: "The Depths of Life. (There is pleasure in all pain.) The fast watch and the majesty of Life: white fingernails and the exact time and fingernails painted with the illusion of Life.""

From between their leaves Eterna picks violets for the little vase on the President's nightstand, violets she leaves without anyone seeing her, with a little card on which she had written:

> Violets . . .
> Violets . . .
> And an Eterna

And on whose back the President will write:

> Love sealed with violets.
> You freed your hand from my hand
>
> And so captured my heart!

Or she sends him a paper flower, with ferns, and on each one of its six petals she has written a letter of her name; and he will respond on the stem of this flower:

> He who lived without seeing her
> Feels himself late
> And now sees Eterna

(Even though one night he had confessed to her that someone who had lost everything in a long life would recover everything in finding Eterna.)

The President and Sweetheart returned from their walk to the swamp by the bank of the river, a grotto formed by six willows, an intriguing place because of its teruteru birds, ducks, and the occasional small snake, and whose profound mystery they hoped to one day penetrate. Sweetheart drove the carriage, the same one in which the President drove everyone to the train station every day, and she let herself be convinced by various ideas or observations.

"The two Murmers I've discovered," the President says, "are Death and Old Age, or the Passing of Time. The inevitability of death and aging are as if time alone could make things slow down, and change. This involves two betrayals: Death, which I've already explained is no betrayal, and that the most intense form of old age, in a large number of cases, is young old age, which occurs between the ages of twenty and twenty-five, when a man must assume all the responsibilities and demands of life, leaving behind the life watched over by his mother and father, which he so enjoyed. Old age is simply not about the years but about the entire relationship of the life's excessive charge with respect to the reactivity of an individual psyche." And also the President made her see the ridiculousness of his life: that he'd studied the same biological time since he was thirty, which is to say, how not to die, and metaphysics, which is to say, how nobody dies.

Then Sweetheart said to the President, in an undertone:

"Why can't we continue like this all of our lives, in this Carriage, without time passing, without losing appreciation for one another, all together, in 'La Novela?'"

"Why not?"

And at this very instant the Traveler (Our Traveler does not go to museums; he looks at what's alive, not at the Past) approaches the beach on the banks of the River Plate, facing the gates of the estancia.

"And can you be happy now, Traveler, with your search at an end?"

"Maybe, because it's an invented quest, it was not imposed."[1]

---

1. From here on the author continues alone. The last readers have dropped him. And, naturally, they plan *to write*.

CHAPTER XIV

(STILL.)

AND THE PRESIDENT? AND ETERNA?

The President, who is only impulsive after he's thoroughly analyzed every facet of his conduct (and whose life has been spent in the resolution of the problem of consciousness), has gone a long time without meditating, in the full sense of the word.

And so it is that after the Conquest of Buenos Aires in the name of beauty, and having returned to "La Novela," he awoke one day with the sadness of having discovered that the city is an irremediable ugliness, which is why it rejects the most accessible, unlimited, and constant recreation and stimulus: Nature.

The Conquest had to be finished for him to feel the vacuum created by this confusion in his work: Should the city exist? Isn't it poor comprehension, uncultivated thought to believe in a beautiful city, to sustain in Beauty what lives in the omission of Nature? Nothing is known without us seeing it, hearing it. Books make it known; facts, thoughts in great citizens, is there anyone who knows something whole, something total?

The contemplation of nature, of savage animal life in its spontaneity, and the spontaneity of humanity's most ancient dwellings and works, with their suggestion of time; human dwellings, not so much pyramids and dolmens; the pyramids want to live for the future, while houses want to live for the present, they live to die, for the actuality of each instant; here are the three incitements and mental suggestions without which nothing, absolutely nothing, can be seen of the mystery.

(At the same time the President realized that the simplest way to suppress war is to suppress cities; since you can't go to war against a nation that's dispersed fifteen million of its cities' inhabitants on farms spread out over a hundred fifty million hectares.)

In the President's spirit, then, the sadness of all unmotivated Action swelled, action that is not intrinsically interesting to the actor (who survives after the enterprise), the sadness that has the same theme as the action: the City versus Nature.

The President and Eterna.

Eterna sees everything on earth except the Mystery; the President sees the Mystery in everything.

Eterna thinks of everyone on earth, and of the nothingness of eternity. Eterna believes in death. She denies Eternity, but believes and accepts love's farewell, which is death. The President believes that death is nothing: that there's no other death than Oblivion (without corporeal annihilation), for those who love each other.

The President gives Eterna little lights, and Eterna gives him the soft, cool pillow of her shoulders, which brings sleep.

Eterna gave everything to love; the President, everything for thought.

Eterna says: that all of her love's present is robbed of the notion that there was a past, in which the President did not know of her existence, he didn't love her, didn't even guess of her presence, could have passed by her without seeing her. This horrifies her. What would you say to this, reader? It's fine to write a novel to respond to what Eterna thinks and suffers. The President has not known until now how to dissipate Eterna's nighttime abyss in their every conversation, when everything seems so perfectly complete, when Eterna's feeling—of not being able to contemplate possession, their love, when it didn't exist before and might not have existed at all—fatally arises. Is there any hope that the President might one day possess the lucidity to convince her?

Eterna has God, and the President does not; Eterna—and not the President—wants a maternal aspect to her love, wants him to rest his head on her breast.

The two nonexistences between the President and Eterna are: one that only Eterna knows, and one that only the President knows. (Meanwhile, there's the nonexistence who doesn't yet know Eterna and he's on his way to meet her, and this is the Gentleman Who Does Not Exist, who reflects: "The author seeks nonexistences and I am very comfortable with nonexistence, as comfortable there as a woman is comfortable in existence, since a man can never get used to existence.")

Already The Lover told you: the President will always be sad, and if you want it otherwise, give him a different past.

And Eterna changed this past, and she also brought him an exchange of Thought for Love. But there was one thing she couldn't do: change her own past, or even other people's pasts where it concerned her. That's her impossibility, that she can't be understood.

And what has the President given Eterna? Since he has not won her full love, because he didn't know how to elevate himself to the grace and tenderness of the Lighted One (who didn't want him to have *forgotten* her, during the time before he met her)—what could he give her?

Eterna possesses a never-possessed power: of changing our pasts, and the greatest impossibility for herself: to tolerate the fact that there was no love in the past, that her lover did not know her: there's nothing to do for this impossibility, which only exists for her. (Another impossibility: to be understood?)

Eterna is greater than the most elevated daydream, and just as real as she is perfect, since that which is totally dreamed, in all its detail and desire, even as an idea, is real, since now, confronted with *the real* we do not find ourselves in a new state of being. The President found all he dreamed of in her, or he dreamed greatly; and everything he dreamed and everything he found was less than the simple, original perfection of Eterna. She is real perfection.

If you would like a new past, Eterna can give it to you. The President, on the other hand, would only be a Historian, changing Humanity's Past, giving it something different than history has given it. He would give to Man a Present, of which History strips him. Presentism: to live only in the Present, without History or future Progress, this could be his slogan. Since to start, or not to start—in—another, not a future, to not resemble anyone, this is what we all are. History and Evolution, two types of emphasis, don't explain anything, since it's not because of the future but because of existing that we are the mystery.

Training, Friendship, Action . . . What did the President lose? Thought?

The President's drama is: thought as passion, because Love is being, is more than Being, and Thought is the seed of the notion (or problem) of Being. Passion is the highest form of being and being is the highest form of thinking. For this reason Thought can be Passion. But in his Thought-Passion the President is unhappy: he is missing the Real of an imagined Eterna, the personification of the Real in thought.

Does Art matter for someone who is mortified by this absence? The President works on his worldless novel, perhaps, in the name of his own liberation; he works, but without joy.

There still remains one hope for the President, and perhaps for us all: the pro-reality transfusion of Eterna; a collection of "life" for Eterna. But the saddest thing is that after having all felt the antipathy and risks of the President's proposal to leave behind Friendship in favor of Action, the characters got excited about Action, and hoped it would bring them happiness; and it's the President himself who has given them this disillusionment with action, which they believed they had done so well and so thoroughly.

So now he gathers them all together to propose that they give Eterna life, so that someone in the novel may be saved from the unreality of being a character.

CHAPTER XV

FOR EVER-CHANGING ETERNA, AN ENDLESS, IMMUTABLE POEM

For Eterna:

At your feet, before either you or I is sure of the first word that says *today begins for you,* bend to me your amiable visage and lucid spirit, either frowning or with forehead serene, so that in it are shown your labors and your reposes; bend towards the grave thought that with my art I inspire; and today, more than the days before, when they made a Today for you of my own, I want severe and rigorous divinings of the mystery pulsing in your being and in the gracious line of your tiny, eternal steps, for now you are Matter, if I am your artist, and you are what I most hope for myself.

For I make your hope my hope. I didn't bring it with me when I came, yet today I know hope, better than my own, your hope in me—I don't want it for myself, nor would I have it without you. Now you know that if you let your faith fail, there will be no point, nothing will be left of me to die, not even hope, since everything of me dies in you.

CHANGES IN YOU.

Agitation, in the immortal, is your fantasy in love. Even if there were death, even if our heartbeats were numbered, you give yourself ardently to life's pressures; your inspired being tries everything, and you call out everywhere so that nothing of your love is untested, so that nothing in it may sleep, even unexpected sleep; even if death could exist! Even if you had to learn and count each grain of sand.

Neither my love nor my mind had any warning of how you were yesterday.

I knew you anew, and loved you as you asked. With everything I already know and love of you, you made yourself a beautiful other: yesterday you wanted to be the being the Night showed you.

I still don't know how to wait for you after you've come: in your genial changes you outstrip me, and even though I eagerly follow, my love cannot guess ahead of you. One day I'll have a feeling for what you will and want to be each morning.

But in your ardent fictions, does it not sometimes happen that you are so far ahead of what I can guess that to see you transformed, stripped of your beauty, is always equally lovely? I love you for the first time with an entirely new love, and am thus unfaithful to the first; you make me unfaithful with your changes, and always in love with what I do not see in you. Is this not a death, the only kind that can happen in the fullness of love, because I love you forgetting what I have already loved?

I am still only an acolyte in the mystery of love, taught by your lighted eyes, and in your mobile accents. I vacillate, unable to recognize you amidst all the enchantments and mutations of your transfigurations, as you avidly renew your eternal beauty.

In the eternal, everything is, and this is how I may find myself bitter that I have ceased to love you, since you are always what I love; "another" love is possible in you, if you change so much that my memory cannot reach you, cannot find you. Let me learn. And later foretell.

NIGHT IS THE BEAUTY IN WHICH IT PLEASED YOU TO DRESS YESTERDAY

As if your eyes had thought themselves a part of the night's vestment: stellar lights in them—but it wasn't that, it was wishes of your soul, hardworking in their adornments and self-transfigurations, your spirit's ardent fictions as it gives itself to fantasy and the force Beauty requires to protect your being from the near and involuntary cosmos—you feigned your eyes' spoiled presumption—truly, you figure their disquiet—your vigilant concern was to live in exaltation, immune to the Forces of the mundane: Night, Beautiful-Sadness: you wanted to be beautiful and so you appeared, to the point that it gave me pain, for to equal you is impossible, and it's impossible for any art to explain you.

You affirm the lights of your spirit—the day has no light, nor the night any purchase without your consent—you are unafraid to lose them, to be Night and to lose yourself in it, immense and untrammeled . . . And night has turned to today, it possesses the enigmatic night, and it possesses Departure, and nearby Dreaming—the departure is in its breast, invisible dreams trip us up—you listen to me with your breath agitated by the flutter of your full, confident heart and the skeins of your fantasy.

You are deep night, with its ebony depths, heights of life in the domed headdress of the Milky Way, brilliant dimples at diverse distances, the immense, ample swing of the celestial vault.

Your thought is honored in your person, your vestments and motions, the statuary of the night, its subtle and magnificent path, and harmonious respiration in its full extension, your nearby step wakes the surrounding air, in the revolving processional towards the dawn your distant pace is congruent with all planes and summits. In you the "word" and the "voice" of the night are one; I heard its voice for the first time and in your hand I knew something even more prodigal: the touch of the night.

The night, which chooses its own precious, sparse, delicate and invariable adornments, not the day, whose oppressive dazzle we cannot avoid; the lunar paleness of your face blues in your black eyes and hair. We are capsized by both nearby voices and broad murmurs, vast ebonies that marble the heights and the depths alike. The night touches us, and we tremble, like its distant lights.

Night is life in beautiful sadness, but with hope's flutterings, with voluntary, ornate, sparse, and elevated thoughts, this is how you made yourself, pale and dark, how you undid the distractions of immortality, how you gave yourself such beauty in the supreme and unhesitating predilections of your being, in spirituality's reborn joys; let these joys defend your eternity and the Desire with which you have chosen to live it.

And you are the Night, as severe of aspect as your heart is lush with fervent invention.

THE DAY AJAR

I know who the "pale one" will be who can defeat me in your heart. He's the one I sometimes meet on the way, who walks before me, fervently advancing along the walls and hedges. He twines roses in the fences; and in the whiteness of a thousand sparks with which the afternoon raises itself in light, he winds a band of darkest shadow around the roots of each tree, and he stretches a narrow ribbon of darkest shadow at the feet of the low fences of the countryside, and along the walls he runs a plank outlined in black, sets it "plumb" in the entire verticality and oscillation of the day, on the lake named Siesta. Little stains of darkness, dappled gray in the dazzling light, secrets kept from the Day at the foot of the rose bushes, as if the roses grew from this secret and the fragrance of the roses were the tears of this secret.

There is another man with the pallor of the artist and lover, another "pale one," more loving, more artistic. He has no more life than what we give him. He's the one who believes he's found in me what I long to be: the Artist, he who even takes the shadows of things in hand, so that the Day does not subsume them, the Real in its transparency of being. The artist is he who loves everything and speaks everything.

He is invisible, if the light of the afternoon Siesta passes through him; dark in the Night, but his face is clear in its pallor and with the pallor of the moon and stars. When you think of him, I think of him.

You have eyes and hair of the darkest shade, they hate the light that lets things dodge the absorption of Siesta; tender things that love their shadows and humble love affairs, let the artist take them in hand, they don't want to be absorbed into the transparent-making power of the Siesta and they wait, holding on to their shadows; they walk towards the Night, catching up their tulle skirts in their hands, skirts that tell them they exist: their shadows.

You intertwine your steps in the present with the Night, and you secret yourself from the call of the Day, of the President; you make your present nocturnal and love your past as dazzlement.

You love the night and sometimes in your pallor you are the night in your bestarredness, your eyes, your sighs, in the silence, in the non-present, in the Remembering. You. I believe in your pallor of love and remembering, not in the pallor that one day death will simulate in you.

> You are the night where I saw my way
> You carry me, you are the guiding night!
> I call you illumined night,
> Because you make the night's light fresh,
> The daylight wounds you, snuffs your world.

You are the night. I only found my way in you.

> And only I
> Discovered you
> In night's shadows.

I will be defeated, but there's only one thought that can give you the entire response to the Mystery of your being and of all being, and it's mine. One day you'll seek me out for it, in the pathways of eternity. I'll tell you the word that only I possess and you'll stay by my side year after year. I have the thought that explains all being, yours included. And now I search your portrait for the trace not of your being, but of how you are, because you are however we see you and know you.

DARLING BEING:

Nothing matters as you do, as we do; no work of man or of the world, nothing has a chance, nothing breathes as it does in you, what lightens or rests or bids farewell, for an instant, to the murmuring memory where recollection sleeps in you, if only for an instant. Not even your quick laugh, so noble, tremulous, and wet with tears; it's my laugh, it is the word you have for me, the word that among all of your words alone finds comprehension in me; may the entire Future wait until I have come, and may it not linger after, Never shall another drink from your throat, from your being, like the artist who speaks to you now, who has found you, who follows you. And I don't want you, the Wellspring, the eternal Child who still finds her first tears in this tender, fleeting laughter which sometimes I can elicit in congress with you and which seems to be the last sob of weeping like petals, opening with the day: tears, tears from the Wellspring, tears of hope, of "weep no more . . ."

IT COULDN'T BE

> You will show me
> Dolorous Eterna.
> Pious, we wound ourselves
> with oblivion's kiss
> it burns memory
> but loveless leave us on this ground
> Without this futile love.
> Let it be when tears' kiss presses
> Our faces in what our bodies knew
> supreme intimacy

When we feel passion's last pain
And its greatest.

We'll forge lethal
the sign
all pain
but with death.
The death asked for love's
Initiation is not
the death lovers fear.
Day through night,
not night through the day.

SUBMISSION

If I cannot stay by your side
you must give me
a lover's talisman.

Faithful as you are strong
you must forge oblivion's kiss
fatality's kiss, impossible kiss
here we submit our destinies.
And let tearing ourselves away
be our departure,
separating ourselves from when we were closest.
Pull our resigned destinies
first step of no return
out of our last caress
when we were the closest.

And we will not await
Love's vanquishment
Tormented.

Your love slept while it could
I didn't fall apart until you awoke.
I already know how it will be.

I've already known my love
impatient in the future's ardent study

pulling us our gullible hands will say: come to me
later . . .

O ETERNA, IN YOUR MOUTH NOTHING MORE BE SAID: I AM FLEETING

Suspense remained, the breath placid
murmuring quiet existence,
placid a faraway gaze, and a thought resting
amused for a quiet while
free from agitation or life's demands
influencing the caring white hand
you placed on me, as if it were a breeze
and this is how I know the new paces of your thought.

Knowing your spirit's ways in the cool pressure of
     your palm
drinking with you the air you breathe,
it just vibrated with your voice, you said:
I am fleeting.
Below, at my gaze's edge,
Your white hand
Like your black pupil wholly ardent, where
I don't look, judging it full.

What you said, just now, without looking at me
Waiting in precious silence
gracious and assured of the answer you know
My enamored mind sought to surrender to you
with all its forces, immense, eternal.
This silence, Eterna, in a mouth subtlely smiling
trusting in love, this silence gentle and clear
only I have discovered this smiling light,
I would like to keep it.
And in my eternal memory I'll have it
eternal as our love's wealth of speech.
This silence
You hold this silence between your lips
so close to my happy contemplation
it provokes me.

To a lover's rage against

the ephemeral
against death, in all my thoughts.
Rid yourself of the silence you toy with in love's security
feigning hopelessness while you expect certainty
I have the answer you know already, it cannot be hidden
no matter the fictions of ceasing, of leaving
we call death.

So close, venturesome, looking at your throat
and your breast alive with respiration's murmur
It comes and goes, is moved and loses itself
in opened mouths' immense signification.
The air we drink in
the sound of rhythmic breathing
our breasts' oscillation in unison with the ocean.

I loved Eterna
though I never hoped to be her lover
and today, how modestly
you gave me a beginning more real more
pristine, more inaugural than birth
when you said "Yes, I love you too."
as if it were nothing
as if the magnificence of Life's creation
didn't light your prodigious words!

Yes, I am as one who trembles
one who trembles happily in a beautiful dream
and, hurt, because wakening robs him
nevertheless reality awaits him
and the wakening that keeps her words,
I am here, trembling
without receiving the gift, not believing it
not intimately receiving it, surest joy of my being
without faith
in your love's present, what before I begged for
with lamentation
this love was given to me so often in dreams
of which wakefulness robbed me.

Even if I could

today the real is more daring for me than any dream
tell me again, call me, wake me
I still haven't the courage
to draw back wakefulness, morning's curtain, make
        this dream distant in exchange for the real.

KEEPING COMPANY

"It isn't that I didn't know
but I was late"
she told you, strangely disturbed me, my voice,
        submerged in contentment
the first time I met you.
Fortune teller, now my foot is on your threshold
it introduced us.
You are wise, but there is no place, no instant
        where you are.
Or how you look, talk, and appear.
only your soul knows love.
and there can't be anything more in it
anything more in me.

Only I was late
because the fences said as I walked
coming here, walking again
"It was never love, it can never be."
and truly there were flowers withering
in the fences, in the hour of siesta, all light.
I told the countryside fences and walls
"I have left it to her, she must give me her love."
I know how to be only love,
neither deity nor knowledge
nor the world, nor human
I scarcely have
her
company.

THE SHADOW IN LOVE'S DAYLIGHT

What is most loving in my love for you is that I think of you as
uncreated, eternal; I see you as fragile, docile, dressed in mortality;

and I think that you too will know a day when your face and hands feign death.

I'm certain that this dream will reach you. This thought—the thought of your Heart going mute, already without what my love heard, without this beat repeating in you, always and only: "my lover"—this thought is pain but not pallor, it torments my earthly existence, but it does not dismay my certainty.

A silence in your breast, a hand that does not reach out to follow mine as it calls to your palm, this is sadness, it's everything lived culminating in the total pain of an instant. Everything we were is made pain, from when your heart forgot all the words that it gave to life, preferring to always and only to beat out: "my lover"—until this terrifying silence!

If you or I has to be the one to hear this last palpation, if you or I has to be the one who first experiences the silence of a heart, either mine or yours, may whoever of us knows the greater pain also die; do not cry out, wishing for one heartbeat more, as if it meant the whole pain of the Earth, all of Life, but instead seek a new encounter, to wake together, it's as close as every waking, every dream

Let's always say so to each other.

> Sometimes, when I'm by your side
> Your eyes close halfway, and forget me.
>
> Forgotten and close to you
> I am like one who watches all night
> at the head of the bed of a sleeping lover.
> But you're not asleep, you've gone; you always love
> But not always me.
> So I keep watch
> over the links forged between our hours
> and unknown to you
> I ardently seek
> a new link, invisible and strongest of all
> but I can't work on it if you've already turned away.
>
> I'll always fear
> your returning past
> this present, when you leave me.

This is your doubting eyes task
to tend an ardent feeling
to sweep your gaze
over all you fear
to think of what you love, even adore,
what might hurt you.
Discover, discover!
I will look where you look.
If you don't find it, who will?
Today if I am found where you are.
You are Totalove, and I am Clarity.

CHAPTER XVI

(TODAY THERE'S MORE PAST THAN THERE WAS YESTERDAY)

So Eterna gave the President a pleat in her skirt to hold and she said, "Take hold here, and follow me, to your penitence."

The President desired this—to be treated like a child punished by his mother—now that he couldn't do anything more with his ill-temper and his depression during frequent conversations when Eterna seemed so sure of herself, although so loving, more certain than him in her coddling and even more certain than he, always, of what could derail, degrade, or dull their love. Sulking, dominated, drunk with her ever-increasing beauty, care, energy, clairvoyance, resigning himself to the subtle, and most intelligent thought that pleased him: "It's enough for me that all beauty resides in her; what does it matter what I am?"

So he followed her.

And Eterna . . .

Suddenly, with a suave attitude, Eterna turns to you, reader, and says in a rich, courteous voice:

"I address myself to you, reader; I am Eterna; a woman who is perhaps noble, perhaps beautiful and strong headed, of generous sentiment and grave destiny, perhaps haughty, with majestic manners, from an old and prominent family, and with a sumptuous house; with a clean and severe past, perhaps unhappy, and capable of an adventure whose exquisite, shuddering, brimming laughter, intrepid laughter that resonates from a deep place within, perhaps is capable of wiping the idea of Death from the face of the earth.

"You read what I've been saying and doing here, and perhaps you think that I've just been passing time with the President. Allow my words to reach you from these corners, that my accent and figure may reach you from the written word, and I'll tell you, come closer:

"Tell me, swear to it, can you feel my breath? Can you hear my voice?

"Every day I've got more of a past; to live is to create a past; so since mine grows every day, which can only happen for someone who's alive, I must be alive and you and I must be in the same current of murmuring, faint, fleeting Time, and so you will have noticed that you learn more of my past in each page.

"But I'll never know what I am; if perhaps what's happened is that I was once real, and an artist with strange plans, tormented with tenacity and determination, turned me into a dream of these word-covered pages, which you hold in your hand.

"And if that's so, I've got you, too: so much that happened to me must have been predetermined by novelistic causality. What you don't have is a shocking sorrow: the sorrow of knowing that what my ambitions are to suffer and achieve is already written, prefigured in these pages; everything I don't know, that will befall me; I don't know anything of myself beyond this page, I know nothing of what fortune has in store for my great aspiration and so I'm even more disconcerted, and I rebel even more if I think about how unconcerned you are, reading, without realizing or thinking that how much you read, and at what speed, is the event that at this moment lacerates me, perhaps, and snatches from me whatever goodness was or would have been given me."

It's true, Eterna, you're perfect, a unique perfection: all of your sensory existence is emotionalized, which is to say, that the slightest occurrence or action or consequence of that action is judged emotionally for itself, for its own tenderness, laughter, or reproach.

That's why the President, who knows you so well—and who hasn't a single emotion of his own—turns instantly and irrevocably into a child. Eterna, who applauds every lover's caress and would give and receive all of them, has until today denied any caress that he would give her or that he conceived; she would be tireless and indiscriminate in caresses, but only with a lover and a beloved who were not perplexed in any way. Her torture, of being so much this way and not being able to accept caresses nor condescend to give advice in giving them, is the greatest and least evident, most unique and irreconcilable, disadvantage from which a human can suffer.

The Lover understands Eterna's love. He, who is a Lover and who was the first to suspect Maybegenius's affection for Sweetheart, and who more than once thought about this love, and Eterna's love, believes that although Maybegenius loves Sweetheart the most, and she also *loves him the most*, that does not make Sweetheart the *most loved* among women, if we can't prove that Maybegenius is the *man with the most power to love* in all the world, since there could be another woman who had *all of the love* of the man who had the greatest force of love possible; and it could also be that a woman was loved by the most amorous man in the world but that she wasn't the only one he loved, or the one he loved the most.

In contrast, Eterna did not want to be the *only one* loved by the *most loving* man, and she didn't find this, nor does she have a splendid, that is maximum, human love. She is what Reality loves: Perfection. Reality has rested from its anxiety to realize a Perfect being, or an identification of the plurality among equals, that is, the annihilation of Plurality. She knows this, that she's Being's beloved, the World's beloved, and this is the reason for the happiness in her face; she doesn't have the total love of an Individual lover, and as proof I have here the immense sadness of her pursed mouth: she's the happiest and the most unhappy of women. She isn't understood. Reality is still unhappy, it can feel her convulse, lost. Even the best lover does not reach the best beloved; he had the love and even the exclusive love of various real individuals, but not the totalove of the best lover. Reality cannot stop itself: the absurd, the stupidity of Plurality continues, it has not been undone.

Author: "Why the devil do I write? What you are doing, reader, and what I'm doing—is it better than sleeping? A reader can define himself as a man who can't sleep without a book in his hand; but it's a minor neurosis, very understandable. On the other hand, the author writes about someone sleeping, or everyone else falls asleep."

Reader: "I seek, and I wait."

Author: "To be an author?"

Reader: "Because I'm resisting the belief that a 'man of letters' is someone who says everything and knows nothing."

Author: "Reader, sometimes your presence is requested in my pages and you are absent: your face comes close, and mirrors the dreaming in these pages, and you are absent. What bothers me is the reader: you're my problem, your existence is invincible; the rest is just a pretext to keep you within earshot of these proceedings."

Reader: "Thank you."

CHAPTER XVII

Sweetheart: "Don't you think the President's a little down?"

Maybegenius: "He undertook the Conquest of Buenos Aires with enthusiasm, and showed a good example of activity, but now I sense a certain enervation in his initiative."

"Maybe it's his memories."

"How the past can weigh on us."

"But many people live on a momentary happiness."

"Is it the past or the future that makes the President sad?"

"What if we ask him? How good he is!"

"Will he guard his secret jealously?"

"I don't think so. If we come at an opportune moment, we may learn what concerns him."

"But let's also speak of ourselves today."

Maybegenius: "Today I have two new storylines, sweetest Sweetheart; do you see how I make good on my promise to invent a story or a plot for you every day? Thinking of lives, almost all of them sad or empty of great inspiration, it pleases me to create destinies that are shaded with the sense that it is preferable to have lived than not to have."

Sweetheart: "The discoloration of not having lived makes me sad, too. To live must be more than just a blast of light before sleep. But I don't want to get depressed, I want to laugh with you."

"I'll have to invent a new plot; I was so happy with you that I wanted to cry."

"It doesn't matter, tell me today's double stories, even if they're not happy."

"If you like. My first invention is merely a novelistic schema. It's called, 'The perfect *third party* or *love's friend*, or *friendship's third party* in a love.' In my opinion, two of the most delicious human attitudes are: the collective sentiment of knowing oneself to be *publically in a state of Passion* and the state of *friendship's third party* with respect to other's loves, or to a dead friend's passion. My novel would be called *The Transparency of the Third Party in friendship of a love,* or *Transparent Third Party,* or *Novel of the Third Party-Transparency of love.* What do you think?"

"If your novel fails, it won't be from a lack of titles."

"It's just that when I look at you, my improvisations get all muddled."

"But your inventions or jokes or great ideas always make me pass the best time with you, and I, on the other hand, don't even know how to show you how much cheer and good company you give me. But I remember your novel; it's melancholy to live in the shadow of others' lives. What about your other story?"

"It's very tragic, maybe it will impress you, it's called 'Every Fear.' It's also just a sketch, the story itself will be a little long. What do you think about leaving it for later?"

"Tell it now. I listen with live pleasure: it could last all afternoon."

"The character says, 'Although I am dying, I must speak . . .'"

Author (to Sweetheart and Maybegenius): "What Maybegenius is relating already happened to me. (To the reader): Seeing Sweetheart's enthusiastic attitude when listening to Maybegenius, it's obvious that in her mind he is the finest and most inventive teller of live experiences. Sweetheart has forgotten that I'm the narrator. While she gets a tray with the ingredients for a *mate,* which she's going to ask Maybegenius to make her so that he doesn't stop telling her a single detail of what happened with his protagonist, I'll tell you my story, reader. Eterna is a deity when she listens: to contemplate her while she listens makes the President fail at every story he tells. I would be equally paralyzed, but I write down my narratives, and perhaps I'm thereby obligated to write competent novels."

Maybegenius: "Do you hear something? Is life trying to get in here? It's always near."

Sweetheart: "Go on, go on, I'm hanging on your every word."

"The dying man removes himself and says, 'Make me stay, since I still have to tell you my great personal secret.' They respond: 'Yes, yes, stay, Substitute. Stay, we all want you to.' So you know that in those days and among that people an abnormal psychology made it so that you could make people stay in life, the way today we make affable or much-loved visitors stay a while longer when they are about to retire or leave the conversation. So it was that this sick-unto-death man jauntily spoke up: 'I will tell you why I was always known by the name of Substitute. I was born and was made to live as an understudy for Dionysius, that beautiful and intelligent man who the abnormal Mutilator of our people had in reserve so as to torture with brilliant mutilations, as if they were surgical models carved with an Extra-scalpel. Everyone here knows that the mutilation-type we love is Pure Mutilation, which is to say without hatred or the filth and vulgarity that Hateful appetites bring.'"

"Continue, please; the narrator of this story has no right to breathe."

"Very well: 'I was living and alert until I encountered my Disembowler, which had not yet been used, since it would be exclusively for me, since like all of us, I wanted its first Action (or anything worthy of that name, that is, anything destructive) to be, naturally, on me. I lived a horror of moral martyrdom when . . . But no, I'm regretting having asked for the prerogative of life: I should remain myself, regardless of the final consequences, I should die with my great personal secret . . .' Substitute begged them to find a death whose effect would be retroactive, occurring the moment when he had been given his prerogative of life in order to make this regretted confession. Death throes have their duties but also their privileges, and the abnormal ones did not want, despite the intrigued anxiety that Substitute elicited in them, to force him to unveil the horrors of his moral martyrdom."

Maybegenius or Substitute: "You must learn not to promise a story whose legitimate ending cannot appear on the record; otherwise you leave a little wound on the curiosity of whoever has legally contracted to hear your story. I am not content to let Substitute carry the greatest secret of the abnormal ones to his grave!"

"I recognize that Substitute has a certain defect, though I think that if he had known you would be so interested he wouldn't have left off in his confession of the secret of the Extra-scalpel. I propose instead that I read you the first chapter of *The man with only one nose* (an incredible novel)."

But Sweetheart can't forget about Substitute so quickly, so Maybegenius has to find a way to absorb her in one of those subtle problems that he likes to cultivate: man's existence or being, from which some other equal creature exists in the world (the secondary man), or man's existence which is alluded to in a correspondence of dialogue between people who know each other and who have heard him talked about but don't know him. But since Sweetheart remained pensive, he opted for trying to cure her mental wound with some mental tickling. So he told her that although in the trajectory from Buenos Aires to Rio de Janeiro a packet ship does not carry an official castaway, the orchestra makes more noise than moving house and would have drowned out the clamor of a hundred castaways. So the captain got great results with the following method: When there wasn't a favorable wind, he had all the hot dishes served, and with all the wind that the thousand occupants of the boat blew in the same direction to cool off their dishes, he had a better than steady wind, and in the end, with this method he arrived in port a day before he would have been late.

"Your inventions and plots are powerful enough, friend, but are they for living people or novel people?"

Reader: "Enough of characters' stories and more story for the novel! It's been motionless for several chapters. It's lazy to make a novel where the reader has to do everything! There's nothing understood here, it has to all be spelled out."

Author: "Please, don't ask me to hide the outcomes from you, it flatters your taste for the all-valiant gunfighter, for the all-knowing investigator, for the dressmaker who marries a millionaire, for the princess who falls in love with the chauffeur, for the injustice neatly avenged; Reader, I ask you not to vulgarize me, since authors are very vulnerable to this and you have to support them when they attempt true art. Didn't you read my prologues?"

"Sure, it's easy to skimp on plot when you lack imagination; how does your novel end?"

"That's all you wanted!"

The rest of the readers: "Get out of here, you ending-reader! We'll give you a 'novelistic rose.' And if this isn't enough for you, one of us will tell you the plot. Or we'll call the characters and free them from your curiosity. Here's one now."

Character: "I'm going to tell what happens in the novel right away; I laugh at hidden endings, unguessable endings, since some call themselves musicians and yet everything they're able to do is an imperfect chord whose resolution the public awaits. My life . . ."

Reader: "Excuse me, I've rectified myself. We'll see whether I'm able to give up caring whether or not this novel ends."

The rest of the readers: "We all hope so."

Author: "Reader, I'm feeling very defeated. I've let you sleep in the margins, now let me sleep."

The rest of the readers: "Let's not bother the author. Any work of art in which an end is expected is not an art work, and has no emotion. Mend your ways, reader. Do not water down our passions.

May this novel never end. There's no more artistic moment than the fullness of reading in the present."

The President (questioning the author): "What are these mutterings? Another page without Eterna? Why don't you show us Eterna, author?"

CHAPTER XVIII

A BRILLIANT LITTLE HEAP OF DELIBERATION SPOKEN IN WHISPERING GUSTS,
BY THE CHARACTERS, WHO RALLY TO GIVE ETERNA LIFE.

Each of the characters tries to do something to give Eterna life. One talks about finding a moonbeam in a rose, another of finding a sparrow wing etching itself across the face of the full moon.

Until one interrupts:

"How can we give a life, when we haven't any?"

The Lover breaks the disconcerted silence:

"What you need, on the contrary, is to not have life; what we don't know is whether Eterna wants it. Until now we haven't thought of that. Only the President can say for sure. Let him tell us. Does Eterna want life?"

President: "Don't torment me further with such a question. She would want life if there were someone in the world worthy of her love. But this hasn't happened, and until then her only mode of happiness is that of the character."

CHAPTER XIX

WHAT'S HERE? PAIN
CHAPTER WITH ITS BACK TURNED
TRUNCATED

They conquered Buenos Aires in the name of beauty and of the mystery and everyone hoped to return to the estancia, that is, to their friendship. The old life in "La Novela" has been taken up again. One wants to work in the garden or restore the paintings, and others initiate a whitewashing project for the house, so that life can continue as before.

The Action has been carried out, and the spirits have not been satisfied; Action without Passion continues to have no meaning for the President. He identified this point with the intention of following through with the action in all of its aspects, with the result that he hoped this would come out of it, but at the same time he felt that his spirit had achieved nothing. There's no contentment in him; his attitudes and conduct presage that life in "La Novela" will not return to how it was of old. There's a bitter feeling in all the characters that comes with knowing something will only last a short while, that it will be cut off or truncated.

And now even this last attempt, to give Life to Eterna, has been frustrated by the President's vacillation.

Their happiness threatens to expire. The President is out of sorts, and again it's feared that he'll change his mind. In the end, he leaves for a metaphysical meditation.

Only the Lover, the Gentleman Who Doesn't Exist, thinks the action just as good as no action at all, and he feels himself just as happy as before, and knows what he's going to do.

AUTHOR TO THE READER:

So what just happened: reunited at the President's request in one of his sessions, he makes clear to them, with great torment, that he will leave "La Novela." And as he saw that nobody wanted to stay there without him, he invited them to an eternal goodbye among all of them, and for each of them to choose a path that would take them farthest from the others, so as to assure, at least, that no one had to experience in another that other farewell, death. And so they were saved all the bitterness of separation because of death, so totally that this collective farewell felt mortally charged.

Only Simple wanted to speak, he's the only one who threatened to rebel, to try and hold on to the possibility of happiness for all. Nobody heard him, surely, but he murmured (any final term of a President should have this infallible threat of uprising, which authenticates every President):

"Why choose Pain, why? We flee unhappiness. Go for the Good!"

But the Lover, the man to whom death had the most to offer, makes his way among the others with a grave expression and takes his leave, saying:

"Please, have pity on a happy man: let me pass."

Death was his Truth.

There couldn't have been more unhappiness. Except for the Lover, everyone whom the President had brought together the previous year in his estancia, "La Novela," has been derailed, since they once knew happiness. Who suffers the most, isn't it Eterna?

All that is seen are the curved backs of the characters as they depart.

FINAL NOTICE

Sweetheart will never resign herself—as she has said—to two things: to the life in "La Novela" and to live that life with the President. She leaves to search him out. Maybegenius is enchanted. He'll give his all to support her.

Hope remains with those who remain in "La Novela."

Happiness. Happiness does not resign. Any citizen can resign from the presidency, but a Novel President cannot resign.

At the time of publication this novel has achieved the dispersion of backs, the farewell without looking, academic death.

CHAPTER XX

All destiny is: a downward gust of wind hitting the crazy swirls of choking smoke from the chimney, and, from heights it sometimes is able to achieve the velocity of an anxious escape.

Nevertheless there's intellectual perfection, and love, clear and warm hearts, limpid mobility, a pulsing clarity, the line made by the waters of the sea, clear souls, always pulsing with some Sentiment— these are the hearts of great matrons, and of the Lover.

There is also the perfection of adversity for the destiny of a full and clear soul. Eterna's sorrow is too much, she wanted totalove, and out of desperation, she made herself a slave to chastity, which is love's frustration. She shouldn't have done so.

Don't love the President, and don't hate him; there is no worse bedfellow for Intelligence than Heat. Intelligence, which has a singular being, should not be curious about the Heartbeat. It's despicable.

Everything's done, but nobody's contented.

ATTEMPT TO HEAL THE WOUND INCURRED

Here's where the readers will agitate for the characters to be resurrected and for the plot to continue, now that they've fallen in love with the novel. (Because my book was as enchanting as Eterna's tresses, a loving enchanter of readers who do not know when, in what page, their hearts were conquered.)

In the final moment of a novel that's been ripped apart, any appreciative reader begs the author for the resurrection of one or more characters, novelistic resurrection, which is to say that they continue to be characters, not novelistic birth, which is to make the character into a person; and since you can't continue being a character without continuing the plot of the novel, the author would have to satisfy the reader by following the character's ongoing trials and tribulations.

The character who I guess the reader would most like to see continue is Sweetheart, and that he would most like to see life continue in "La Novela." Eterna's sadness has such a halo of grandeur that the reader doesn't have the stamina to continue reading her, he doesn't want to know any more of this sublime and pain-stricken destiny. On the other hand, since the reader is just as smart as the author, he can imagine that if I have given him advance events in this novel in the person of Eterna and the enviable environment of "La Novela," Maybegenius won't be long in sniffing it out and making a second appearance to fight for Sweetheart's love. Not even if he himself urged me to could I keep him separated from Sweetheart. The reader's state of mind is this: he would bet that if Sweetheart and Maybegenius are able to stay together in "La Novela," that there would be not only insuperable stories and dialogue like the ones through which they got to know Maybegenius, but also that both characters would be immensely and imperturbably happy, and the reader would thus have at the same time the picaresque pleasure of seeing an author who otherwise specialized in total misfortune obliged to portray unbreakable happiness. He would thus craftily put in my hands an "indestructible happiness," and he would guarantee himself a lot of laughs at my expense, seeing me fail at breaking it, since I'm a slave to my pessimist's instinct. If he does it, I'll sign it; but for me to describe a felicity, knowing that none was ever immortal in art and that only some tears, sobs, and some unhappy "Ay, poor me!"s are what people read centuries later, I won't undertake the task while I still have to invent at least a dozen situations in which my characters must sally forth into life.

Isn't it sad, reader, that the living adventurers of the estancia "La Novela" are dispersed so far afield, never to return to that innocent existence?

Even with the few details I've given you of what life was like there, I'm certain that you envy it; and once there, no one would have pulled you away from there, since there was no sudden imperative to save Eterna from humiliation, or to save Sweetheart from the President when he involuntarily takes a brusque tone with her.

It hurts me, the author, more than anyone to interrupt this life; no one had more aptitude than I for the warm society of mutual affection.

No author has had the vision to torture the reader after the words THE END. No one took charge of that moment. I do it here for the first time, since I know that when the reader falls in love with a book he always wants two pages more, despite the words THE END. With the book gone, they stay with the reader.

Finally, grant me this merit (it chokes me to think of any merit), grant me that this novel, because of the multitude of its inconclusions, has been created largely in your fantasy, in your capacity and necessity to contemplate and give rise to finales. Except me, no novelist existed who believed in my fantasy. The complete novel, which is the easiest kind to write and the only kind that was previously used, is made entirely by the author. It kept us all like children, spoonfeeding us. Let us all enjoy the compensation that my novel provides for this irritating omission, which is in very poor taste.

THE NOVEL IN STAGES

The artistic school that shall soon dominate, to reign over art's maximum severity, will only tolerate the novel in stages, a kind of melody without music in which it unfolds in stages that mirror the chapters, like a metaphor of what is felt in each moment of the novel.

Prose will be like music: a succession of states without being long-winded in motivation, which can be understood by reflecting on a Beethoven sonata. In a quarter of an hour we hear the totality of the feeling in a four-hundred-page novel, which we would need many hours to read.

In what follows, I give a summary example, using my own novel as a first attempt.

This is the same novel you just finished reading, in stages.

—There was a human plurality that lived in mutual sympathy (Estancia "La Novela").

—They appear without a past: faced with a happiness that they never dreamed they could hope for but considered impossible, they cut off their pasts so as to feel it was more real, and made themselves dreams; family bonds and memories were forgotten.

—In the midst of the sorrow of forcing this oblivion, they were as happy as they could be, without passion. The President, who had gathered them there, urged them on.

—A stasis of the happiness of cohabitation, which was the first moment in which insecurity insinuated itself.

—To escape from this first tremor in their fragile happiness, everyone— the President, Eterna, Sweetheart, Maybegenius, the Lover, Father, Simple, the Andalusian—all threw themselves crazily (and at the orders of the President) into training for happiness, a rare act of rehearsal in active withstanding.

—Everything is concluded; the characters have proven themselves, and they return to live in the estancia with high hopes.

—But happiness did not entirely return. They worried as the President worried, whether they should throw themselves into Action.

—*The plan is to suffocate the long and obstinate battle between the Jubilants and Romantics in which Buenos Aires has been destroyed, a blind discord that the President believes was engendered by Ugliness's long reign in the city.*

The President and his friends dominate in the engagement and abolish civil ugliness.

—*So it is done and accomplished, all by means of novelistic miracle.*

—*The melancholy satiation from a triumph that was erroneously believed powerful enough to return happiness to the inhabitants of "La Novela."*

The happiness in Friendship that the President gave them was real, but it delicately did not allow itself to be felt. But there were unhappy shadows that made Action necessary for him; later, again discontented, he will invite them to disperse, to die simultaneously.

He was unhappy because he couldn't be what he should have been, a Thinker alone, and he made Eterna unhappy that he was what he should have been. And that obliged him to be a writer and reader of the melancholy.

—*Backs, which are the curves of a Deathless pain, fade away in the distance.*

TO WHOEVER WANTS TO WRITE THIS NOVEL

(FINAL PROLOGUE.)

I leave it an open book: perhaps it will be the first "open book" in literary history. Which is to say that the author, wishing it were better or even decent, and convinced that with its demented structure he has committed a terrific blunder with the reader, but also convinced that it is rich and suggestive, authorizes any future writer who is so inclined and who enjoys circumstances favorable to intense labor to liberally edit and correct it, with or without mention of the book, or his name. It won't be easy. Surpass it, amend it, change it, but please, leave something of the original behind.

By offering this opportunity I insist that the true execution of my novelistic theory can only be achieved by various people, who have gotten together to read a different novel, to write it—so that they are reader-characters, readers of the other novel and characters in this one, will incessantly create themselves as existing persons, not "characters," as a counter-shock to the figures and images in the novel that they themselves are reading.

This plot of characters who are reading and read with characters who are only read, will, if systematically developed, achieve a uniform and consistent doctrine. The plot of the double novel.

A dialogue to confess that my book is very far from the formula of belarte of written characters. There's this, too, the "open venture."

I thus leave the perfect theory of the novel, an imperfect execution thereof, and a perfect plan for its future execution.

Notice that there's real possibility in the adhesion of the double plot, for someone who is able to give life to a character-reader, by means of an alchemy of consciousness—thus invigorating the existential nothingness of the read-character, who becomes much more of a character because of this accentuation of his frank non-being with an emphasis on nonexistence, which purifies him and carries him far from any promiscuity with reality; and in his own time the reading character's existence will resonate for the real reader, who writes himself out of existence as a counter-figure to the character.

This deliberate confusionism is probably the result of a fertile urge towards liberation in the consciousness; it's a genuinely artistic labor; artificiality is fertilized by the consciousness in its attempt to undermine the notion and the certainty of being, from which follows the universal intimidation of the equally absurd and vacuous verbal notion of non-being. There is nothing more than not-being; the character's non-being, the non-being of fantasy, or of what's imagined. He who imagines will never know non-being.

Macedonio Fernández is considered one of the greatest Argentine writers of the twentieth century. He was a close friend of Jorge Luis Borges, and Macedonio's metaphysical and aesthetic ideas greatly influenced Borges's generation. The mythical life of Macedonio is almost as interesting and fun as his books. Some of the stories about his life include: his campaign for president, which consisted of leaving notecards with the word "Macedonio" on them throughout Buenos Aires' cafés; his attempt to found a utopian society, only to be thwarted by pesky mosquitoes; and his belief that he shouldn't publish, instead allowing his work time to "age." He passed away in 1952, and the first edition of *Museo de la Novela de la Eterna* was released in 1967.

Margaret Schwartz is Assistant Professor of Communication and Media Studies at Fordham University. She was a Fulbright fellow in Argentina in 2004, during which time she researched the life and work of Macedonio Fernández. In addition to translating and teaching, she is also developing a book based on her dissertation, which analyzes representations of the embalmed corpse of Eva Perón.

Adam Thirlwell's first novel, *Politics*, was translated into thirty languages. In 2003, Granta chose him as one of the Best Young British Novelists. His much-praised book *The Delighted States* won the Somerset Maugham Award in 2008. He lives in London.

Open Letter—the University of Rochester's nonprofit, literary translation press—is one of only a handful of publishing houses dedicated to increasing access to world literature for English readers. Publishing ten titles in translation each year, Open Letter searches for works that are extraordinary and influential, works that we hope will become the classics of tomorrow.

Making world literature available in English is crucial to opening our cultural borders, and its availability plays a vital role in maintaining a healthy and vibrant book culture. Open Letter strives to cultivate an audience for these works by helping readers discover imaginative, stunning works of fiction and by creating a constellation of international writing that is engaging, stimulating, and enduring.

Current and forthcoming titles from Open Letter include works from Catalonia, France, Germany, Iceland, Russia, and numerous other countries.

www.openletterbooks.org